Donna
Lawrie

Bathsheba

A story of sin and redemption

Pacific Press® Publishing Association
Nampa, Idaho
Oshawa, Ontario, Canada
www.pacificpress.com

Cover design by Gerald Lee Monks
Cover design resources from iStock.com
Inside design by Steve Lanto

Copyright 2008 by
Pacific Press® Publishing Association
Printed in the United States of America
All rights reserved

Additional copies of this book may be obtained by calling toll-free
1-800-765-6955 or online at http://www.adventistbookcenter.com.

Library of Congress Cataloging-in-Publication Data

Morgan, Tracy A., 1973-
Bathsheba : a story of sin and redemption / Tracy A. Morgan.
p. cm.
ISBN 13: 978-0-8163-2242-8 (paper back)
ISBN 10: 0-8163-2242-2
1. Bathsheba (Biblical figure). 2. David, King of Israel.
3. Israel—Kings and rulers. 4. Women in the Bible. I. Title.
PS3613.O7485B38 2008
813'.6—dc22
2007028798

08 09 10 11 12 • 5 4 3 2 1

Dedication

This book is dedicated to my three *T*s. You are my song, the laughter in my stories, and the joy in my heart. I love you.

A special thanks to . . .
Grandma (Patricia) Morgan for your encouragement and prayers. You are the spiritual backbone of our family and a true prayer warrior. Happy eightieth birthday!

To our dear friends, the Glenn family. Thank you for the time and support you've given me during the writing of this book. Friends like you are truly more precious than gold. I'm so glad we have you in our lives.

And to the rest of my family (you know who you are). You've cried with me and celebrated with me, but more important, you've been there for me—through everything. There aren't enough words to tell you how much I appreciate you.

God bless you all!

Characters — *Starred characters are fictional; all others are mentioned in the Bible.*

Bathsheba	Daughter of Ammiel and Shiran
Ammiel	Bathsheba's father
***Shiran**	Bathsheba's mother
Uriah	Bathsheba's first husband
King Saul	the first king of Israel
Jonathan	Saul's son
***Atarah**	Bathsheba's half sister
***Zeev**	Shiran's first husband
Ahithophel	Bathsheba's grandfather
***Bilah/Mili**	Mean girls from Bathsheba's childhood
***Rivka**	Bathsheba's friend, Uriah's cousin
***Zabad**	Rivka's husband
***Adina**	Bathsheba's pet lamb
***Nadav**	Atarah's husband, the chief baker to King David
***Jotham**	Bathsheba's oldest nephew
***Kaleb**	Bathsheba's second nephew
Joab	David's nephew and commander in chief

Absalom	son of David and Maacah
***Barak**	Bathsheba's cousin
***Ronen**	Rivka and Zabad's son
Amnon	David's oldest son
Ahinoam	Amnon's mother, second wife of David
Chileab	son of David and Abigail
Abigail	David's wife, former wife of Nabal, mother of Chileab
Maacah	David's wife, mother of Tamar and Absalom
Tamar	daughter of David and Maacah
Adonijah	son of David and Haggith
Shephatiah	son of David and Abital
Ithream	son of David and Eglah
Michal	first wife of David, daughter of King Saul
***Matana**	Bathsheba's servant, half sister of Michal
Mephibosheth	Jonathan's son
Phaltiel	Michal's second husband
Nathan	prophet and friend to David and Bathsheba
Oded	David and Bathsheba's first son
Jonadab	David's nephew
Shammua, Shobad, Nathan	sons of David and Bathsheba
Solomon	David and Bathsheba's son, also called Jedidiah
Gad	a prophet
Ziba	Mephibosheth's servant
***Ayala**	Levite girl, lesser wife of Solomon

*Donora	Ayala's younger sister
Naamah	Ammonite princess, first wife of Solomon, mother of Rehoboam
Abishag	David's Shunammite nurse
Abiathar	Levite who served David and later Adonijah
Zadok	David's loyal priest who anointed Solomon
Basmath, Taphath	Solomon's daughters
Rehoboam	Son of Solomon and Naamah

Definitions

Abba	affectionate Hebrew term for *father*
Eema	affectionate Hebrew term for *mother*
Sav	affectionate Hebrew term for *grandfather*
Sava	affectionate Hebrew term for *grandmother*

Chapter 1

Darkness still filled the small room as she rose from her mat. She quietly stepped over the sleeping figure of her mother and walked out the door and up the stone staircase to the roof. Today of all days, she needed to have this time alone to sort out her spinning thoughts. It was the last morning she would spend in this house as the daughter of Ammiel and Shiran. In just a few short hours, she would become the wife of Uriah the Hittite.

She was glad for the blanket she had brought and quickly wrapped it around her shoulders once she reached her favorite place on the roof. It was a hidden corner where she had a panoramic view of the town below. The sky was still splashed with stars, and the moon was a waxing crescent low in the horizon, making way for its brighter companion. She tried to savor every moment of the morning, knowing everything would be different tomorrow. It's not that she was unhappy about her upcoming marriage; she didn't really feel anything, just numb. She didn't dislike Uriah, but she didn't love him either. He had simply been in her life as long as she could remember, just lingering in the background. He was a friend of her father and grandfather and had served in the army with them for years. He was much older than she, but that was not unusual. What she found strange was that he never even spoke to her. Sure, she would catch him looking at her from time to time, but he always quickly looked away when their eyes met. She was so surprised when her mother told her she was to be his wife. Maybe it was because she didn't really feel like a woman yet, even though she was only a year younger than her sister had been when she was married. She had technically been a woman for several months now, which made her eligible to be married, but she just couldn't imagine herself as a wife. Part of her was afraid Uriah would look closely enough at her to discover she really was only a child and call the whole thing off. Then, she decided, it would be a good thing if he did. She could spend the rest of her days in the comfort of her parents' home, surrounded by the familiarity of her youth. Deep down, she knew that would never happen. If it wasn't Uriah and it wasn't today, it would happen eventually. She heard the way people talked about her. Even at her young age, she was called a great beauty. People always said she would grow to be a stunning woman. She remembered a conversation between her parents that she overheard shortly before her father announced the engagement.

"Ammiel, just be patient." Her mother had tried to reason with her father. "Imagine how lovely she will be in another year. We will get an incredible bride-price for her if we just wait. How can we waste that beauty on a poor soldier? He is not worthy of her. She should be in a palace."

"Quiet, Shiran!" Her father snapped. "Uriah is my friend, and we made this arrangement years ago. He is a good man and will treat her well." His voice softened. "Besides, my love, would a palace really be such a good place for her? Remember Asreal's daughter who was taken to live in King Saul's harem. Do you want that for our little flower? I would rather her be the only wife of a poor man than one of the king's many playthings. If she is married, she will be safe."

Bathsheba didn't understand what others saw in her. Sometimes, when she went to the well early on a quiet morning, she would look at her reflection in the water. Yes, her eyes were large and bright and her hair was as black as a raven's wing, but she didn't think there was anything exceptional about her face. There certainly wasn't anything special about her body. She had started changing, but she still didn't have the curvaceous figure of her sister, Atarah. When she looked at her sister, she felt very boyish and gangly, yet Mother hadn't hesitated to take the first offer of marriage Atarah received. Why would she want to delay her marriage to Uriah? How could she think her worthy of a king?

Just then, her thoughts were interrupted by her mother's approaching footsteps.

"Shalom, Flower. I thought I'd find you up here. Did you sleep well?"

"Yes, thank you."

"You have a very big day today. We should get started on the preparations."

"Oh, Eema, I just don't know if I'm ready." She replied holding back a sob.

In one graceful motion, Shiran embraced her daughter and held her close. Both women cried quietly for a moment then sat in silence while Shiran stroked Bathsheba's flowing hair. "My little beauty, oh, the things you could have become," Shiran said more to herself than to her daughter. "From the moment you were born, I knew there was something special about you. I know every mother says that about her babies, but this was different. You were blessed with something extraordinary that the other girls don't have. The first time I held you in my arms, I made an oath that I would do everything in my power to help you achieve greatness. That is why I named you Bathsheba, meaning 'daughter of oath.' If only your father wasn't so devoted to that dull man Uriah, you could have been betrothed to a great man, a powerful man. I've seen how that wealthy merchant Uzziah looks at you when we go to market. They all look at you, Bathsheba. Why, you could even have King David himself if you wanted."

"Eema, why do you say such things? I'm nothing but a skinny girl!"

"How can you be so blind, my darling, and deaf too? Don't you hear people talking about you? Flower, the sooner you recognize your gifts, the sooner you will be able to use them to your advantage. Oh, if only we could have waited!" She sat silently for a moment then continued with new fervor. "Bathsheba, even though you have to marry that worn-out soldier, you will still need to be aware of your power over men. Uriah has fought many battles, but he knows little of the wiles of a beautiful girl. You must use your body and your mind to get what you want out of this world."

"Why do you talk like this Eema? Uriah will be kind to me, just as Abba has been to you. Why do you act as though married life will be so bad?"

"There is much you don't know, little one. I was not always your Eema, you know. I was once young and beautiful too. But your Sava was jealous of me and had me married off to a very cruel man."

"No, not Abba!"

"No, love, not Abba. I've never told you this story, but you are old enough now. I was married before I married your Abba. My Eema was not a pretty woman, but she was clever. She saw men looking at me, and she used it to her advantage. There was a man named Zeev, who worked for the Philistine blacksmiths. You don't remember, but there were no blacksmiths in the entire country, so all of our tools had to be taken to the Philistines for repairs. He would transport the tools and take a large percent of the profits for himself, as if we weren't paying those filthy Philistines enough," she said bitterly as she spat over her shoulder.

"My Eema saw him staring at me in the market one day, so she paraded me before him. I was very embarrassed but, of course, could not refuse. She held me out in front of him for months and even tried to create competition by exposing me to other eligible men in town. Abba was unaware of all of it, so when a high bride-price was offered for me, he took it without question. Eema knew the man's reputation for cruelty, but she didn't care. All she cared about was getting rid of me and getting as much gold for her pouch as possible.

"It didn't take long for me to realize what type of man I was married to. I will spare you the details, but my life was very unhappy. It only got worse when your sister was born. Zeev was very angry that I had not given him a son. As Atarah grew older, he became even crueler. I feared for both of us, but mostly for my daughter. I spent every moment of every day trying to protect her from him. At night I would cry myself to sleep and pray the Lord would deliver us from this man, but when I awoke in the morning, nothing had ever changed. I realized God was not listening to me, so I took matters into my own hands. I knew I was pretty, even though my Eema told me I was as ugly as a hog. It was all I had, so I used it. When I was in the market, I would subtly expose my arm to a man or walk near him to make him notice me. Sometimes the men would try to grab me, and I would cry out. To save his honor, Zeev had to fight to keep the men from touching me. Finally, my salvation came when Zeev got into a fight with a traveling merchant from Kadesh. My husband was badly beaten and died in his bed three days later." Shiran paused for a minute noting the shocked expression on her daughter's face. "I know my relief at Zeev's death sounds awful, but you don't know what it was like. You will be a mother someday, and then you may understand what a woman sometimes has to do for her child."

Shiran took a deep breath and continued with her story. "Even on his deathbed, Zeev hurled insults at me and tried to hurt me with words since his fists were no good. After he died, Atarah and I returned to my parents' house. It wasn't much better there. My Eema was still as nasty to me as ever. My Abba had aged quickly due to illness, so he was unable to secure a match for me. I wasn't about to leave it in Eema's hands again, so I tried to find myself a husband. I met your father shortly after he returned from battle in Ziklag. He had acquired modest wealth while fighting with David's band of rebel soldiers. His father, your Sav, had already made quite a name for himself as an advisor to David during his hiding. Saul had just died, and David was named king in Hebron. I knew once the throne was well established, both Ammiel and his father, Ahithophel, would be well rewarded. I thought if I could capture the eye of Ammiel, I would live in comfort at the palace for the rest of my days, but, unfortunately, your Abba hasn't proven to be as ambitious as his father." Shiran smiled slightly then continued.

"It wasn't easy for a widow with a young daughter to secure a match, especially without the help of her parents, but I used the only tool I had. Ammiel had been away in the wilderness so long, all I had to do was lure him with lingering looks in the marketplace and in no time at all, he asked for my hand. He had also been married before, but his wife and baby had died years earlier in childbirth. I did not love your father, but I needed him, and he was kind to me. What was even more important was how well he treated your sister. She has some memory of Zeev, but Ammiel has been so good to her, she has always thought of him as her father. A year later, you were born. It was a difficult labor, and I almost died. The midwife told me I would never have another child. I wept at the thought of never having a boy, but your Abba was so delighted with you. He never showed the slightest bit of grief over not having a son to carry on his name, and he never rebuked me for my inability to give him more children. I could not have asked for a better man. I don't deserve his love."

"Then why don't you want me to be married to his friend?"

"Because you don't love him. You will be doomed to the same fate as your poor Eema. You will never know true love or passion. You are too beautiful to spend your life in a clay hovel married to a soldier. I know I should be happy for you. You will never have to face the cruelty of a man like Zeev, but you have so much fire, so much beauty. You should have wealth and power, but above all, you should have love! No, I mustn't go on so. You will be happy, my flower. Uriah will treat you well. Besides, he will be easy to control. He knows much of battle, but little of domestic life. You will have power, even if it's just in your own home. You will be happy." Her voice faded as though she were trying to convince herself more than her daughter.

"But, Eema, does he love me? I see him look at me sometimes, but I don't see love in his eyes."

"I think he loves you in his own way. He has waited patiently for you since you were a little girl. I just think his passions have all been spent on the battlefield. But, that may be a good thing. Passionate men can be dangerous. Just use your head—and your body if you have to—and you will be fine. Now, we have a lot to do, child. We had better get to work."

The two women shared one more glance into each other's dark eyes before descending from their rooftop hideaway into the day that lay waiting for them.

Chapter 2

The morning sun had taken its rightful place in the sky, chasing away the chill Bathsheba had felt only a short time earlier. Without a moment's hesitation, she grabbed the water pots by the front door and began her morning routine. Minutes later she was approaching a small crowd of women gathered at the well. This was the part of her morning she liked the least. For some reason, these young women, with whom she had spent most of her childhood, always treated her like an outsider. Many of their families had moved here from Hebron when David took the city of Jerusalem from the Jebusites. Their fathers fought battles together, their mothers shared recipes, but the daughters did not accept Bathsheba as one of their group. When she was young, they would call her Sticks because she was taller and leaner than the others. Sometimes they would pull her hair and tell her she looked like a crow with all that black hair on her head. They ran in circles around her, flapping their arms and cawing at her like a flock of birds trying to take down their prey. Not knowing how to handle the girls, she always tried to remain composed and quiet. This response seemed only to anger them more, but it gave them less ammunition to attack her with. Even now that she was a woman in the eyes of many, she still felt small and insecure around them.

Bathsheba approached quietly with her eyes downcast. She was shocked when she noticed warm smiles on the faces of some of the young women as she drew nearer.

"Shalom, Bathsheba. Today is the day, huh?" one familiar voice asked.

Struck dumb by the girl's kindness, she simply smiled and assumed her place in line. Most of the women completely ignored her and continued talking about the latest gossip.

"Did you hear King David has put out an inquiry, trying to find if any of Saul's relatives are still alive?" one woman asked.

"Why, does he plan to have them put to death?"

"No, that's the strange part. He said he wants to show them kindness out of respect to his friend Jonathan—but it must be a trick."

"David would not play a trick like that!" another woman jumped into the conversation to defend her beloved king. "The late King Saul may have been very cruel to David, but Prince Jonathan loved and protected David until his dying breath."

"I guess we'll see. Ziba, one of King Saul's former servants, answered the inquiry. Apparently, Jonathan's son Mephibosheth is still alive and has been in hiding ever since his father and grandfather died."

"You don't think he'll try to take the throne from David, do you?"

"No, I hear he's a cripple, so he would be of no use to anyone. Why David would want to help him is beyond me. It would be better to just leave him on the other side of the Jordan River."

"That just goes to show you what kind of man David is. Not only is he brave and strong, but he's kind too."

"Not to mention handsome," another woman joined in.

Bathsheba thought the conversation was getting silly, so she tuned out the sound of the chattering while her mind wandered to her own thoughts until her peace was interrupted by an all too familiar sound.

"Out of the way, Sticks. I was next in line."

It was that awful girl Bilah and her little flock of scavengers squeezing their way into line in front of Bathsheba. Just seeing them brought back all of her childhood insecurities.

"You're not in a hurry are ya, Sticks? It's not like you have anything important to do today."

They all giggled and pushed the bewildered girl aside.

"Maybe we should let her go, Bilah. After all, her husband is very old and may not have many good years left in him. We really shouldn't keep his little beauty from him." Mili, a girl with a long sharp nose, jumped into the banter.

"Have you seen her little foreigner?" another girl interjected. "I don't even think he's as tall as you, is he Sticks? And that scar on his face, yuck, I'd hate to see what the rest of him looks like."

"I think they're perfect for each other!" exclaimed Bilah, trying unsuccessfully to control her giggles.

Their cruel laughter stopped suddenly when the group saw the figure of an older girl standing behind Bathsheba.

"I believe it's my cousin's turn to draw water. If you little hens would kindly step aside, we have a busy day today. Oh, and watch your step, with all the cackling, I'm sure one of you has laid an egg."

Bathsheba turned quickly to see the smiling face she loved so well. It was Uriah's young cousin Rivka. She was brought here with her mother three years before when her brother and father were killed by Amalekites. Uriah, being their closest relative, didn't hesitate to bring the two destitute women into his care. Rivka caught the eye of a soldier named Zabad, and when Uriah found out the two were in love, he immediately made plans for them to wed. Rivka obviously adored her cousin, so she immediately became the friend and protector of his betrothed. She must have known even before Bathsheba did that they would someday be family because she had been calling her "cousin" right from the start. Even though she was only a few years older than Bathsheba, she seemed to have so much confidence and strength. The other girls respected her and never had an unkind thing to say behind her back. Rivka was a very devout girl with a peaceful spirit, making it impossible to dislike her.

"Let me help you with that water. I brought extra jugs in case you forgot. We need extra water for your bath," Rivka said with a glimmer of humor in her eye.

"Oh, cousin, thank you—for everything. I get so shaken when

those girls taunt me. I just don't know what to say or do when they're around."

"They're just jealous. Not one of them is even betrothed to be married, and here you are on your wedding day glowing like a sunrise. Envy can be an ugly thing. That is why the Lord warns us against it." Rivka's hands moved swiftly while she talked and before long she had the jugs full of water. The two gathered their load and headed back to Bathsheba's home.

They had to slip around the back of the house to avoid the crowd of men starting to gather around the front. They were immediately accosted by Bathsheba's mother, who had been running around in a tizzy ordering servants here and there.

"Where have you been? We have much to do girls. Get that water warmed up and get yourself washed, Bathsheba. Rivka, be a dear and help her get ready. You were just a bride yourself not long ago. You will be a big help to her today."

"Yes, Shiran, I am here to serve you both in any way I can," Rivka answered respectfully.

Shiran impulsively hugged the younger woman then glided off to tend to the other details of the day.

The day wore on and Bathsheba had been scrubbed, perfumed, and draped with veils, prayed over, kissed, and hugged until she thought she couldn't stand it anymore and the wedding ceremony hadn't even started. Women she knew well, and others she hardly recognized fussed over her for hours until she heard the sound of her name being yelled from the front of the house. The men who were gathered there began to whoop and yell. Uriah had arrived. As was the custom, he stood down the street and called for his betrothed.

"Bathsheba, my bride. Come to me!" she heard his voice off in the distance. She could feel the excitement running through the group of women as they pulled her ornate veils over her face and hair. A group of men came to the back of the house and hoisted her onto their shoulders and carried her to meet the bridegroom. She saw Uriah approaching her parents' house riding on the shoulders of another group of men. The couple was gently placed under the canopy that had been erected for the occasion. The shelter was a simple white sheet that was held in place by four poles, one at each corner. It was just large enough for a few people, so only her parents were able to stand with them. One of her father's friends, a retired soldier who was now an elder of the city, stood between the couple and offered the prayer and vows. Uriah held his outer garment over their heads during the vows as a symbol of the spiritual and physical protection he would provide for his new wife. When the ceremony was over, the crowd erupted with cheers.

For the evening meal, she was placed at the main table next to her new husband. She sat silently while those around her feasted on the best food and wine her father could provide. As plates filled with lamb, fish, fruit, and bread went by her, she couldn't help wondering how her father could pay for all of it. The guests all commented on the quality of the wine as well.

At one point, when everyone had probably had too much to drink, her grandfather, Ahithophel, stood up to make a toast. She would have been proud of him standing there in his fine linen robe, looking much more regal than the soldiers and merchants that filled the room, but he had obviously had too much wine, and he looked a bit foolish. He held his cup up over his head and exclaimed, "Uriah, you are a fortunate man. Our little Bathsheba is the most beautiful girl in all of Israel, and I know beautiful girls. I'm surrounded by a palace full of them," he tried to give a teasing elbow to the man sitting next to him but missed and almost tipped over. "But none of them can hold a candle to our Bathsheba. She's a beauty all right." He stammered something else then fell into his chair, sloshing wine on the front of his robe. Everyone laughed good-naturedly and drank to Bathsheba's beauty. For the first time all day, she was thankful to have her face covered with the veil so no one could see her embarrassment. Uriah must have sensed she was uncomfortable, because he gently took her hand and gave it a little squeeze. She wondered if it was the wine that made him suddenly brave around her, but she didn't care. She appreciated the gesture and smiled at him even though he couldn't see it.

Chapter 3

The next morning, Bathsheba's eyes fluttered open, and it took her a moment to realize where she was. When she noticed the thick arm of her husband resting gently across her stomach, it all came back to her. This was now her home, and this man sleeping next to her was her husband. It was strange that after so many months of planning and anticipation, the wedding was over in what seemed like the blink of an eye. Uriah stirred next to her but didn't awaken. Bathsheba realized she didn't even know what he looked like. Sure, she had seen him many times before, but she had never really looked at him. She studied his face, which even in sleep looked firm and hard. His hairline was receding, and he had a tan line from wearing his helmet in the sun. She wondered what color his eyes were. Bathsheba liked to look at people's eyes and hoped she would be brave enough to look at them when he was awake. His nose looked as though it had been broken, but it wasn't unattractive. He had a long scar on his left cheek that she assumed was from a battle long before. His thin lips were circled by a long dark beard that was beginning to turn gray. She wondered for the first time how old he was. He couldn't be as old as Abba, whose beard had been gray as long as she could remember, but Uriah was definitely much older than she. His arms and chest were bare, which caused her to blush for a moment. She looked again at the arm draped across her. It was strong and hard with a calloused hand at the end of it. She noticed how clean his nails were and this made her smile to herself. She disliked unclean men and was glad her husband took care of himself. *Her husband . . .* The thought made her stomach flip. She was the wife of Uriah. Maybe soon she would be the mother of his sons. She had never given much thought to having children. As of yesterday, she had still considered herself a child, but now everything was different. How wonderful it would be to hold a baby in her arms. Her sister already had two boys and another baby on the way. Oh, if God would give her a son, how happy she would be. Her thoughts were interrupted when she sensed Uriah looking at her. Perhaps it was the first time he had really seen her as well. She turned toward him, and he gave her a sleepy smile. His eyes were brown—and they were much sweeter than she thought they would be. They seemed out of place on such a rugged face.

"Good morning, my little lamb. Did you sleep well?"

"Yes, thank you." She wasn't sure what to do now. She knew she had to prepare the morning meal, but didn't want to leave the protection of her blanket. He seemed to read her thoughts.

"I have some business to take care of this morning. Rivka said she would be by later to help you settle in. Knowing her, she'll probably have breakfast with her, so you won't have to worry about a thing. Just take your time unpacking. I'll be back soon." He washed his face in the basin in the corner and dressed while he talked. He then headed to the door to leave. "Bathsheba," he added, "this is your home now, I want you to be happy here, so if there is anything you need. . . ." He seemed suddenly shy and left quickly.

Bathsheba smiled to herself after he left. What had she been so afraid of? It was obvious Uriah did love her, and she was sure they would be happy here forever.

She found her belongings neatly packed in the corner of the small room. Her mother must have had them sent yesterday. She began unbundling her clothes to find a place for them among Uriah's things. When she lifted one of her robes, a small wrapped bundle fell to the floor. When she opened it, she was shocked to see a little wooden idol. The head and body looked like a shapely woman, but the legs resembled the trunk of a tree. Bathsheba's parents weren't very spiritual people, but she knew her father would never allow such a thing in his home. Her mother would speak of God, but only when it was fashionable. She was much too independent to actually believe in Him. She did remember hearing her mother talk of fertility gods used by people in neighboring countries; maybe this was just her way of ensuring another grandchild. Surely she didn't mean any harm. Before Bathsheba could decide what to do with the little goddess, Rivka walked in the room.

"Shalom, cousin. How does it feel to be a married woman?" Her voice trailed off when she spotted the Asherah.

Bathsheba didn't know if she should try to conceal it or just pretend she didn't know what it was. Fortunately, she didn't have much time to think about it.

"Oh no. This can't be here. Please, Bathsheba, don't bring this thing into my cousin's home. We must get it out of here."

"I, uh, didn't know it was here. I'm so sorry. What should I do with it? I don't want Uriah to be angry."

Rivka's face softened. "It's OK, don't worry. I didn't mean to frighten you. Here, let me take it. I'll just throw it in the fire outside. No one will even know you had it."

Bathsheba was relieved that she didn't have to destroy it. She didn't believe it was anything more than a piece of wood, but it was still a little risky destroying a god.

The two women went outside, and Rivka tossed the idol into the stone oven as though it were nothing more than kindling. That is when Bathsheba noticed the food that had been set out for her. There were two plates with fresh barley loaves, dates, figs, and grapes sitting next to a basket filled with even more food. Her stomach rumbled loudly and both girls laughed.

"What a disappointment I must be, my first morning as a wife, and I don't even prepare food for my own husband."

"Oh, don't worry about him. He and Zabad were stuffing their faces at my fire before I left. He's been taking care of himself for a long time. Anything you do for him he will appreciate, but give yourself time to get settled."

Bathsheba enjoyed the food and company until she saw her husband approaching the house with a very serious look on his face.

Did he know about the Asherah? Was he angry to find her sitting idly by the fire? What could possibly be wrong with him? Rivka noticed the look too and immediately grasped Bathsheba's hand.

"Uriah, what's happened?" Rivka asked.

"The Moabites broke the pact they made with David when they gave his parents asylum from Saul. They are mobilizing their troops for attack. The Lord has instructed David to go out and defeat them. We march in the morning." With that he walked in the house to gather his gear.

"Rivka, what is going on? He can't just leave. Can't he tell the king that he was married just yesterday? Can't he get out of this?"

"Uriah could do that, but he never would. He takes his responsibilities very seriously." She squeezed the young bride's hand. "You don't need to worry about him. He is an incredible soldier; besides, the Lord is leading them into battle, so he is in good hands. Now, I must get home to my husband before he leaves. They will spend the night at the palace gate tonight with the rest of the king's servants. I will come back later to check on you."

Moments later, Uriah came out of the house with his quiver full of arrows and a bow and shield over his shoulder. His chest was covered with armor, and he wore a helmet. It was the first time she had seen him in armor, and it filled her with pride and fear. She had seen her father head off to battle many times, but there was something different about sending her husband off to fight. Without any thought, she ran into his arms. Uriah held her tight for a moment then kissed the top of her head and released her.

"I'll be back soon. If you are afraid to stay alone, you may stay with your mother or Rivka."

"I'm not afraid," Bathsheba answered, sounding braver than she felt. "I will be here when you return." And with that her husband left.

Chapter 4

Bathsheba busied herself around the house for the next few hours. Uriah's home was larger than her father's, but it lacked the homey touches a woman brings. Everything was very clean, but she went through the motions of sweeping the clay floors in both rooms and shaking out the mats just to keep herself occupied. When the afternoon heat made it uncomfortable inside, she moved outdoors to the cooking area. Uriah, or more likely Rivka, had everything neatly organized. She found the grinding stones and barley right away and began making loaves of bread. She didn't realize until she was finished kneading the dough that she wasn't hungry and there was no one else to feed. Not knowing what else to do with her time, she continued with the task and decided she would take dinner to Rivka to repay her kindness. When the small round loaves were baking in the clay oven, she combined lentils, onions, and herbs in a pot she found. She placed this over the fire and waited.

The streets were unusually quiet this evening. She knew the routine well. The night before the soldiers departed for battle was generally spent close to the family. Only the Mighty Thirty, the king's elite fighting men, spent the evening at the palace in preparation for the battle ahead. Her father always remained at home as long as possible. She wondered if her father loved her mother more than Uriah loved her. She tried to suppress the feelings of abandonment that rose up in her heart. He was only doing his duty. She must not take it personally. What did she expect? She had been his wife for only a day; maybe things would change once he grew more attached to her. The conversation she had with her mother on the roof yesterday came back to her. Should she have used her charm to persuade him to stay with her for the night? How would she ever have a baby if he was off at the palace or on the battlefield? She immediately realized how ridiculous these thoughts were. Uriah had been gone a few hours, and she was already worrying about not conceiving a child. She laughed at her own foolishness as she resumed the dinner preparations.

Once everything was ready, she set off to Rivka's house with the warm bread and stew. It took her a moment to decide on the best route to take. She had been to Rivka's house many times, but always from the direction of her parents' house. Bathsheba got her bearings when she noticed the palace on a hill just north of her home. It saddened her to realize how close her husband actually was to her, yet he felt so far away. The first street she approached looked slightly familiar, so she decided to turn left to see if that would get her where she wanted to go. The streets were narrow and lined with houses similar to Uriah's. It was much more congested near the palace than it was farther out of town where her parents lived. Everywhere she looked she saw new buildings in various stages of completion. There had been so many recent changes to the city, it was hard not to get lost. She knew the palace was visible from Rivka's home too, so she kept the hill in sight and made her way through the streets until her surroundings became more familiar.

At last she arrived at Rivka's house, but she was nowhere to be seen. Bathsheba quietly peeked in the door and was surprised to see her friend sleeping soundly on her mat. She didn't want to disturb her, so she started a fire and began setting up the dinner dishes. The short walk and the smell of the food made Bathsheba hungry, so she decided to eat by herself. Halfway through the meal, Rivka stepped out the door and stretched. She saw her friend and smiled, looking a little embarrassed.

"Oh, how long have you been here?" she asked.

"Not long, I didn't want to disturb you, but I brought dinner."

"I'm glad you did. I can't believe how hungry I am. I haven't done a thing since Zabad left this afternoon. I don't know what came over me. I haven't taken a nap in the middle of the day since I was two years old." Rivka took her place by the fire and began to eat heartily. Bathsheba smiled at her friend and finished her meal as well.

"Would you like to stay here tonight so you're not alone in your new house?" Rivka asked while the two women cleaned the dinner dishes.

"Thank you for the offer, but I think I'll go back home. I guess I should get used to being alone if Uriah will be pulled away like this for every battle the king calls him to," Bathsheba answered with just a hint of bitterness in her voice.

Rivka sensed Bathsheba's resentment and tried to soothe her. "It's not so bad, cousin. With the Lord's direction, it will not be a long battle."

"How can you have so much faith, Rivka? Aren't you afraid Zabad will be taken from you?"

"I can't worry about tomorrow. I can only live in the moment and trust that the Lord will take care of things," Rivka replied solemnly.

"But, what about your father and brother? God allowed the Amalekites to take them. And when all you had left was your mother, He took her too." The words burst out of Bathsheba's mouth before she could stop them.

"Yes, but God impressed Uriah to take care of my mother and me until she died. He brought me the love of a good man, Zabad. Tragedy will befall us all at some point in our lives, but with faith, we can endure anything."

"I wish I had faith like that. I've never heard anyone talk of God the way you do. My family is faithful in tithes and sacrifices, but there is nothing more to it than obedience. Why are you so different?"

"Bathsheba, God loves you. He created you. Yes, He wants your obedience, but more than that, He wants your love. He doesn't care about burnt offerings or money. Those things we give Him to show our trust and understanding of His plan."

"What plan?"

"His plan for redemption, of course."

"What's redemption?"

"Well, you know the story Moses told of Adam and Eve, right?"

"Sure, I've heard it since I was a little child—the Garden, the serpent, the Fall. What does that have to do with me?"

"It has everything to do with you. When Adam and Eve sinned, they brought destruction upon themselves and their offspring. The wages of sin is death. But rather than killing Adam and Eve, God allowed them to offer a lamb as a substitute for their blood."

"Yes, I know. And that is why we have to give offerings to the Lord, so we won't be killed."

"No, not exactly. Death is the penalty of sin. But God in His mercy allows us to offer the blood of a lamb rather than our own blood. But, there will come a time when we won't have to sacrifice animals anymore. He will send a Redeemer who will be the Sacrifice for all people."

Bathsheba listened intently. This information was all new to her, and she felt as if a whole new world was opening before her.

Rivka continued, her face glowing, "God told Abraham on the top of Mount Moriah that the Promised Seed would come from his lineage. We are a very privileged people, Bathsheba. The Lord's Lamb will be one of us. One of our children could be the Redeemer of the world."

"Not us, Rivka. Have you forgotten that you and Uriah are Hittites, not Israelites?"

"It doesn't matter. We've accepted God as our Creator and Lord, which makes us His children even if we were not biological descendants of Abraham. Isn't it wonderful? To be a child of Israel means only to be a child of God!"

Rivka's happiness was contagious, and for the first time in her life, Bathsheba felt real peace.

Chapter 5

That night, Bathsheba slept soundly and awoke before dawn feeling refreshed and rested. She quickly washed, dressed, and grabbed a loaf of bread to eat later. She wasted no time heading to the palace gates to catch a glimpse of her husband before the troops marched out against the Moabites. It wasn't the first time she had made this trip. Her family had risen early in the morning to see her father off before battle many times. They usually walked together and said their goodbyes at the gate. Taking the walk alone made her feel homesick for the first time since leaving her parents.

When she reached the gate, she saw several groups standing around waiting. There were little family groups huddled around their men, some hugging, some crying, some praying. There were women standing alone and in clusters. There were soldiers bustling about attending to last minute details. Bathsheba stood alone watching the scene.

The stars were growing dim in the sky, and the crowd began to grow. She spotted her parents in the distance and made her way through the people to get to them. Her father embraced her then held her at arm's length, looking at her as though he hadn't seen her in years.

"Is this our little flower? Could it be you are more beautiful than when we last saw you?"

"Oh, Abba," Bathsheba replied, feeling like a child.

"Shalom, darling," her mother said, taking her turn hugging her daughter. "It sure is quiet around the house without you. Won't you come stay with me now that the men will be leaving?"

"I don't think so, Eema. I'm still trying to settle in. You are welcome to stay at Uriah's house with me if you are lonely."

"I may just do that. I'd like to be closer to the palace anyway in case your sister has her baby. You know the midwife recommended she stay in bed until her time comes. She is having pains too early, and there is some concern the baby will come too soon. Now that Nadav has been made chief baker, I doubt he has much time to spend with her and the boys. We really should go see her—after the men leave, of course."

"My Shiran, remember when you used to weep for me before I went to battle? Now you can't wait to be rid of me so you can get on with your day," Ammiel teased.

"Don't be silly. You know I miss you when you're away. I guess I'm just too old to get worked up over every little battle."

Bathsheba enjoyed watching her parents' playful banter until the sound of trumpets summoned her father to take his place in the ranks. Men quickly kissed their families and scrambled into the gates to find their regiments. Within moments, the procession began. First through the gates came the priests in their linen robes and ephods, their high turbans making them seem taller than the people around them. The musicians followed closely behind blowing their horns and trumpets. Next, riding on a large white horse, came King David dressed for battle. Bathsheba had seen him many times before, but he always stirred in her a feeling of awe. He was a valiant warrior whose victories over giants and men had become legendary, but what Bathsheba admired most about him was his skill as a musician. She had always loved to sing, and many of her favorite songs were written by David. All the women admired him for various reasons—some for his looks, some for his skills, and others for his position of power. Though he already had seven wives, most of the women and girls at the well would have jumped at a chance to be number eight. She saw the looks of adoration on the faces of those around her and knew she wasn't the only one moved by the presence of the king.

The chariots and cavalry followed David in the military procession. Then came the foot soldiers. There were so many of them it took her several minutes to spot Uriah. He was not a tall man, so it was difficult to see him over the others, but at last their eyes met. His face was hard and determined. Any trace of the softness she had seen in his eyes the previous morning had disappeared. He gave her a slight nod then turned his face straight ahead. He was no longer her husband; he was a soldier in King David's army.

Chapter 6

When the men were out of sight and the dust had finally settled, Bathsheba and her mother made their way through the crowd toward the palace. They passed several people they knew and stopped to visit with them on the way. Some of the women gave Bathsheba a look of pity, as if she were the only one who had sent her husband off to war. She tried to ignore them and act as if it didn't bother her to be alone so soon after her wedding.

Once inside the palace gates, the women made their way toward the servant's quarters on the east side of the compound. Though King David was not as extravagant as the rulers of neighboring nations, he still had a lovely palace. All of his servants lived comfortably within his walls. Atarah and her husband Nadav had an attractive home located near the kitchen. Though it was smaller than her house, it was much more beautiful. It was made of stone rather than clay like the homes outside the gates. The floors were covered with tiles instead of mud, which made it feel very luxurious. Her sister had exquisite taste and was able to decorate her home to reflect her love of art and pottery. Unfortunately, her two energetic boys didn't appreciate her fine things and were forever knocking them over. Nadav finally built shelves on the walls for her to display her favorite breakables.

When Bathsheba and Shiran approached the house, a young servant girl they did not recognize greeted them.

"Shalom, may I help you?" she inquired respectfully.

"We are here to see my daughter Atarah," Shiran replied, feeling a little put off that she had to answer to a servant.

"Oh, yes, certainly. The mistress is resting right now, but I'm sure she will see you. Please follow me."

The three entered the home and were immediately greeted by Atarah's two sons.

"Sava, Sava!" they yelled as they jumped into their grandmother's arms. "What did you bring us?"

"Oh, now I have to bring gifts every time I want to visit my grandsons? You don't love your Sava, only the sweets I bring," Shiran pretended to pout, but the children hugged and kissed her until she laughed and pulled out the bundle of honey cakes she had brought.

"What am I, invisible? I don't bring treats, so I don't get hugs!" Bathsheba teased the boys. They rewarded her with smothering kisses.

"Eema, Bathsheba, is that you?" called Atarah from the back room. "Please send the children out to the courtyard with the maid so that we can have some peace."

The young servant quickly gathered the children, nodded respectfully to her mistress's family, and left the house. A sudden quiet filled the space when the door closed behind them. Once in the back room, Shiran and Bathsheba were able to sit comfortably and visit with Atarah. Previously she had had a voluptuous figure, but now she was just plain round. She looked so miserable trying to position herself on her mat so she could see her guests over her belly, that Bathsheba felt sorry for her. She quickly went to her to try to help but was brushed away by her impatient and moody sister.

"How are you feeling, darling?" her mother asked.

"How do you think I'm feeling, Eema?" she answered tersely.

"I've brought you some herbs to help give you comfort."

"If I have to drink one more of those silly potions, I just don't know what I'll do." Atarah sounded as if she might cry. "That midwife is in here every day trying to force that stuff down my throat. And making me lay here all day. I feel like I'm going to go crazy."

Bathsheba didn't understand why her sister was getting so emotional over an herbal drink, but she refrained from saying anything.

"Darling," her mother tried to soothe her, "you have the best midwife in the country. She attends queens and princesses. How fortunate you are to have her. Please listen to her and try to be patient. It will all be over soon enough."

"I know, Eema. I'm sorry. I just get upset so easily these days. I don't know what is wrong with me. I don't remember getting so emotional when I had the boys."

"Oh, it must mean you are going to have a daughter. I was very sensitive with both of you girls."

Bathsheba thought the whole conversation was getting ridiculous, so she decided to turn it in a different direction.

"We missed you at the wedding, Atarah. I'm so sorry you were unable to attend."

"Yes, I'm sorry too. Nadav had a lovely time and brought back all the details for me. He was a bit drunk though, so I don't know how accurate his retelling was," Atarah joked.

Bathsheba was glad to see her sister happy again, even though she wasn't sure how long it would last.

"How does Nadav like his new position?" Bathsheba asked.

"Oh, he's happy with it. It really isn't much of a change in his duties, just his title. He has been running things in the bakery for a long time. I'm just glad he is finally getting noticed for it."

Just then, what looked like a small pile of wool in the corner got to its feet and walked over to Bathsheba, making her jump.

"What is that?" Shiran exclaimed.

"What does it look like? It's a lamb, of course," Atarah replied, laughing at the women's reaction.

"Yes, I know it's a lamb, but where did it come from?" Shiran replied, irritated by her daughter's response.

"That husband of mine! You think I have two children; well, it's more like three the way he acts sometimes. For some reason, the lamb's mother rejected her. She was too small and sickly to be any good to the butcher, so Nadav brought her home to me. He said he thought she would keep me company while I'm waiting for the baby. Silly man! That's all I need, something else to take care of! The poor little thing is terrified of the children, and it stays huddled there in the corner most of the time. I guess I'll just give it back to the butcher to see if he can use it for soup or something."

"Oh no, please!" Bathsheba exclaimed without thinking. "Let me take her home. I'm sure Uriah wouldn't mind if I had a pet to keep me company while he's gone."

"Fine with me," answered Atarah. "There is a jug of sheep's milk in the corner. You have to hand feed her until she is able to take care of herself."

Bathsheba found a rag and dipped the corner into the jug. The lamb licked the dripping milk from the rag and tried her best to grab hold of it between her lips. Bathsheba laughed and felt an immediate connection to the little creature.

She held the lamb on her lap while the women visited and chatted about the latest news. Exciting things happened at the palace all the time, and Atarah always knew what was going on. There were so many princes and princesses and queens, it was difficult for Bathsheba to keep track. Her mind wandered back to her conversation with Rivka. She wanted to talk to her mother about the idol, but didn't know how to bring it up. She waited for a break in the conversation and then ventured a question.

"I have to ask you both something," she said tentatively. "Do you believe in the God of our forefathers?"

"Sure." They both replied automatically.

"No, I mean it. Do you really believe that He is the Creator of all? That He is really all powerful?"

Her mother looked over her shoulder to make sure they were alone before she replied, "All I know is there were times in my life when I needed Him, and He was not there for me. My Eema, that evil woman, warned me countless times that His eyes were always on me, just waiting for me to sin so He could punish me. I know it's not true, because I would have been killed ten times over if it were." She tried to laugh to lighten her words, but it sounded forced.

"You don't pray to idols, do you, Eema?" Bathsheba asked, hoping not to push it too far.

"I wouldn't say I pray to them really, but I have a few stashed around here and there. It can't hurt, right? Are you asking this because you found the Asherah I sent you? It's really harmless, dear; don't get worked up over it. I have a friend who prayed to her and made loaves of bread in her image when she couldn't conceive and it worked for her. I just thought it would be nice if you and Uriah could start a family right away, like your sister, that's all. It's no big deal."

"It's not just that, Eema. It's just something Rivka told me, about God caring for us and wanting our love and obedience. I just wondered what you thought about it."

Atarah was obviously getting uncomfortable, not just with the conversation, but with her bulky abdomen as well. Bathsheba dropped the subject, set her sleeping pet on her mother's lap, and went to help her sister. This time she was allowed to help roll her onto her other side. Her eyelids were getting heavy, and it was apparent that she needed to rest. The two women took the lamb and the jug of sheep's milk and stepped outside.

"Darling, if you are sure you are going to be all right by yourself, I think I will stay here with your sister. I have a feeling that baby will arrive any day now. Perhaps I can be of some assistance to the midwife. The poor thing will probably need as much help as she can get."

"Who, the midwife or Atarah?" Bathsheba laughed. "Don't worry about me; I'll be fine, Eema. Besides, I won't be alone. I'll have my little friend here to keep me company." She wrapped the animal into her robes like a mother swaddles her baby. "That's what I'll call her, Adina, my gentle little friend."

Her mother kissed her cheek and returned to the house. Bathsheba and her new companion headed home for the first of many evenings alone.

Chapter 7

The days passed slowly. Bathsheba kept herself occupied by visiting her family and her friend, Rivka, who didn't seem to have much energy lately. She took frequent trips to the market, mostly just to look at the new items brought in by the traveling caravans. Sometimes she purchased things for her home, hoping Uriah would not want to leave her again so soon if she could make his house more comfortable. Her little lamb, Adina, required a lot of her time as well. She was glad to have the distraction and the company. Sometimes her mother would come spend the day with her when she couldn't bear the noise and chaos at Atarah's house. Bathsheba occasionally felt annoyed with her mother for dropping by so often without warning, but it gave her the incentive she needed to prepare regular meals, just in case she had another mouth to feed.

One evening, after Bathsheba and her mother finished eating dinner and cleaning up the dishes, they went to the roof to enjoy the breeze. The sun was nearing the western horizon, and the sky was glowing with pinks and oranges. Bathsheba loved to spend her evenings on the flat roof, playing with her lamb and watching the sunset. Uriah's house was set back from the road slightly, so the roof was very private. The people below could only be seen if she stood right by the edge, which she never did for fear of falling off. She was able to set up a comfortable sitting area in the center of the roof, which afforded her a beautiful view of the palace above and kept Adina a safe distance from danger.

"You've made your home quite lovely, Bathsheba," her mother commented as the two reclined on the comfortable new cushions. "You seem to be in a hurry to get it decorated, though. Shouldn't you wait until Uriah comes home before you make too many changes? He may be angry with you for spending so much money without discussing it with him first."

"He doesn't seem like the type to get angry about money, Eema."

"How can you know what type he is? You didn't even get to spend a full day with him before he left. I heard he went off the night before battle and slept at the palace. Did you do something to displease him?"

"No, Eema. He is one of David's Mighty Thirty. It's what they do. Rivka's husband does the same thing before battle."

"I would never allow such a thing. Your Abba is one of the best soldiers out there, but he spends his last night sleeping with me, not praying with the king."

"What can I do? I'm only a woman."

"Only a woman, hah! Have you forgotten everything I told you? You have more power than you think. You could make that man do anything just by batting your eyes at him. Trust your old Eema; I know what I'm talking about."

"It's only one night. Why should I bother him with such a little thing?"

"Bathsheba! How will you ever have a child with that attitude? You must keep your man close to you. If he was so eager to leave his fresh new bride, what will happen when he has tired of you? You must get a better hold on your husband, or he will never give you a baby."

Shiran's words stung like a slap. Bathsheba picked up Adina and nuzzled her close to her face, using the soft wool to wipe away the tears she could not hold back.

"I don't mean to upset you, my little flower. I only want to see you happy. You must help Uriah understand that he is no longer a bachelor. You must become his first priority. Nothing should be more important to him than his beautiful wife." She rose from her cushion and kissed her daughter's head. "Now, I had better get back to your sister. Hopefully those wild children of hers are tucked into bed so I can get some sleep. I'll send word if she has the baby so you can come see her."

Shiran proceeded down the stairs looking over her shoulder once to see the breathtaking figure of her daughter bathed in early moonlight. She felt a twinge of jealousy rising in her heart but quickly pushed it down. She would do better for her daughter than her mother had done for her. After all, she had made an oath.

Chapter 8

Early one morning, a messenger came to her door. He was a young boy, barely ten years old, wearing the robe of a royal messenger. It was much too big for him, making him look absurd. For a moment, Bathsheba's heart sank, thinking the message was bad news about her husband, but when she looked at the boy, she knew he would not be the one to carry such a message.

"Shalom, Ma'am, I have a message from your sister, Atarah." He bowed to her respectfully as he spoke. She almost started to laugh at him because he really wasn't much younger than she, and here he was calling her ma'am. But instead of laughing, she played along.

"Speak, boy," she said in her haughtiest voice.

"Your third nephew arrived before dawn this morning. Your sister and mother request your presence at the palace at your earliest convenience." He bowed again, then departed in a very royal fashion. She smiled at the boy's back as he marched away.

Now that Adina was getting bigger, she could take care of herself for a few hours. Bathsheba found a rope to tie around her neck and put her outside with a bowl of water and some scraps of food. As she walked away toward the palace, she heard the lamb cry for her a few times. Bathsheba almost turned around to go back for her, but knew she had to leave her alone eventually.

In no time at all, she reached her sister's home, which was bustling with activity. The boys were pulling the young maid in circles, but they stopped spinning when they saw her approach.

"Shalom, little ones. I hear you have a new brother today," she said as she hugged the children.

"Yes, but he's very ugly," Kaleb, the younger of the two said.

"You can't say stuff like that; you were ugly, too, when you were born, and I didn't go around telling everybody!" his older brother, Jotham rebuked.

"Now boys, I'm sure he's beautiful, just like you both were when you were born. I'm going to go see him and your mother. You give this poor maid a break and go play in the courtyard for a while. I'll see you later." The servant girl smiled at her gratefully as the boys ran off.

When she got past the women milling about in the sitting room and approached her sister's sleeping mat, the picture she saw overwhelmed her. Atarah sat propped against the wall, looking absolutely radiant. Her newborn son lay against her breast gazing up at her with his glassy gray eyes. Her husband, Nadav, sat by her side looking as if he would burst from pride. Her mother was bustling about the room, preparing another of her famous herbal drinks.

"Come, Bathsheba, look at our boy!" Nadav's deep voice bellowed. "Three sons! Can you believe it? What a rich man I am. What a good wife your sister is, giving me a quiver full of boys!"

She looked at her nephew. He was pink and wrinkly with a full head of dark hair sticking up in every direction.

"Isn't he the most beautiful baby you've ever seen?" boomed Nadav.

"Yes, he is," she replied softly. "He most certainly is."

"Nadav, you should go back to work. This is no place for a man. You can go back to the kitchen and crow all you want there," Atarah teased her husband. He took her advice and left, but not before kissing every woman he passed on his way out. They all giggled at the proud father, but deep down, Bathsheba felt empty. Would Uriah behave like that if she were ever able to give him a son? Would he ever love her so openly?

The day drew on, and she knew her sister needed rest, so Bathsheba decided to leave. She didn't really have anything to do, so she took her time walking through the palace grounds on her way out. Certain areas were forbidden to visitors, and guards stood by to ensure no one went where they weren't allowed. Of course, the guards were mostly gray-haired, tired men who were too old to go to battle, but no one challenged them. There was a small kitchen garden near her sister's house filled mostly with herbs and vegetables, but she followed the path into a larger garden she had never seen before. Overhead, there were almond trees in full bloom. Along the path, she saw lily of the valley and rose of Sharon almost ready to display their flowers as well. Shrubs of camphire, or henna, grew wild along the edge of the garden, producing a smell sweet enough to be made into perfume for queens. It was the most beautiful place she had ever seen. Occasionally a well-dressed woman would stroll past her. She saw eunuchs in various places around the garden and realized she had wandered into the women's quarters by mistake. She envied the women who lived here and had this garden to walk in every day. Filling her lungs one more time with the scents that surrounded her, she walked back down the path to more familiar grounds.

As she was leaving the palace, she heard a commotion coming from the area surrounding the watchtower. Something exciting was happening and the word seemed to spread from the guards to the people passing by. She tried to get information from those around her, but everyone was so agitated it was hard to get a straight answer. Finally, a woman near her yelled, "They're back! King David and his men have returned from battle!" A shout rose from the others nearby, and before long a crowd had gathered. She couldn't have left the mob if she wanted to, so she stayed where she was, waiting to find out more. Before long, she heard the sound of men on horseback shouting cries of victory. King David and his commander in chief and nephew, Joab, rode side by side through the parting crowd. David held his sword over his head and shouted, "The Lord has done great things through His people! The defeated Moabites have surrendered and are now subject to Israel. Shout praises to the Lord Most High! To Him give all the glory!"

The people raised their hands in the air and shouted, "Glory to God in the highest!" Some men leaped and danced for joy. Others sang and rejoiced. The king spurred his horse on as the rest of his victorious army followed him home.

Bathsheba craned her neck to try to catch a glimpse of Uriah. She saw Rivka's husband, Zabad, who usually fought alongside Uriah, but there was no sign of her husband. A sick knot started forming in the pit of her stomach. Just when she thought she was about to collapse, Bathsheba saw him walking toward her, looking very stern. She wanted to run to him, but felt suddenly awkward. Instead, she greeted him as she would a stranger, which aside from one night together, is really what they were. "Shalom, husband. Welcome home."

"Oh, Bathsheba, I've missed you," he said breathlessly, his hard exterior crumbling before her eyes. He reached out his arms to her, and she gratefully took her place against his chest. After a short embrace, he took hold of her upper arms and held her out in front of him so they were standing face to face. "I have some sad news for you, my lamb," he said, looking serious again. "Your father was killed by an enemy sword. I was not in his regiment, but am told he died bravely and was able to kill several Moabites before he fell."

Bathsheba's legs went limp, and she would have crumpled to the ground if Uriah hadn't been holding her arms. Unable to speak or even cry, she just stood there looking into the soft brown eyes of her husband.

"I personally saw to his body on the journey home. It is outside the city walls and will be prepared for burial first thing tomorrow. I sent a man to your father's home to inform your mother, and I've made arrangements . . ."

"Eema!" she exclaimed interrupting Uriah's carefully thought-out words. "She's not at home; she is with Atarah and the new baby. Oh, what will become of my Eema? With no sons to care for her, she will surly be turned out by one of my uncles. Oh, poor Eema."

"Darling, don't worry about a thing. We will bring her home with us. I will take care of her. She is my family now, just as you are."

"Uriah, you are too kind. What did I do to deserve such a man? I know you are eager to get home, so please go ahead. I should go to my sister's house to tell them what happened, so they don't have to hear it from a stranger."

"It is too heavy a burden for you to bear alone. I will go with you and tell them, if you would like. A few more hours away from my fire will not hurt me, especially since I am by your side. You are my home now."

Bathsheba fell into his arms again, now weeping openly. She remembered what Rivka said about the Lord taking care of His people even in times of tragedy. Even in her despair, she felt safe in Uriah's arms. Surely the Lord was with her, giving her strength to endure this.

Uriah gently led his wife through the palace to the homes nearest the kitchen, and then he let her take over, because he wasn't sure which door to go to. When Bathsheba's knock was answered by the young maid, she was unable to speak. Uriah stepped up and asked the maid to bring Shiran outside. In a moment the woman appeared at the door. When she saw the couple before her, she smiled broadly but immediately looked past them to find her husband.

"Shiran, he is not here," Uriah spoke calmly.

"Oh yes, of course, he does not know about the baby. He must be at home." She turned to gather her belongings so she could leave, but Uriah stopped her.

"I'm afraid he did not make it this time, Shiran."

"What? Of course he did. He's been fighting for years. You don't know what you're talking about, Uriah! Where is my husband?" She was starting to shake and lose control.

"Eema, he is dead," Bathsheba said plainly, as she took her mother in her arms.

Her mother cried uncontrollably for several minutes. When she finally stopped, her grief had turned to anger.

"How could you let this happen, Uriah? You were supposed to be his friend. Where were you when my husband was killed? Where were you?" She screamed in his face. "And where was the mighty King David? How many men have to die serving him? Didn't he say the Lord was leading them to victory? What kind of God leads good men into battle only to let them fall to those wicked heathens?" Uriah tried to move her back indoors to protect her from the stares of the crowd that was starting to gather, but this only made her angrier. "Let go of me, Uriah; get your hands off of me. I'm going to see the king! He sent my husband to his death, and he has to answer to me!"

This was too much for Uriah. "Silence, Shiran. Do not let your grief take over your better senses. You must not speak of King David like that within his own walls."

Shiran stopped abruptly and stared at Uriah, her dark eyes full of fury. "Get out of my sight. I never want to see your ugly scarred face again." She spat at him and turned to enter the house.

After being stopped briefly at the palace kitchen, Uriah and Bathsheba walked home together in silence. He left her for a moment to speak to a soldier on the street but soon returned to her. How was he able to behave normally after what just happened? Bathsheba had never seen her mother so hysterical. She grieved not only for her lost father, but now for her lost mother as well. How could she live her life torn between parent and husband? Uriah seemed absorbed in his own thoughts as well. It was impossible to tell if he was suffering from the death of his friend or from the harsh words spoken to him by his mother-in-law. They both kept their feelings to themselves.

Neither of them was in the mood to deal with what they found when they got home. Adina had been very busy in their absence. She had managed to chew a hole in a sack of barley and made a terrible mess in the process. She had fallen asleep in the pile of scattered grain, getting the pieces stuck in her thick wool. Under other circumstances, it would have been a comical sight to see her look up at them with her big sleepy eyes, her face all spotted with grain. But, the couple did not see the humor in it, especially Uriah.

"What is that little beast doing here?" he exclaimed, rushing to scoop up the lamb to get it away from his house.

"Uriah, no! She is my pet. My sister gave her to me. Please don't hurt her."

"Your pet!" he practically shouted at her. "I don't want this creature in my house! Get it out of here!"

She was about to react with tears and begging, but she stopped herself and thought about her mother. She couldn't stand the thought of losing Adina, so she turned on the charm to convince her husband to let her stay. She lowered her eyes and stuck her lower lip out just a bit. She gracefully moved toward him and put her hand on his arm.

"Darling, I was so lonely without you. I needed someone to keep me company. What will I do if you are called away again? I just can't bear to be alone. Please let my little Adina stay." She nuzzled up against him and felt his body relax slightly. "Just think," she purred, "when we have children someday, they will have fresh sheep's milk to drink."

He gently set the lamb down then kissed his wife's cheek. "All right. I suppose you can keep her. I guess it would be nice to have fresh milk. Just try to prevent these messes in the future. I'm going to get cleaned up, and you should do the same. We will host the funeral meal here tomorrow evening."

"What? How can we host it after what Eema just said to you?" she said, unable to enjoy her victory.

"Who else is going to do it? Your sister just had a baby and can't leave the house during her time of purification, and your mother is obviously in no condition. I made arrangements before we left the palace," Uriah explained.

"You mean even after she talked to you like that and humiliated you in front of all those people, you are still willing to help her?" Bathsheba couldn't hide her surprise.

"How can I expect forgiveness if I am not willing to forgive others?" Uriah said calmly and walked into the house.

Chapter 9

Bathsheba awoke before dawn the next day. Rather than washing in the usual way, she observed the traditions of mourning and only did what was hygienically necessary. She dressed in sackcloth instead of her linen robe and left her head and feet bare. Uriah, being a faithful Jew, also respected the mourning period. Knowing he could not have relations with his wife for a week after her father's death, he moved his sleeping mat into the other room. She went in to wake him, but found he was already dressed and ready to go. He took care of a few last-minute details while she saw to Adina. This time Bathsheba was sure to find a better place to tie the lamb before leaving her alone all day. Once everything was in order, the two walked together in the direction of the palace. Uriah left her at the gate for a few moments and returned with the group of hired mourners. When they saw her, they began to wail and cry dutifully. There were several soldiers with their families who came to show their respect as well. Then Bathsheba saw her brother-in-law, Nadav, and her grandfather, Ahithophel, walking on either side of her mother. She wanted to run to her mother and give her comfort, but the look on Shiran's face told her this was not the time.

Just outside the walls of Jerusalem, they found a small band of soldiers who had the body already prepared for burial, as Uriah had instructed them. There lay her father, motionless, covered completely in grave clothes. A litter had been made on which to carry his body the short distance to the Kindron Valley, where King David had tombs reserved for his honored soldiers. The procession renewed its wailing and headed east toward the caves.

During the journey, some of the mourners sang songs. They were sad, solemn songs, but there was an underlying message of faith in God that kept Bathsheba from breaking down. She also found strength in the quiet dignity of her husband, who walked by her side. She was still amazed that he would do so much for her family, especially after he had been treated so poorly. Her mother did not look in their direction at all during the walk. Of course, she did not really look at anyone. Bathsheba had never seen her look so old and frail as she walked slowly between the two men at the head of the procession. Her mother had told her once that she did not love her father, but looking at her now, Bathsheba found that hard to believe.

A few hours later, the group reached the mouth of the family cave. Her grandfather stepped forward and said a few words about his son. He offered a prayer, and then the soldiers took the body inside and buried him with his ancestors. Once the large stone covered the entrance, the wailing began again with new fervor. This time Bathsheba joined in, not because she had to, but because she was filled with genuine grief.

When they returned to Uriah's home that afternoon, Rivka was waiting for them by the fire. The food had been delivered from the palace kitchen, and her friend had it all set out for her, waiting for the guests to start arriving. Bathsheba was exhausted after the long day, and she was so grateful to have this one task taken care of.

"Oh, cousin, I am so sorry for your loss. I am also sorry I could not go to the tomb with you today, but I was not feeling well this morning. I hope I can make it up to you by helping with the feast," Rivka said as she hugged her friend affectionately.

"Please don't do so much, Rivka. If you are ill, you don't have to stay here and help me."

"Oh, I'll be fine. Whatever is wrong with me seems to come and go, and I feel just fine now. Besides, I would feel ashamed if I could not be of help to you today."

With that settled, the two women busied themselves until the first guests arrived.

Bathsheba was shocked to see her grandfather and mother approach the house first. Ahithophel led Shiran to a place by the fire and set her down in a rather gruff manner. It was obvious it took a great deal of persuading to get Shiran to come, but she was there, and that made Bathsheba feel hopeful.

"Ah, my little Bathsheba," Ahithophel said as he embraced his granddaughter. "You look tired, dear. You should go sit by your Eema and rest for a few minutes. It will be a while before the mourners arrive. I think I will go have a talk with your husband. If you ladies will excuse me," he said as he made his departure into the house.

Bathsheba took a seat next to the fire but did not know what to say to her mother. Both women sat in silence. Rivka excused herself for a few minutes to find her husband.

Shiran begrudgingly spoke first, "I, uh, I don't know what to say, Bathsheba. My behavior yesterday was unacceptable. Can you find it in your heart to forgive me?"

"Oh, Eema, of course. I was never angry with you! It's just Uriah . . . It hurt to hear you speak to him in such a way. He doesn't seem angry with you either, but Eema, he is really the one you should apologize to."

Before Shiran could reply, a small group of guests arrived. When Ahithophel and Uriah heard the men's voices outside, they came out to join the group. Everyone sat around on the mats that had been prepared for them while Bathsheba served the food. Rivka returned and helped with the handwashing. Then Uriah offered a prayer for the meal. It was the duty of the family to make the guests feel comfortable, and since her mother looked so sullen, Bathsheba had to work extra hard to keep the conversation light. More people arrived and the mood of the group eventually became less somber. Men told stories about the mischief Ammiel had gotten into in his younger days. Others talked about his bravery in battle. There were some tears, but mostly just happy reminiscing.

After the last guest left, Rivka and Bathsheba began cleaning up. Shiran had spent the day sitting quietly observing those around her, but not saying or doing much else. Both of the young women were surprised when she got up from her seat and helped them with the dishes.

"Your Abba, he was a good man, wasn't he?" she stated quietly while the three worked.

"Yes, Eema, he was a very good man. He was loved by many."

"Yes, he was loved," Shiran replied simply. This brought tears to both of their eyes, and they held each other and cried for a few minutes feeling completely reconciled.

"Eema, where will you stay?" Bathsheba asked after the tears had subsided.

"Well, I guess I will go home. There is no room for me at Atarah's house and there is no peace for me there either. It will be nice to go home."

"But, Eema, won't you be lonely there?"

"No, I will have my memories to keep me company. I want to be surrounded by the things I shared with your Abba."

"Won't you stay here with us? I'm worried about you."

Shiran laughed bitterly. "Flower, you may think a great deal of your Uriah, but no man would allow a woman to stay under his roof after she spoke to him the way I did."

"Oh, but he would, Shiran," Rivka jumped into the conversation. "Uriah is a very forgiving man. I can assure you, he harbors no ill feelings toward you."

"How would you know, Rivka?"

"I have known him all of my life. He is not a perfect man, but he knows the Lord has forgiven him much. How could he not forgive your little imperfections?"

"You are both naive girls. Besides, even if Uriah is so willing to forgive, perhaps I'm not."

Chapter 10

The week of mourning passed quickly. Bathsheba spent her days visiting her sister and making sure her mother had food and water. The time she did have at home was spent receiving guests who stopped by to offer condolences. As the sun was setting on the seventh day after her father's death, she finally sat down with Uriah to enjoy some peace and quiet. The official mourning was finally over. All Bathsheba could think about was taking a bath and washing the week of grief off of her skin. She tried to think of a place she could go where she could have privacy, not just from the crowded streets, but from her new husband as well. They still behaved like strangers most of the time, so she did not know how to broach the subject. Uriah sensed she had something to say, so he broke the silence.

"Is there anything you need, my lamb?" he asked kindly.

"Well, there is something, but I'm not sure if it's even possible."

"What is it?"

"I would really like to take a bath, but, I'd like to be . . ." she hesitated for a moment.

"You'd like to be alone, of course." He finished her thought. He looked around for a moment trying to decide the best way to accommodate her.

"Would it be possible to take some water and a tub to the roof? I know it sounds silly, but it's one of my favorite places, and it's very private," she asked shyly.

"Yes, of course. I'll take care of everything," he answered, jumping up to get the jars of water inside the door.

They heated some water over the fire, then the two of them carried up the supplies she would need for her bath. Apparently, he hadn't been on the roof since his return from battle because he looked surprised to see all the changes she had made.

"Where did all of these things come from?" he asked, sounding a bit confused.

"Oh, I bought them in the market while you were gone. You didn't seem to mind the little changes I made inside the house. Does this bother you?" she asked, trying to sound innocent.

"No, it's just so much. How did you pay for it?"

"Easy. I just told them I was the wife of Uriah the Hittite, one of King David's soldiers, and that you were off at war. They were very accommodating and opened accounts for me in your name."

"Bathsheba, I am not a rich man. How will I pay for all of this?"

She picked up the strain in his voice and decided this would be a good time to put her mother's advice to practice. "Oh, husband. I'm so sorry I've displeased you." She watched his face carefully for signs of softening and when she saw none, she tried harder. "Please don't be cross with me, not tonight. It will be our first night together since our wedding, and I just couldn't bear it if you were angry." She saw the effect this was having on Uriah, and she enjoyed her power. She poured water into her small tub, lifting the sleeve of her sackcloth robe so it wouldn't get wet. His eyes traveled to the soft skin of her wrist. "It must have been a difficult week for you, having to sleep all alone. I know it was not easy for me." He seemed to melt with each word she spoke. She let her hair slip gently over her shoulders as she moved closer to him. "Now, let's not fight over a few cushions. Why don't you go downstairs and move your mat next to mine, and I'll be down in just a few minutes."

Uriah nodded and started down the stairs. When he had left, Bathsheba almost laughed out loud. She couldn't believe how much fun that was. She had turned that strong soldier into a lump of soft clay in her hands. Her mother was right. She did have power in her home. If she could control Uriah so easily, she wondered what else she was capable of. The notion frightened her for a moment, so she redirected her thoughts to her bath. She slipped off the scratchy robe she had been wearing all week and lowered herself into the tub of warm shallow water. All of her worries seemed to slip away as she sat looking up at the early stars twinkling overhead. She lingered in her bath as long as she was able. The night air grew cooler, and she knew she would have to return to the realities that awaited her downstairs. She suddenly felt frightened of what she may have started with Uriah. For the first time, she realized the game she played with him would have to end sometime, and the time was now. She dressed in a clean linen robe and slowly descended the stairs. She hoped she would find him asleep, but knew she wouldn't. She wasn't sure what she was afraid of. Uriah had never been anything but kind and gentle with her, but she had never tried to stir his passions before either. Would she find he had turned into a beast waiting to attack her? She pushed down her fears and quietly entered the house. She reminded herself that this was her husband, her sweet husband with the soft brown eyes. He could never hurt her. She listened carefully to his breathing to determine if he was still awake. He didn't move or speak, but she could tell he had not fallen asleep. She waited for him to jump up and grab her, but he didn't. He just waited patiently for her to lie down next to him. She felt the strangest mixture of relief and disappointment when she realized he was still in control of himself. She had not driven him out of his mind with desire. Perhaps she had overestimated herself.

Chapter 11

Bathsheba enjoyed a few quiet days of married life until early one morning she heard a knock at the door. She was surprised to see her grandfather and mother standing there. Her mother had torn her robe, and her soot-covered face was streaked with tears. When she saw Bathsheba, she threw herself on the ground and grabbed her daughter's ankles weeping loudly.

"Oh, Shiran, get up!" Ahithophel snapped. "Stop being so dramatic." It was obvious he was annoyed at having to deal with all this excitement so early in the morning.

"What is going on?" Bathsheba asked, showing obvious concern for her mother.

"It was just a matter of time. We all knew it would happen sooner or later. Why she has to carry on so, is beyond me," Ahithophel answered.

"Sav, what happened? Please tell me." Now it was Bathsheba's turn to get annoyed.

"Your cousin, Barak, and his family arrived from Arad this morning. As you know, your uncle has several sons, and the property of your father now belongs to them. They are staying with me at the palace until we can get Shiran's things moved out."

Her mother spoke for the first time, "Oh, what will become of me? A poor widow with no man to care for her. I'll be turned out onto the streets."

"That's enough, Shiran. Uriah has offered to take you in. I spoke to him about it days ago. Now stop howling before you wake the neighbors," Ahithophel snapped.

Uriah heard the commotion and came to the door. "Shalom, family. Please come in and make yourselves comfortable. I will get you some bread while Bathsheba washes your feet."

The small group sat on mats in the sitting room while Bathsheba cared for her guests. The footwashing seemed to calm their nerves a little. When everyone had cleaned their hands, Uriah blessed the food, and the four of them nibbled on day-old bread.

"Shiran, I am sorry this has happened to you, but you are welcome to live here with us," Uriah said gently. "I have already given it much thought. You can either sleep here in this room, or we can build you a shelter on the roof—wherever you would be more comfortable."

Bathsheba held her breath, not knowing if her mother would spit at him in anger or throw herself at his feet. Shiran did neither. She sat quietly, obviously planning her next move. After a moment, she spoke calmly. "All right, Uriah. I accept your offer. I will sleep on the roof."

Bathsheba almost expected Uriah to thank her, but he didn't. He simply continued eating his breakfast in silence. She was a bit stunned at her mother's lack of appreciation and gratitude. Was she still nursing a grudge against Uriah? Did she really hold him responsible for Ammiel's death? Fortunately, her grandfather was more polite.

"Uriah, you have done a wonderful thing. It is very kind of you to take this poor woman under your care. May the Lord bless you for your compassion." No sooner did her grandfather finish his sentence than her mother was up and headed for the door.

"I am going home to gather my belongings. I will send them over later. I'll spend the night there to give you time to prepare my room." Without another word, she left.

Bathsheba and the two men sat in stunned silence for a few minutes. Then Uriah and Ahithophel began making preparations for the shelter. Bathsheba considered going to her mother's house to help her, but then decided against it. She was feeling hurt and confused by her behavior and just didn't know what she would say to her. Instead, she went to Rivka's house so she could be out of the men's way while they worked.

When Bathsheba approached her friend's house, she saw Rivka and her husband, Zabad, eating breakfast by the fire.

"Shalom, cousin, join us," Rivka called out to her.

"Oh, no thank you. I've already eaten," she responded.

"You sure have an early start on the day," Zabad teased.

Bathsheba told them both about the events of the morning. Zabad finished eating, kissed his wife, and left to go help build the shelter. Bathsheba expressed her gratitude as he departed.

"You look sad, cousin. Are you upset about your mother's staying with you?"

"No, it's not that. I just don't understand why she is so unkind to Uriah. She yelled and screamed at him when he told her of my Abba's death. She spat on him and humiliated him in front of the palace servants. Now she acts as though she is doing him a favor by moving into his house. I don't imagine things are going to be very comfortable with the two of them under the same roof."

"Uriah will be kind to her," Rivka answered gently.

"Yes, I'm sure he will. But the question is, will she be kind to him?"

Chapter 12

The men erected a small open tent on the roof, just large enough to cover Shiran's sleeping mat. This gave her the shelter she would need to protect her from the hot afternoon sun but a large enough open area to sit and enjoy the breeze. It must have been comfortable enough because when Uriah was home, Shiran spent most of her time there. Uriah didn't seem to mind the silent treatment. In fact, it almost seemed that he would rather not have to deal with Shiran. Bathsheba decided to leave it alone and see if her mother's behavior would improve with time.

The men spent several hours a day at the palace, either discussing fortification of the city or just keeping their skills sharp in case they had to go to battle again. Uriah also went to the tent that housed the ark of the Lord every day to pray. This gave the women plenty of time to visit. Rivka had good days and bad days, but when she was feeling well, she liked to call on Bathsheba and her mother. One morning, after breakfast, Rivka approached the house looking quite healthy.

"Shalom, ladies," she said merrily.

"Shalom, cousin. You look wonderful this morning. What have you done to yourself?" Bathsheba asked.

"I don't know what you mean," she replied with a slight smile on her face.

"Rivka, you're positively glowing. Do you have news for us?" Shiran asked, seeming to already know what was going on.

Bathsheba felt as if she had missed something very obvious. "What is it? What do you two know that I don't know?" she said, feeling like a child left out of a game.

"Oh, cousin, I'm going to have a baby! I've been feeling so poorly for the last few weeks. I finally figured out what was going on and called for the midwife. She said the child should arrive by the end of the year."

"Rivka, that's wonderful!" Bathsheba exclaimed, hugging her friend.

"Yes, Rivka, congratulations. I'm very happy for you," Shiran added. "Now, Bathsheba, when are we going to get some good news from you?"

"Eema! I've only been married a few weeks. Besides, this is hardly the time," she scolded.

"Yes dear, you're right. I'm sorry. Now, let me think if I have anything I can make for you, Rivka." She rummaged through a small box of herbs she kept near the kitchen supplies. "Ah, yes. This will get you through the next few weeks until the sickness passes." She steeped what looked like dried leaves in a small jar of warm water and gave it to Rivka to drink. "If you can't stand the taste, just add some honey to it."

Rivka drank obediently, trying hard not to make a face. When Bathsheba saw her friend struggling, she quickly got the little pot of honey and dripped some into her cup. "Thank you, Shiran. It's delicious," she said, trying hard to make it sound convincing.

"Now for you, my daughter. Yes, here it is," she said as she went back to her box of potions. "Mandrake root! This should do the trick."

"What trick, Eema?" Bathsheba asked, sounding a bit frightened.

"Sometimes a woman just needs a little help, that's all," Shiran answered cryptically.

"Help with what?"

"Well, you want a baby, too, don't you?"

"Of course I do, Eema, but please just give it time. Besides, drinking that stuff is not going to get me a baby!"

"But it could help. There are plenty of things a woman can do to help things along a little bit." When she saw she had her daughter's attention, Shiran continued. "If you watch the moon to keep track of your cycle and drink this root, you'll find yourself glowing too, my flower."

"Shiran, the Lord will provide Bathsheba with a child in His own good time," Rivka said as respectfully as she could.

"Yes, yes, but what if He is too busy to be bothered? I would hate to see my little Bathsheba in the same predicament as me, with no sons to care for her. Besides, what if something were to happen to Uriah? We would both be homeless. If I had a grandson, I know I would be safe. And so would my daughter," Shiran added quickly.

Bathsheba took the cup her mother offered her and drank it without further argument. As the warm liquid slid down her throat, she silently prayed that God would give her a son. Not just for her own sake, but for her mother's, who seemed to want a grandson so badly. Perhaps a baby would bridge the gap in the family. If only Uriah could give her a child, maybe then her mother would be happy.

Chapter 13

The next few days were spent preparing for another battle. Uriah received word while at the palace that King Hadadezer of Zobah, a powerful Syrian state, was trying to gain control over the territories along the Euphrates River. King David told his soldiers to spend the Sabbath with their families and then march out early the first day of the week. Uriah prepared his gear while Bathsheba did her usual Sabbath preparations. Shortly before sunset, a priest stationed on the palace wall blew the shofar to notify everyone that the Sabbath was approaching. Every man and woman put away his or her work to observe this holy time. Some people of Israel were devout Jews, others were not—but everyone stopped what they were doing when they heard the deep, resonant sound of the priest's horn.

Uriah's family sat inside the house on the mats Bathsheba had arranged for them. It was customary for the wife to light the candles while the husband said the blessing. Bathsheba had seen this done every week of her life, but only recently was she allowed to participate. It was very strange for her to take the part her mother formerly played, while Shiran sat idly by watching.

When the evening meal was completed, Uriah read from the scrolls his father had given him when he became a Jew several years earlier. She had heard the stories many times before, but Uriah added something new to the old tales. When he read about the Flood that covered the entire earth, he said it as if it were a fact, not just a legend that had been handed down through the generations. When he read about Abraham on Mount Moriah, holding the dagger over his precious son, Isaac, he got tears in his eyes and had to stop for a moment to compose himself. Bathsheba wondered how someone who was not born a Hebrew could feel so connected to the history of the Jewish people. She looked over at her mother, whose mind was obviously elsewhere. How could this woman, who could trace her lineage all the way back to Adam, be so far away from the Lord? For that matter, why didn't she herself have the spark that Uriah had? Something was missing in her own life, something that Uriah had found without the benefit of heritage. Maybe she would go to the tent of the ark in the morning with Uriah to see if it could be found there. She had been before, but only for social reasons. Maybe tomorrow she would try to see things through Uriah's eyes.

The next morning, Bathsheba and Uriah ate a light breakfast of day-old bread and fruit. She dressed in a yellow-and-brown mantle with a darker yellow girdle and matching headscarf. Shiran, as usual, did not feel up to attending worship, so she remained on her roof-top hideaway, petting Bathsheba's little lamb, Adina, while the couple walked the short distance to the tent. The streets were bustling with people all headed in the same direction. Many of the faces were familiar, but there were new families moving into the City of David every day. Several people greeted them by name as they entered the area that housed the tent of the ark. Uriah gave his wife a smile and then headed off to the front were the men worshiped. Bathsheba found Rivka, and the two went to the women's section. As they waited for the prayers to begin, Bathsheba reminisced about one of the most memorable days of her life—the day King David brought the ark to Jerusalem. Though she was only a young girl at the time, it was a day that was burned into her memory forever. The king danced through the gates of the city followed by throngs of people, all leaping and shouting praises to God. Four Levites carried the shrouded chest on their shoulders using golden poles slipped through rings fixed on the corners of the ark. Only three months earlier, David had made a fatal mistake when he tried to move the ark on an ox cart. When one of the animals pulling the cart stumbled, a man named Uzzah reached out and put his hand on God's sacred object to steady it. He was struck dead on the spot. David was afraid to try to move the ark any farther, so the ark stayed at the home of a man named Obed-Edom for three months. After studying the laws concerning the ark, David decided to try again. This time he followed God's commands, and the ark came to Jerusalem amidst much celebration and rejoicing. When the ark was placed inside the tent for the first time, the entire area shone with a light so bright it was hard to look at. Even the most hard-hearted were in awe of the presence of the Most High. She remembered David's blessing the people and giving everyone a loaf of delicious soft bread and cakes filled with fruit. Her mother had tried to duplicate the recipe many times, but never got it quite right. She even remembered the hymn the priest sang that day; it was a favorite of the people, and they sang it frequently.

A priest had begun reading, but Bathsheba did not hear a word of what he was saying. Her thoughts were interrupted when she felt someone shake her shoulder gently. "Are you all right, cousin? You have a strange look on your face," Rivka asked softly.

Bathsheba blinked several times until the childhood memory faded. When everything came back into focus, she noticed the service was over.

"Yes, yes, I'm fine," she managed to stammer. When she finally came to her senses, she looked her friend straight in the eyes and said, "I really am going to be just fine."

Chapter 14

Bathsheba was sorry to see the day end. It had been one of the nicest Sabbaths she could remember, and she was afraid her new-found peace would vanish with the setting of the sun. When the candles had been extinguished and put away until next week, Uriah gathered his gear and prepared to leave for the palace. Bathsheba wasn't surprised he was going to spend the night there, but she was disappointed. Rather than trying to coerce him into staying with her, she kissed him goodbye and tried to remain as cheerful and support-ive as possible. When he was out of sight, her mother came down the stairs from the roof, carrying the sleeping lamb under her arm.

"Bathsheba, why would you let him go like that? Haven't you been paying attention to the moon like I told you? If you ever want to have a child, you need to keep track of things like that, and above all, you need to get a better hold on that man of yours."

Bathsheba was in no mood for her mother's nagging, so instead of arguing, she just went up to the roof to enjoy the evening. Shiran followed her, but sensing her daughter's mood, she let the conversa-tion drop.

"Eema, it's so beautiful up here. Are you comfortable enough? Do you have everything you need?"

"Yes, it's very nice. So many of the new things you bought are up here with me. You and Uriah should have more for yourselves. I think maybe we should go to the market tomorrow to find some nice cushions and rugs for the house."

"The house is fine, Eema. Besides, I don't think Uriah was happy with all the purchases I made. I will just wait until he returns before I buy anything else."

"I was thinking a new loom would be nice," Shiran continued as if she hadn't even heard her daughter. "Just think of the beautiful things we could make if we worked together. Do you remember that cloak I made for your father when you girls were young? He wore it so much it practically unraveled right off of his body."

"Yes, I remember. When he held me on his lap, I liked to twist the frayed threads together. Atarah used to tease him and tell him he looked like a beggar. But it didn't stop him from wearing it. He loved that cloak very much. He loved you very much, Eema."

The two women sat in silence, enjoying their memories and the twinkling stars overhead. They spent many evenings together in the same way while the men were away. Shiran's mood seemed to improve with every passing day. Bathsheba hoped the domestic peace would continue when Uriah returned from battle.

The war with the Syrians went on longer than anyone had expected. When the Syrian king of Zobah had been defeated, reinforcements came from Damascus, expecting to be able to easily defeat the tired Israelites. But God was with His children, and He brought them victory on all sides. David and his men had to establish strongholds in the large Syrian cities of Damascus and Zobah. Several of the Israelite soldiers were temporarily left in the cities to ensure peace. When the rest of the troops came home, Bathsheba went to the palace gate to greet her husband. The earth shook beneath her feet with all the horses and chariots the soldiers had captured and brought back to the city. The chariots were filled with large quantities of bronze and other precious metals. Several of the higher-ranking soldiers carried golden shields that had been taken from the Syrian officers. Bathsheba tried to spot Uriah in the crowd, but she didn't have to look long. Zabad, Rivka's husband, was one of the first soldiers through the gate. He walked right over to Bathsheba, who happened to be standing beside his wife. Surprisingly, he did not greet Rivka first; instead he talked to Bathsheba.

"I bring word from your husband. He has been asked to stay in Damascus a little longer to help oversee the troops. He asked me to give you this to take care of any needs you may have." He handed her a small bag filled with coins.

"Forgive me for asking, Zabad, but why didn't you stay, too? The two of you are usually stationed together."

"Actually, I was asked, but I thought I should be here to make sure Rivka is all right. You did hear about our news, didn't you?" Zabad asked, beaming with pride.

"Yes, congratulations," Bathsheba was able to say without sounding too distressed. "I'll leave you two alone now. I'm sure you have a lot to talk about." She didn't wait for a response, but practically ran away.

When Bathsheba arrived home, she didn't see her mother at first, but when Adina trotted out to greet her, Shiran was close behind.

"Where is Uriah?" she asked.

"He has to stay in Damascus a little while longer."

"Don't be too upset about it, darling. After all, it is his job."

Shiran immediately noticed the tears in her daughter's eyes.

"Yes, but I don't think he had to stay. You should have seen all the men coming through the gate today. Zabad came home to his wife! Why couldn't Uriah ask to come home to me? Doesn't he love me?" Bathsheba realized she was losing control of her emotions, but she didn't care. "It seems like nothing I do makes any difference. I try to make his home nice, and he reminds me that he is not a wealthy person. I try to cook good meals for him, but he never says a word about it. Everything I do, I do to make him happy, and yet he practically volunteers to stay away from me. What am I doing wrong, Eema? Why doesn't he want to be with me?"

Shiran embraced her daughter and tried to soothe her. "My beautiful flower, there is nothing you can do. I knew all along Uriah was not the man for you. The only thing that matters to him is duty. He will never appreciate you the way he should."

Something about her mother's tone made Bathsheba bristle. Even if she was angry with Uriah, she didn't want to hear her mother criticize him. After all, he was still her husband, and there was nothing Shiran could do to change that.

Chapter 15

The hot summer days dragged on. Bathsheba spent most of her time on the roof with her mother, trying to catch whatever breeze was available. They were both thankful for the shelter to protect them from the blazing afternoon sun. Despite the heat, Rivka seemed to grow stronger and healthier every day. She came over often, sometimes with her husband, to make sure the women had everything they needed. Zabad would give them news about the troops stationed in Syria. More and more soldiers were coming in and out of the city every day—some going to Syria for long-term assignments, others being deployed to various previously conquered areas. It wouldn't be much longer until Uriah would be relieved of his duties in Damascus and he could come home. Bathsheba tried to be patient, but she felt the disapproving looks her mother gave her whenever the subject came up.

Occasionally, she went to the palace to visit with her sister. The baby looked different every time she saw him. He was starting to make amusing expressions, so the new pastime of the family was to try to see who could get the best reaction from him. What usually ended up happening was that the adults made foolish faces and the baby just stared at them, looking confused. Her older nephews were still as active as ever. One afternoon, she felt so sorry for their poor maid that she offered to take the boys for a walk with her and Adina. They led her to a courtyard where several of the palace children played. It was a beautiful grassy area shaded by large trees. She found a spot where she could sit and watch the boys while Adina grazed on the sweet grass. Bathsheba watched the groups play and found it interesting how they interacted with one another. She could tell from the robes they wore that some were royalty and others, like her nephews, were the children of servants. Jotham and a boy who was probably one of the king's sons were using sticks to sword fight. He seemed impervious to the prince's size advantage and went at him with the ferocity of a warrior. When Jotham claimed to have won, the other boy started stomping his feet and yelling. When this didn't work for him, he pushed Jotham to the ground, hit him with his stick, and stormed off. Bathsheba ran to Jotham to make sure he wasn't hurt.

"Jotham, are you all right?" she asked, kneeling down to check for injuries.

"Yeah. He always acts like that. If I did that, my Abba would skin my hide, but those kids get away with everything."

Almost instantly, a woman dressed in a very fine robe and holding a young girl on her hip was standing over Bathsheba and her nephew.

"Kindly remove your son from the area. He has no business treating my child, the son of King David, in such a manner."

Bathsheba stood to her full height and looked her directly in the eyes. Who did this woman think she was, speaking to her like a common maid? She was the granddaughter of the king's closest advisor and the wife of one of the Mighty Thirty. How dare this royal snob talk to her like that? She didn't care who her bratty little son was!

"I beg your pardon, Madam, but your son was entirely at fault in the situation. My nephew was playing fairly, and your son pushed him down."

The woman was obviously flustered. She thought she was dealing with an average commoner, but Bathsheba proved to be anything but. She shifted the girl onto her other hip and called for her son.

"Absalom, this woman said you pushed her boy down. Is that true?"

"Of course not, Eema. He is smaller than I am. I would never do such a thing." When the boy spoke, he stared up at Bathsheba with a fiery challenge burning in his eyes. She was a little frightened by what she saw, but her anger was taking over any other emotions she may have had. But before she could dispute the account further, Jotham walked over and bowed low before the prince and his mother.

"I'm sorry, Absalom. It was my fault. Please forgive me."

Bathsheba was in shock, but the queen seemed satisfied. "What is your name, boy?"

"I am Jotham, son of Nadav, the chief baker."

"Very well, Jotham, son of Nadav. You are forgiven. Just make sure you are more careful in the future, or you will be allowed to play only in the kitchen gardens." She gave Bathsheba a sneering smile as she collected her children and walked away. Jotham took her hand and looked up at her with brave eyes.

"Auntie, there are certain things you must learn if you're going to spend time at the palace, and one of them is not to make the royals mad."

"You are wise beyond your years, little nephew," Bathsheba said as she ruffled his hair. "Now, let's find your brother and Adina and get back to the house before we all end up in the prison."

Chapter 16

When Uriah finally returned home, he brought with him two small bags of gold coins. The king had rewarded him well for his time served. He also brought with him an elegant bracelet made of tiny gold strands woven together to make a thicker rope. "I thought of you when I saw it. It's beautiful and delicate, but the man who made it said it's very strong."

"Oh, Uriah, it's perfect. I'll never take it off." After he slipped it on Bathsheba's wrist, he handed her a small bag of coins.

"Now, this is for you to take to the market tomorrow. I don't like to be in debt, so I want you to pay off all the vendors you opened accounts with. And if there is anything you would like to get for yourself, there should be a little left over."

Bathsheba went to bed that night feeling happier than she had in weeks. It didn't even bother her that her mother disappeared to the roof as soon as Uriah came home. Maybe a trip to the market would make her feel better, especially if they were able to get a new loom.

After breakfast the next day, Bathsheba and Shiran headed to the market. It was a large open area just outside the city walls. Early in the mornings, the vendors would set up their wares. There were booths selling fruits, vegetables, oil, almonds, grain, and other food items from local farms. There were others selling everything from raw wool to the finest dyed fabrics money could buy. Bathsheba especially loved to see what came in on the caravans. There were tapestries and pottery from all over the area, silk fabric so soft, it felt like the petal of a flower, and spices that she didn't even know how to pronounce, let alone cook with. She went to the vendors with whom she had accounts with and one by one, she closed them.

She stood looking at looms with her mother when a young man she did not recognize approached them. He was tall and gangly with a greasy beard and dirty hands.

"Shalom, Shiran. And could this be little Bathsheba? My, how lovely you are." He stood gaping at her for a moment until Shiran's voice brought him back to his senses.

"Bathsheba, you remember your cousin, Barak. He is the man who took my house from me," Shiran said coldly.

She did not recognize him but smiled anyway.

"I hear you are recently married, cousin. It is too bad our fathers were not more prudent in making a match for you. If we were to-gether, your mother would still be living comfortably in her own home. Well, what's done is done. Of course, if anything ever happens to your little soldier, I could always use a second wife." He stared at her again, licking his lips as he talked.

"What a kind offer, Barak," Bathsheba replied steadily, "but my mother and I are quite comfortable where we are. We've grown so accustomed to our larger home that we would feel cramped living in your house. Oh, but I'm sure you and your first wife will be very happy there. Now, if you'll excuse us, we have several purchases to make today." She removed the bag of coins from her girdle and walked into the booth looking more like a queen than a soldier's wife.

Other than the run-in with her cousin, the shopping trip was very enjoyable. She was able to purchase a loom small enough for her and her mother to carry home. They also bought several different colors of thread, not knowing exactly what they wanted to make first. As they approached the house, they were both chatting merrily until they saw Uriah in his battle gear. Bathsheba set the loom by the road with her mother and ran to confront him.

"Why are you dressed like that? You just got home. You can't possibly be leaving again so soon."

"I'm sorry, but I must go. The Edomites are headed toward the city. We must go out and fight them before they get any closer."

"And I suppose you're going to spend the night at the palace again," she said heatedly.

"Of course, darling. Why are you getting so angry? You know it's my job. If the king calls, I must obey."

"You can't even spend your last night here with me? What, did you find a cute little maid at the palace to keep you company before all your battles? You probably have women planted all over the country for your long stints in conquered territories." The bitter words flew from her mouth before she could stop them.

"How dare you accuse me of such a thing? I've never given you any reason not to trust me. I have a duty and that's all there is to it! Where do you think that gold comes from that buys you the pretty things you want? I am just a poor man, but I'm doing everything I can to give you the things you want. If that means I have to stay on in a strange city longer than the others, than so be it." Uriah's face was turning red as he spoke. "I am a soldier, Bathsheba, and if I have to spend every day of my life fighting for my king and my God, then so be it." He picked up his shield and quiver and left without another word to his wife.

The troops marched out early the next morning. This time Bathsheba was not there to see them off.

Chapter 17

The Edomites were quickly defeated in the Valley of Salt. David and his men killed eighteen thousand of the enemy soldiers. Most of the troops returned to Jerusalem amidst songs of praise and victory, but Uriah was not one of them. He stayed on in Edom to ensure peace while a new transitional government was set in place.

There were times when Bathsheba regretted the way things went with Uriah before he left, but then she thought about his staying in Edom, and she became angry again. She pictured him stepping forward to volunteer for extended service in the territory, just to stay away from her. He was probably trying to punish her. Well, she'd show him. She didn't need him around. She was just fine on her own. But, there were the nights when Bathsheba cried herself to sleep clutching the bracelet Uriah had given her.

The days were easier to bear. There were the tasks that had to be completed such as fetching water, cooking, and cleaning. She worked with her mother on small weaving projects so they could get a feel for the loom. She took long walks with Adina, exploring the new parts of the city. Every enemy the Israelite army subdued brought more wealth through taxes into the country. It was an exciting time to live in Jerusalem.

One morning, an entourage entered the city gates, causing quite a commotion. The word spread throughout the streets that King David was receiving a delegation led by Prince Joram of Hamath. Bathsheba and her mother, as well as most of their neighbors, ran to the palace gates to catch a glimpse of the wealthy prince from the north. Joram was sent by his father, King Toi, who had been fighting their southern neighbor Zobah for years. When David and his army had successfully defeated the Syrian city, there was much rejoicing in Hamath. The prince arrived with gifts of gratitude to bestow on King David. Rather than hording the gold, silver, and bronze for himself, David immediately dedicated the gifts to the Lord and His future house. He invited the entire city to a dedication ceremony at the tent of the ark. After he offered sacrifices to the Lord, he thanked Prince Joram for his gifts and discussed his plans for the future of Israel. The king began with a song that he had written. The crowd was silent as he sang in his deep, strong voice:

> My heart is not proud, O LORD,
> my eyes are not haughty;
> I do not concern myself with great matters
> or things too wonderful for me.
> But I have stilled and quieted my soul;
> like a weaned child with its mother,
> like a weaned child is my soul within me.
>
> O Israel put your hope in the LORD
> both now and forevermore.*

The congregation responded to the song by shouting praises to God. Once the noise died down, David spoke again. "Our God is so good to us Israel. He kept the promise He made to Abraham when He said his descendents would be as numerous as the sands of the sea. He kept the promise He made to Moses and our ancestors living in bondage under the Egyptians when He led them to the Promised Land that we now enjoy. And He is keeping His promises to me. He has given us victory over our enemies and will continue to protect us and keep us in His loving care.

"I wish with all my heart that I could begin building a house for our Lord now, but it is not to be. My hands have seen too much bloodshed. But, He has promised that there will soon be a time of peace and that my son will build the temple we all dream of. We know the Lord will keep this promise."

Another shout rose up from the people. David waited for the crowd to quiet down before he continued. "The gifts that King Toi sent to us through his son Joram will be used by my son to build the Lord's temple. We will also use the taxes and riches taken from our conquered neighbors to further this great work. People will come from far and wide to see the magnificence of our God and to worship Him with us. O Israel, put your hope in the Lord both now and forevermore."

The people cheered for David as he left the tent. They were very proud of their king. As the departing groups congregated in the streets, they all spoke of the great things he was doing for them. Many of them remembered King Saul and his moodiness and disobedience to God. How much better David was turning out to be.

"What a good man he is," Bathsheba heard a woman nearby say to her friend. "With him leading us, we have nothing to fear."

"Yes, so brave and strong and godly. He's exactly what we wanted when we cried out to the Lord for a king," an older woman replied.

"And he sure is easy on the eyes too," another said, giggling.

"He really is ideal, if you think about it," a wise-looking woman remarked. "Remember the rules God established through Samuel for the future kings of Israel? David's just about perfect. He doesn't stockpile riches for himself—he gives his best treasures back to God. He didn't even keep all those warhorses the army brought back from Syria. Did you hear he cut the hamstrings on all but a hundred of the horses?"

"Why in the world would he do that?" asked a young woman in the group.

"Samuel instructed the future kings not to build up a large number of battle horses for their armies. He wanted them to be dependent on God alone for victories in war."

Bathsheba and her mother moved closer to the women so they could hear the conversation better.

"Yes, but what about all his wives?" the old woman asked. "Didn't the Lord warn against taking too many wives? David already has seven, not including his concubines."

"He works so hard. He should be entitled to a little leniency in his personal life. Besides, that doesn't affect the kingdom."

The crowd of women continued walking, and Bathsheba lost the rest of their conversation, but somehow what she had overheard made her feel uneasy. *If David was being so careful to follow God's orders for a king, why didn't he obey when it came to his personal life? Perhaps it really didn't matter. The country was thriving, the people were happy. What's the harm in having a few extra wives*, she reasoned as she continued on her way home.

---

*Psalm 131, NIV.

Chapter 18

When Uriah finally returned home, there was a great deal of tension between everyone in the house. Shiran retreated to the roof to avoid any contact with her son-in-law unless it was absolutely necessary. Bathsheba was too proud to apologize, so she acted cold and aloof. Uriah, who was used to dealing with men who were far less emotional, didn't know what to do with the two of them. Unable to handle things at home, Uriah spent as much time as possible at the palace, which only made Bathsheba angrier with him. It finally all came to a head one evening at dinner when the three were sitting around the fire eating in silence. Bathsheba couldn't stand it anymore, so she blurted out the first thing that came to mind, "Well, you've been home a few days now, when are you leaving again?" It came out much harsher than she intended, but she couldn't take it back.

"There's no talk of war right now, but if you would like me to stay at the palace, I will."

"It must be very comfortable there. Perhaps you like it better than your own home?"

"Though my home has not been the most comfortable place for me lately, I would still rather be here."

"Why?" she said, trying to hold back tears.

"Because I missed you, my lamb. I hate being away from you. Why must you punish me so for doing my job?"

With those words, she crumbled. She slipped into his arms and cried against his chest. It was hard to tell whether her mother was annoyed with the scene or just wanted to give the couple privacy, but she quietly slipped up to her room. Uriah held his wife and let her cry until her tears were spent.

"Oh, Uriah, I'm so sorry. I don't know why I behaved so poorly. I'm just a stupid little girl who doesn't know how to act like a proper wife. Please forgive me."

"You're not stupid, and you're certainly not a little girl. I've been all over this country, and you are still the most beautiful woman I have ever seen. Now, whether you know how to act like a proper wife or not, I guess we'll just have to see about that," he said, teasing her to lighten the mood. The couple sat by the fire holding each other and talking until late in the evening. By the time they went to bed, the rift between them was completely gone; in fact, they felt closer than they ever had before.

There was a short time of peace in Israel, and Bathsheba was able to enjoy the company of her husband for several uninterrupted months. She was glad her friend, Rivka, had her husband home as well. As the year drew to a close, Rivka was getting nearer to the arrival of her baby. Once she made it through the first few months of nausea and fatigue, she handled the rest of her pregnancy with ease. Bathsheba and Shiran tried to be as helpful to her as possible, but Rivka would not allow anyone to do too much for her. Her husband, Zabad, was always hovering around her as though he expected her to break in pieces at any moment. It was obviously starting to annoy Rivka, but she tolerated it with as much patience as her condition would allow.

One morning at the well, Bathsheba tried to help her friend carry her water jugs, but as usual, Rivka would not permit it. As they were walking back home, she noticed beads of sweat forming on her friend's forehead. It wasn't a hot morning, so Bathsheba grew concerned.

"Rivka, are you OK? You don't look well."

Rivka stopped and took a few deep breaths before she could respond. "I'm not sure what's wrong with me today. I just can't seem to catch my breath. Maybe I will let you carry my water today—but just this once." She handed over the jugs and tried to continue walking home, but had to stop again moments later.

Bathsheba's arms were getting tired from carrying all the jugs, but she stood patiently with her friend every time she had to stop. At last they made it to Rivka's home where Zabad was cleaning up the house. The sight of the large soldier clumsily sweeping the floor almost made the women laugh, but Rivka was too uncomfortable to enjoy the scene. When he saw his wife's face, he dropped the broom and ran to her.

"Darling, what's wrong? Are you ill?" he asked, ignoring Bathsheba and her huge load of water.

"I think it might be time, Zabad. Will you please go get the midwife for me? I'm going to lie down for a little while."

"Yes, yes, of course," he stammered as he walked around in a couple circles, trying to figure out what he was doing. "Bathsheba, you'll stay with her, won't you?" he asked, noticing her for the first time.

"Of course I will, Zabad. Don't worry about a thing. I'll take good care of her until you get back." She tried to hide the fact that she was terrified of what might happen while he was gone.

She managed to set the water down by herself without spilling too much of it then she went in the house to help her friend lie down on her mat. Rivka was breathing harder and was obviously hurting.

"Is there anything I can get for you, Rivka?" she asked.

"No, just sit with me." She winced for a minute then her face relaxed. "And to think, all this pain because of a little piece of forbidden fruit," she said, trying to smile. Bathsheba didn't know how she could joke at a time like this. Didn't she realize she could have a baby at any moment and there was no midwife anywhere to be seen?

The minutes dragged on like hours while they waited for Zabad to return. Bathsheba didn't know the first thing about delivering a child, and she was terrified she would have to learn if someone didn't come help her soon. Rivka was calm and endured the contractions well; in fact, she was probably doing better than Bathsheba, who was on the verge of tears when Zabad walked into the house with the midwife.

"Oh, you're back!" she exclaimed, almost hugging them both. "You'd better hurry. Here, let me help you with your things," she said to the midwife as she grabbed her bag and the small wooden stool she was carrying. "I don't think you have much time, you really should get over there." She was practically pushing the woman across the floor.

"Relax, dear. It's her first child. We may be here all night. Just set those things over there in the corner for me; then you two can step outside while I check her. I'll call you if I need anything." The midwife was chuckling when she sat on the floor at Rivka's feet.

Bathsheba and Zabad paced in circles around the outdoor kitchen area. It was a wonder they never collided. When the sun was directly overhead, they saw Uriah approach.

"There you are, Bathsheba. I was worried about you. When you didn't return from the well, I thought something happened to you. Is everything all right?" He saw the worried looks on their faces and immediately figured out what was going on. "Oh, it's time, huh? How wonderful. Come on you two, stop looking so glum. Let's sit down and relax and celebrate with a cup of water. I'm parched." He laughed a little and got cups of water for all of them. "Here, dear, why don't you take some in for Rivka and the midwife?"

Bathsheba was afraid of what she might see when she stepped into the room, but nothing had changed. Rivka was lying on her side, trying to keep her breathing steady, and the midwife sat next to her looking as though she were waiting for bread to bake.

"I brought you some water," she stammered, handing the midwife both cups.

"Oh, thank you, dear. Here have a seat. You can keep her company for a while. You know, help pass the time. I'm going to go stretch my legs." She rose to leave, and Bathsheba felt panic rise up in her throat.

"Wait, you can't go," she almost yelled. "What if . . . what if something happens?"

"Well, if a baby comes out, just catch it," the midwife said, laughing as she walked out.

Bathsheba was horrified at the thought, but quickly tried to calm herself for her friend's sake.

"How are you feeling, Rivka?" she asked timidly. "Would you like some water?"

"Oh yes, thank you. Could you please help me sit up?"

Bathsheba propped her up against the wall and sat with her while she drank sips of water between contractions.

"Is it very painful?" she asked when her friend seemed relaxed.

"*Painful* isn't a strong enough word for it. I just can't believe so many women do this. Our mothers did this! Well, if they can all do it, so can—" she broke off when the pain swept over her again.

This went on for several more hours. The midwife was in and out the entire time, leaving Bathsheba to look after Rivka when she was gone. The time finally came for Rivka to move to the birthing stool. Bathsheba was sent out to boil water. The men were still outside waiting. They had managed to pull together some sort of dinner but they both stopped eating when Bathsheba came out.

"I think it's almost time," she told them, as she put a pot of water on the fire. Zabad stood, his meal forgotten, and started pacing again. She was glad she had something to do to keep her from joining him. Before she could get the water off the fire, they heard the sound of a baby crying from inside the house. The three of them stared at each other, not knowing what to do next.

The midwife stuck her head out the door and called to them, "Congratulations, Zabad, you have a son!"

Chapter 19

Just before little Ronen's second birthday, the men were once again called to war. The Ammonite king Nahash, who showed David kindness during his time in hiding from Saul, died and his son Hanun succeeded him. David sent a delegation with a message of sympathy to Hanun at the loss of his father. Hanun did not believe David was sincere, so he insulted the messengers in order to provoke the Israelites. When David received word that his delegation had been sent from the city of Rabbah with half of their beards shaved off and their robes cut at the hip, he was furious. This reaction was exactly what the new king had counted on. Immediately after he sent the shamed Israelites out of his city, he hired thousands of mercenaries from recently defeated Syria, as well as men from Maacah and Ishtob. They positioned themselves in the open area several miles outside of the fortified city of Rabbah and waited for David's men to attack.

When it was time for Uriah to leave, Bathsheba did not complain. Her sense of patriotism had taken over any personal feelings of neglect she may have had. The entire city was irate at what the new Ammonite king had done to their people. Every citizen, from the highest ranking soldier on down to the lowest maid, was ready to take on the enemy if necessary. When the military procession left the palace gates, everyone was surprised to see Joab, rather than David, leading the men. David's commander in chief had proven himself to be an exceptional general time and again, but a shiver of doubt crept up Bathsheba's spine, knowing that her husband was not under the direct command of the king.

Commander Joab and his army quickly overwhelmed the Syrians and their mercenaries and sent the Ammonites running home, but he did not completely defeat them. When the Israelites were heading back to Jerusalem, the formerly defeated King Hadadezer of the Syrian city Zobah rallied troops from the other side of the Euphrates and sent them after Joab. When David heard about this, he personally went out to fight them. This gave everyone in the city new hope and confidence.

Within weeks, the victorious Israelite army returned to Jerusalem. Syria, as well as the cities of Maacah and Ishtob had finally completely submitted to David and agreed to pay taxes to Israel. Bathsheba was relieved to have her husband back from the grueling battle. His first night home, she made him a special dinner and put on her finest robe. Shiran went to the roof after the meal, giving the couple some much needed time alone.

"I don't know why, but I was so worried about you during this battle. Was it very bad?" Bathsheba asked while she cleaned up the dishes.

"No worse than usual. It was a little unnerving not having King David with us in the beginning, but I guess he's entitled to a break every now and then. Joab is a fine commander, it's just . . . ," he trailed off not wanting to speak poorly of his superior officer.

"What?" Bathsheba urged.

"I don't know. There's just something about him that makes me uneasy. Well, it doesn't matter anyway. I know he would do anything for King David, and that's what is really important."

"Do you think we'll finally have a time of peace? It seems that we are always at war with someone."

"It won't be much longer. We've subdued our enemies all the way to the Euphrates River just as the Lord said we would. We just have some unfinished business with those despicable Ammonites. It still makes me sick to think of the way they treated David's ambassadors. Those poor men are still in Jericho waiting for their beards to grow back so they can return to their families. No, we won't have peace until the city of Rabbah is taken; then at last we will be able to rest."

Chapter 20

The following spring, David ordered Joab and his men to attack the Ammonites and besiege the city of Rabbah. Uriah seemed almost happy to go. *Is it because he can finally get back at the Ammonites, or is he tired of spending time at home?* Bathsheba wondered. She tried not to sulk as she gathered the supplies he would need for the long siege. When she had finished everything at her house, she went to Rivka's to see if she needed help. Her son Ronen was now walking and getting into all kinds of mischief, which made it difficult for Rivka to get much done. When Bathsheba approached the house, she saw her friend trying to wrap a bundle of bread and cheese while her little imp untied another bundle and started eating the figs and dates out of it.

"Ronen, no!" Rivka scolded him. He quickly dropped the bundle and looked at her innocently with his cheeks puffed out from the stolen food.

Bathsheba laughed and scooped the little boy into her arms.

"Are you giving your Eema trouble today, Ronen? You must go easy on her, she has a lot to do." She cuddled the child close to her neck as he finished his snack.

"Oh, Bathsheba, I'm so glad you're here. I just don't know what has gotten into him today. One minute he's playing with Zabad's sword, the next he's trying to grab a loaf of bread from the fire. I don't know how I'm going to keep that child alive to see manhood." She wiped her forehead with the back of her sleeve and continued packing the food for Zabad. Bathsheba offered to take Ronen for a walk to her house so he could say goodbye to his Uncle Uriah. Rivka was grateful for the break.

When Bathsheba and her little friend approached the house, they saw Uriah polishing his shield. Ronen ran to him and threw his chubby arms around his neck.

"Unca Uri, you go bye-bye too?" he asked in his babyish talk.

"Yes, Ronen, Uncle Uriah has to go with your Abba to fight the Ammonites. You stay here and take care of your Eema and Auntie Bathsheba."

"No wanna stay wif girls. Ronen go too," he said, trying to sound grown up.

"Not you, little man. You won't have to fight. Your Abba and I will make everything safe so you won't ever have to go to war."

"Me wanna fight!" Ronen said, sticking out his lower lip.

"OK, OK, here, you go get that little scoundrel over there." He put his huge helmet on the child and sent him off to do battle with Adina, who ran at the sight of him. Ronen tried to chase the sheep, but the helmet blocked his vision, and he just walked into the side of the house.

For some reason the scene brought tears to Bathsheba's eyes. Watching her husband with the little boy made her want a child of her own even more. She had prayed and prayed that God would give her a son, but He didn't seem to listen to her. Now, with her husband leaving again, she felt as though she would never have a baby. Uriah must have known what she was thinking, because he walked over to her and kissed her.

"It won't be much longer, my lamb. When this battle is over, we will have time to start our own family."

Bathsheba looked up at the soft brown eyes of the man she loved so much. She wanted with all of her heart to believe him. Perhaps this really would be his last battle.

Chapter 21

The weeks wore on, and the siege of Rabbah continued. The city was well fortified, so Bathsheba knew it could be months before her husband returned. She tried to keep herself occupied, but grew more and more restless as the days passed.

The women around the well chattered about King David's absence from battle. Some thought he stayed home from Rabbah because he considered himself above a drawn-out military blockade. After all, he was a great warrior and king, why should he sit back with the common soldiers waiting day after day for the Ammonites to surrender? It didn't require any great skill to keep supplies out of the city. Besides, the king of Israel shouldn't have to sleep in a field when he had a palace full of comforts waiting for him. No one really blamed him for staying home, but they did talk.

As the spring rolled into summer, the days grew increasingly warmer. One balmy evening, Bathsheba and her mother sat on the roof enjoying the slight breeze. Shiran seemed distracted and kept looking off into the distance.

"Today is your day of purification, is it not? Shiran asked nonchalantly.

Bathsheba thought about it for a moment, "Yes, I guess it is. You know, you keep better track of my cycle than I do," she joked with her mother.

"Why don't I set up a bath for you? I'll take Adina for a walk if you would like some privacy." Again she glanced over Bathsheba's shoulder as though someone else was with them on the roof.

"That does sound nice. It's such a pleasant evening."

"Yes, and the moon is full. It's just perfect," Shiran responded.

The two women warmed some water and filled the shallow tub. Shiran set out a clean linen tunic for Bathsheba to put on when she was finished, and then she left. Bathsheba washed her hair then lowered her body into the water. She felt cool for the first time all day and enjoyed the feeling of the breeze on her wet skin. She leaned her head back to look up at the stars and was startled by what she saw. There was a balcony off the palace that was clearly visible from her roof. She had seen it many times, but it had always been empty. But tonight she could plainly see a man watching her. If it wasn't for the light of the moon, he would have been just a shadow in the distance, but tonight she could easily make out the figure of the king. She quickly jumped from the tub and covered herself with the linen robe, her heart pounding in her throat. The king didn't turn away in embarrassment, but continued watching her. Even from this distance, she sensed she stirred something in him. Without any effort, she did to him what she had been trying for years to do to her husband. The thought filled her with a sense of power. Perhaps her mother was right. Perhaps she was good enough for the king. She boldly looked at him, this man she had seen all her life but never dared to make eye contact with. They shared a moment just watching each other with the stars and moon between them until he broke the spell and returned to his palace. Just like that, it was over. Bathsheba suddenly felt ashamed of herself. What was she, a married woman, doing naked in plain sight of another man? Her face burned with embarrassment as she descended the stairs and went inside the house. She lay down on her mat and covered her head with a blanket. What was the matter with her? She felt her entire body shaking—but from what she did not know. Was it fear, shame, or something else?

When her heart finally slowed down, she heard her mother outside talking to someone. She couldn't make out the other voice, but it sounded like a man. Bathsheba lay frozen in place, a feeling of dread engulfing her body. Her mother entered the room, obviously excited about something.

"Bathsheba, get up. They've come for you. Get up."

"Who, Eema? Who's come for me?" she asked, terrified of the answer.

"Why, the guards from the palace, of course. Now, get up. The king wishes to see you."

"Oh, Eema, he already has!" she managed to choke out the words.

"Yes, yes, I know. I've seen him stand on that balcony many times the last few weeks. He's restless. He's looking for something. He wants you, Bathsheba. I've always told you, haven't I? I always told you that you could have a king! Now get up!" She pulled the blanket off her daughter and lifted her to her feet. Bathsheba just stood there numbly while her mother combed her wet hair and covered it with a scarf. She put Bathsheba's finest robe on her and pushed her toward the door.

"Eema, I can't, what about . . ."

"Hush, girl. You can't say no to him. He's the king of Israel. Now cover your face so no one recognizes you."

When she stepped out the door, she saw the two men. They were older, like the other guards she had seen at the palace, but she knew they were still strong enough to take her by force if commanded to do so. The senior of the two looked at her sadly then quickly turned his face. She thought she recognized him from her father's funeral, but couldn't remember his name. She suddenly felt very conscious of what she was doing. For a moment, she considered refusing to go with them. All she had to do was run back into the house and bar the door. She was sure her father's friend would give up his unpleasant task if given the opportunity. But then she realized she didn't want to run away. King David was the most handsome, talented, powerful man in the country, and he wanted her. How could she say no? She struggled with herself for a fleeting moment then made her decision. She stepped between the two men and allowed them to take her to the king.

Chapter 22

The evening was warm, so there were still a few people outside. The sight of two guards escorting a woman through the streets did attract attention. Bathsheba kept her head down and hoped no one would recognize her robe. Perhaps her neighbors would think she was in trouble. Maybe she was. Maybe the king summoned her to chastise her for her immodesty. He was known to be a very devout man. It was possible he just wanted to talk to her about her behavior. But, deep down, she knew the man watching her from the balcony did not have a reprimand in mind.

The guards led her through the familiar gates of the palace, then through the doors into the inner court. Her grandfather worked here, but as a woman, she never had reason to come to this part of the building. She was in awe of the beauty she saw all around her. Every tile beneath her sandaled feet was decorated with intricate details of leaves and vines. The ceiling and all the walls were made from the best cedar in Tyre, and the smell of the wood filled her nose with a deep earthy smell. The walls were covered with tapestries embroidered with the finest gold threads. She wanted to stop and look at everything, but the light was not good and the guards urged her on up a long staircase and into the private quarters of the king. She was escorted to a bedchamber, and the guard she had recognized opened the door for her.

"The king is waiting for you inside. If you need anything, all you have to do is call," he said cryptically.

She knew immediately what he meant. There were laws protecting women in Israel, and even the king was subject to them. All she had to do was scream for help and someone would come to her aid, but she wasn't sure she wanted to be rescued.

She stepped into the room, and the door closed behind her. She felt her heart pounding and was afraid to move. When she realized she was alone, she relaxed a little and looked around. There was a thick, soft mat on the floor with red and gold cushions neatly placed against the wall. The floor was covered with richly colored rugs spun into unusual designs. Other than a few comforts, the room was surprisingly simple. The curtains covering the window fluttered, drawing her attention to the balcony beyond. That is when she realized she was not alone. King David stepped in through the drapes and walked to her boldly. Her breath caught in her chest when she saw him standing directly in front of her. She was accustomed to men who were close to her height, but David stood a full head taller than she. His dark hair and beard had a touch of silver, but he didn't look old. She had been around soldiers her entire life, but he exuded a strength and power she was not accustomed to.

"Bathsheba," he said breathlessly and reached a hand out to touch her face. She wondered how he knew her name, and if he knew her name, what else did he know about her? Did he know she was married? Did he know who her husband was? Despite the turmoil in her mind, her body responded to him instantly. She felt her face flush as the blood in her veins rushed to meet his touch. For a moment, she considered crying out to the guards, but something stopped her. Suddenly, she realized she was not afraid. Her pulse was racing and her breath was short, but it was definitely not fear she was experiencing. He untied the scarf from her still damp head and seemed mesmerized by the flowing dark hair that cascaded over her shoulders.

"Oh, Bathsheba," he said again, "you are even more beautiful up close."

She blushed at his reference to seeing her on the roof and lowered her eyes. With both hands, he cupped her face and lifted it so she was looking into his intense gaze.

"You will stay with me tonight?" It was more a question than a command, and again she was reminded that she did have a choice. She made an attempt to bow to him, but he grabbed her shoulders and lifted her back up. "Do not think of me as your king tonight. I am just a man."

"Yes, David," she spoke slowly, savoring the sound of his name on her lips, "I will stay with you tonight."

Chapter 23

Bathsheba awoke before dawn the next morning but hesitated to open her eyes to face the coming day. The events of the previous evening came back to her in a rush, flooding her with guilt and embarrassment. She finally opened her eyes and saw David sitting on the floor next to the bed. He must have been feeling the same way, because he sat with his face buried in his hands. When he realized she was awake, he looked over at her, his eyes full of pain and remorse. It was hard to believe this broken man was the great king who once leapt with joy before the ark of the Lord.

"Bathsheba, you must go," he spoke softly. "If anyone should find out . . ." His voice broke, and he again lowered his head into his hands.

She wanted to run away and cry. Just hours ago, she had felt like the queen of Israel, but now she felt like nothing more than a common prostitute. She quickly dressed and left the room without even looking over her shoulder. On her way to the stairs, she saw the two guards who brought her to the king the night before. Her father's friend quickly looked down when he saw her approach. He couldn't even look her in the face. *What have I done? I am a fallen woman, worthy of death! And my husband, oh, Uriah. What will he do if he ever finds out? How can I bear to look into those soft brown eyes again?* A sob escaped her throat as she bolted down the stairs and through the palace. She was almost to the gate when she practically ran into her grandfather.

"Oh, Sav," she gasped when she saw him.

"Good morning, Bathsheba. What are you doing here so early?"

She couldn't speak; she couldn't even look at him. Instead, she lowered her head and quickly walked the rest of the way home, trying not to draw attention to herself.

When she approached the house, her mother came down from the roof to greet her.

"Oh darling, you're home. I couldn't sleep a wink all night." Shiran seemed happy enough despite her lack of rest. "Why are you crying, Bathsheba? What happened? Wasn't David pleased with you?"

"Eema," she sobbed, "what have I done? I will be stoned. And Uriah, oh, poor Uriah. How could I do this to him?" Her entire body shook with emotion, and she collapsed to the ground. Her mother quickly lifted her up and took her into the house.

"Get ahold of yourself right now, Bathsheba!" she snapped. "What did you do to the king? Why did he send you home so soon?"

"What did you think would happen? Did you think he would keep me? I have a husband! What would people say if they found out the king took another man's wife? We would both be stoned!" Suddenly Bathsheba's fear and regret turned to anger. "You did this!" she shouted. "You set this all up. How could you do this to me? Not just to me, but to Uriah and David, to the whole country! Why did you do this awful thing?"

"Enough!" Shiran hissed at her hysterical daughter. "You ungrateful girl! Don't you know I want only what is best for you? Do you really want to spend the rest of your life in a passionless marriage, living in a clay shack when you could be a queen?"

"I am not a queen! I am an adulteress. There is a big difference," Bathsheba cried as she sat down on her sleeping mat.

"Maybe you're not the queen yet, but just wait. I'm sure you made an impression on David. You're more beautiful than all of his wives put together. Mark my word; he will send for you again.

And, as far as Uriah goes, don't worry about him. If King David wants you badly enough, he'll find a way to make you his own." Shiran sat beside her daughter and held her close, stroking her soft hair. "There, now, don't worry about a thing. It's all going to be just fine."

Bathsheba closed her eyes tightly and allowed her mother to rock her like a baby. She wanted to send up a silent prayer to the Lord to ask for help, forgiveness, anything, but she knew she could never expect God to listen to her now.

Chapter 24

Bathsheba slept fitfully on her mat for a few hours until she heard the sound of Rivka and her son outside. She quickly washed her face in the basin of fresh water her mother had brought in while she slept. She tried to scrub away the feeling of filth from her skin, but didn't feel any cleaner when she finished—only raw and exposed. She put on a heavy mantle and covered her head with the hood even though it was much too warm. When she stepped out into the late-morning sunlight, she felt blind for a moment. She had to blink several times to adjust to the light.

"Shalom, cousin. Are you well?" Rivka asked, sounding slightly suspicious.

"Yes, I'm fine, thank you. Good morning, little Ronen." She held her arms open for the child and tried to give him a smile, but he did not accept either. He only glanced at her for a moment then ran after Adina.

"Is everything all right, Bathsheba? I heard some women talking at the well this morning. That busybody, Bilah, said she saw guards take you to the palace late last night. Is your grandfather ill?"

"Don't you silly gossips have anything better to do with your time than stand around that watering hole making up stories about people? Why don't you all just mind your own business?" Bathsheba didn't know why she was snapping at her friend, but it seemed beyond her control.

"Oh, I'm sorry. I didn't mean to intrude." Rivka looked as if she had been slapped across the face. "Ronen, please leave that poor animal alone. We really must be getting home. Say goodbye to your auntie Bathsheba." She took her son by the hand and pulled him away from his fluffy playmate. He managed to wave a dimpled hand at Bathsheba before they left.

Shiran witnessed the entire scene from her perch on the edge of the roof, and as soon as Rivka was out of sight, she flew down to her daughter. "My flower, you really must be careful how you behave right now. People will talk. You must keep your head up and act as if nothing has happened. Otherwise, it could be disastrous for all of us." She prepared a plate of bread and raisins as she spoke, then selected herbs and brewed two cups of warm liquid. She sat down next to her daughter and tried to get her to eat. Bathsheba picked up the bread, but before she got it to her mouth, she noticed something unusual about it. It was shaped like a voluptuous tree-woman. It was made to look like Asherah!

"Eema, what is this?" she exclaimed, feeling exasperated.

"Would you please just stop worrying about every little thing I do? I'm only trying to give you something to eat. Why do you have to make such a big deal about it?"

"That's it!" Bathsheba practically yelled as she threw the small loaf on the ground. "Get out! Get out of my house!"

"Where will I go? You can't throw me out onto the street," Shiran gasped.

"I don't care where you go. Go to Atarah's; go back to Hebron. Just get out of here!" She stormed into the house and slammed the door.

Bathsheba lay on her mat sobbing long after her tears were spent. She must have fallen asleep at some point, because when her eyes opened, the sun was gone. She stepped outside on weak legs and saw nothing had been done for dinner. She went to the roof to find her mother and found all of her belongings were gone. Even Adina, Bathsheba's pet sheep, had disappeared. Now she was completely and utterly alone.

Chapter 25

The days passed and Bathsheba spent most of her time sleeping, though she never felt rested. She went out only when necessary and tried to avoid talking with anyone. No matter how hard she tried, she couldn't avoid the stares and whispers wherever she went. One morning while she was waiting her turn at the well, she heard a pair of older women talking.

"That's the girl I was telling you about. People say she is the king's mistress," the short, round woman whispered loudly.

"Isn't she married to that foreign soldier?" her tall, skinny friend asked.

"Yes, but my daughter said she saw her sneaking into the palace late at night."

The stocky woman clicked her tongue and shook her head. "What a shame. She was such a pretty child, but just look at her now. Lower than even a concubine."

Bathsheba gave up her place in line and went home quickly, trying hard to hold her head up and act as if she hadn't heard the gossip. After that, she made her trips to the well earlier in the morning, sometimes even before the sun was up, just to avoid contact with all the wagging tongues. Even in the market, Bathsheba felt as if complete strangers were judging her. She began to feel as if she were going crazy with paranoia. It didn't help that she spent all her time alone now and had no one to help keep her sane. Occasionally, Rivka would come over to visit with her, but the wall Bathsheba built around herself was impenetrable, even to her closest friend.

One afternoon, there was a knock at the door. Expecting it to be Rivka, she called for her to come in. Bathsheba was surprised to see her sister enter, looking very upset.

"Shalom, sister," Atarah said as she looked around at the mess that had taken over the once-spotless home.

Bathsheba didn't get up from the mat to greet her, so Atarah helped herself to a seat on the floor next to her sister.

"Bathsheba, we have to talk."

"Where are the children?" she tried to quickly change the subject.

"They're at home with Eema. Bathsheba, why did you kick her out? The women around the palace are talking about you, but Eema won't say anything. She just frets and paces around the house snapping at the children all day. What have you done?"

"I don't know what you mean. Eema and I weren't getting along, so I suggested she stay with you for a while."

"I can't have it!" Atarah exclaimed, probably more passionately than she had intended. "You must take her back. We don't have room. I have three small children, a husband, a maid, and now Eema and that silly ewe. You have to take her back."

"Oh, Adina," Bathsheba sighed, feeling relief for the first time in weeks.

"Adina!" she practically screamed. "You care more about that pile of wool than you do your own mother! What is the matter with you?"

"Nothing!" she shot back, feeling her emotions rising out of control.

"Bathsheba, what happened? One of the baker's wives said she saw you leaving the palace early one morning, and then the next day Eema was at my doorstep crying. You have got to tell me what's going on."

"Atarah, I don't know why people insist on talking about things they know nothing about, and as far as Eema goes, I can't have her here. I just can't forgive her!" she blurted out the words without thinking.

"Forgive her for what?"

"It's none of your business!"

"It is my business. You're my family, and people are saying awful things about you. Your disgrace affects us all. If Eema has done something to dishonor you, tell me and I may be able to help. We could talk to Sav, and he will know what to do. Sister, you must talk to me."

Bathsheba's wall crumbled, and she spilled the entire story. She was so consumed with emotion that she didn't hear Rivka enter the house. When she finally looked up through tear-blurred eyes and saw her friend standing in the doorway, she felt as if the roof had just collapsed on top of her.

"Rivka, how long have you been standing there?" she asked almost in a whisper.

"Long enough," Rivka said through clenched teeth. "How could you do this to my cousin? He has treated you like a queen." She winced at her own words.

"Oh, Rivka, please don't blame me. It wasn't my fault. My mother . . ."

"Your mother! How can you even try to blame her? You did this, Bathsheba, no one else."

"Rivka, you have to believe me. She set the whole thing up. I love Uriah, I really do. I didn't mean for all of this to happen. Please don't be angry with me."

The look on Rivka's face was worse than any words she could have spoken. Bathsheba could see her own guilt mirrored in her friend's eyes, and she wanted to die. All she could do was hang her head and weep. When she was able to look up again, Rivka was gone. Atarah still sat by her side looking pale.

"She will tell your husband, and you will be stoned to death. The entire family will be shamed. What will become of us?"

Bathsheba was still reeling from Rivka's response and was in no mood for her sister's self-pity. "You must go now, Atarah, and you have to keep Eema with you. I just don't know what I would do if I had to see her right now."

Atarah seemed to understand—either that or she just wanted to escape. With a glance over her shoulder, she left her sister still sitting on her sleeping mat and returned to her home at the palace.

Chapter 26

Bathsheba tossed and turned on her mat, trapped in an inescapable nightmare. In her dream, she was walking through the desert with the sun beating down on her. She saw nothing for miles except sand. Suddenly, she approached an altar with a man standing behind it, whose face she could not see. Over his robe, he wore the ephod of the Levites. She could see the vivid richness of the blue, purple, and scarlet linen held together by onyx clasps on his shoulders. Over the ephod, he wore a breastplate with twelve precious stones embedded in it, each stone engraved with the name of a tribe. On his head, he wore a turban made of fine linen. A blue cord held a gold engraved plate to the front of the headdress. She glided closer to the priest and looked at the writing on the gold plate. On it she clearly saw the words *Holiness to the Lord.* Her attention was then diverted to the altar between her and the priest. On it lay a perfect little lamb. It did not cry or try to get free from the Levite's grip. It only looked up at Bathsheba with large, sad eyes. She saw the priest lift a knife over his head and kill the lamb, its blood running down the side of the altar and collecting at the bottom. She looked again at the little ewe and realized it was her pet, Adina. She gasped in horror and shook herself out of the terrible dream.

When Bathsheba awoke, she was drenched in sweat. The cool evening air had not yet chased the heat of the day out of the house, and she felt as if she were inside a clay oven. She picked up her mat and went to the roof to get some air. When she reached the top of the staircase, her eyes automatically went to the balcony in the distance. It was empty. She sat on the soft cushions that had been left by her mother and looked up at the sky. The moon was once again full, and the stars seemed so close she reached her hand out to try to touch them. When she raised her hand, the gold bracelet Uriah had given her slid down her arm. She held it between her fingers and caressed the delicate strands. Tears again sprang to her eyes, but this time she did not weep or sob. She sat silently and let the tears slide freely down her checks.

"Oh, Uriah, please forgive me," she whispered softly to herself. With a bolt of realization, she remembered her dream. Maybe it wasn't Uriah's forgiveness she really needed right now. She recalled the conversation she had with Rivka years earlier when her friend had told her about the Lamb of God, who would take away the sins of all humankind. Was it possible? Could God really forgive her? Would His blood make even her clean? Again she turned her face to the heavens.

"God of my fathers, I have sinned against You and my husband. I am so sorry." Though her words were no more than a whisper, her voice broke as she tried to speak. "Lord, please forgive me. Cover me in Your blood. Please God, please . . ." She had no other words to speak, so she allowed her tears to say the rest.

Bathsheba awoke in the morning, feeling better than she had in weeks. Though she still had many challenges to face, she seemed to have the strength to do what was necessary. She went downstairs to wash and dress, then combed her hair and tidied the house before leaving. Before eating her cold bread, she offered a prayer of thanks to the Lord. When the kitchen area had been cleaned, she headed to Rivka's house.

When she arrived, she found her friend sitting by the fire eating breakfast with her son. They both looked up at her when she approached, but neither of them moved to greet her.

"Shalom, Rivka," Bathsheba spoke slowly and with more courage than she thought possible. "I have come to beg your forgiveness. You are right to cast the blame on me. My mother did not do this awful thing. I did. I have sinned greatly in the eyes of the Lord, and I've wronged both you and your cousin. I never meant to hurt Uriah. I really do love him. I was selfish, prideful, and stupid. Please forgive me."

Rivka looked up at her with tears streaming down her cheeks. She could not speak, but Bathsheba could tell by the look in her eyes that even if Rivka could not forgive her now, she eventually would. That was all she needed.

Chapter 27

Three more weeks passed before Bathsheba noticed she did not need to gather straw for her monthly blood. She was fairly certain why, but she needed to know for sure before making any decisions. Not knowing whom to turn to, she knelt inside her house and poured her problems out to God. She waited for an answer, but heard nothing. She spent the next several days praying and waiting for some response, but when none came, she decided it was time to take action. Girls were rarely taught to read and write, but because Bathsheba's father had no sons, he shared his knowledge with his daughters. Thinking she would never need to use the skills he tried to teach her, Bathsheba didn't pay as much attention to his lessons as she should have. She wished now that she had been a better student. She found a few sheets of papyrus, a quill, and a pot of ink that Uriah used when sending correspondence to his family in Canaan. Her penmanship was shaky, but she managed the simple message: I am pregnant.

When the letter was complete, she folded it in thirds then fastened it closed with wax from a candle. With her thumb, she pressed the warm wax down, creating a seal. She covered her head and face, tucked the letter into her belt, and headed to the palace. If neighbors stopped to stare at her, she didn't notice.

Once at the palace gate, she looked around for a messenger. She finally spotted a young man in royal robes passing through the gate.

"Excuse me, sir," she spoke respectfully with her head bowed. "Can you take a message to the king?"

"Yes, of course," he said, smiling at her like a wolf eyeing a lamb.

She handed him the letter then quickly went home feeling his gaze burning into her back. Everyone knew David communicated with God; perhaps he would know what to do.

Bathsheba spent as much time as possible on the roof, hoping to catch a glimpse of David on his balcony. Night after night, she watched the moon grow rounder and knew every passing day brought her closer to exposing her sin to the world. All these years she had hoped and prayed for a baby, and now she was finally going to have one. She should have been filled with joy, but instead she was terrified of what would happen. What if David ignored her letter? What if he didn't care? She couldn't allow herself to worry. She put her trust in God and in her king and focused instead on the life growing inside her.

One evening, she watched the sun slipping lower in the sky, leaving behind it streaks of pink and orange. Out of habit, she turned to look up at the palace and was surprised to see David watching her. It was a warm evening, but it looked as if he were wrapped in a blanket. It must have been the distance or the strange shades of color in the sky, but he seemed like a different man than the one she knew just a few weeks earlier. He appeared so old and worn. For a moment, she wondered if it was someone else until he held his hand out to her in greeting. She did the same, and they stood looking at each other for a few moments. He must have received her message. Surely he had a plan; after all, he was the king of a great nation and a man after God's own heart. He had to know what to do.

The next day, Bathsheba worked at the loom, trying to weave the threads into something that looked like a cloak. Her clumsy fingers frustrated her, but she needed the distraction. While picking at a knot, she heard a knock at the door. It was a messenger from the palace carrying a large basket.

"Is your husband in?" the boy asked.

"No, he is off fighting in Rabbah with the other soldiers. Can I help you with something?"

He looked puzzled, but continued with his message. "King David has sent this gift to you and your husband, Uriah. It is a token of the king's appreciation for Uriah's loyal service."

"I just told you, my husband is not here," Bathsheba said, feeling as confused as the boy looked.

"I'm sure he'll be along shortly, ma'am. I was told he was sent home by the king to spend the evening with his lovely wife." He blushed slightly as he spoke.

At last, she understood what David had in mind. "Oh, yes. I'm sure he'll be here soon. Thank you so much. Shalom." She took the large bundle from his arms and closed the door. Once inside, she opened the basket, hoping to find a note. There was none. Instead she found loaves of soft bread, a jug of wine, a package of meat wrapped in cloth, and several other fine delicacies from the palace. Even without direction from David, she knew what he intended. Uriah had been pulled from battle to report to the king. As a reward, he would be sent home to his wife. They could lie together, and in a few weeks, she could safely announce that she and Uriah were going to be parents. Then no one would ever know about the result of the indiscretion. Even Rivka would hesitate to tell Uriah if she knew they were going to have a baby together.

Bathsheba practically flew around the house preparing for Uriah's arrival. She dressed in her finest robe and brushed her hair until it shone like black onyx. Once she looked her best, she began the meal preparations. Meat was a luxury soldiers' wives seldom enjoyed. She had prepared plenty of Passover meals, but now, without bitter herbs, she wasn't sure what to do with the meat the king had sent. She started with garlic and onion and added a little salt. She felt confident that Uriah would be pleased with the meal regardless of what seasonings she used. As she cooked, she pictured in her mind the reunion with her husband. He would walk up to the house and smell the food cooking. He would see her from a distance, and they would rush into each other's arms. He had been away from the comforts of home for a long time, and she was sure he would be eager to be with her.

The day wore on, and Uriah did not come home. Smelling the cooking meat for so long turned Bathsheba's stomach, and she couldn't eat it. She did break off a few pieces of bread and dipped it into watered-down wine. Eventually she put away the leftover food and banked the fire. She sat outside of the house long after the sun went down, but when she kept nodding off to sleep, she decided to go inside and go to bed.

Chapter 28

The next morning Bathsheba awoke expecting to see her husband by her side, but he was not there. Perhaps she had misunderstood David's message. There must have been a mistake. Surely Uriah would have come home to her if given the opportunity.

She was relieved when her sister approached her home a few hours later. Atarah always knew what was going on around the palace. Perhaps she could help her figure things out.

"Shalom, sister, what news do you bring?" She stopped sweeping and motioned for her sister to sit with her.

Atarah smiled slightly at her sister's directness. "I see you got the basket Nadav prepared for you and Uriah. King David himself came to the kitchen yesterday to order it. Everyone was in a tizzy at the sight of him in the servants' quarters."

"Yes, I got the basket, but my husband did not arrive as expected."

"I know. I heard he slept at the palace gates last night, even after the king told him to go home to his wife. You can't really be surprised. Sometimes I think he'd rather be off fighting a war than here with you."

"You can be as mean as Eema!" Bathsheba snapped at her sister.

"Oh, who cares? It was a nice gesture, but David can't really think he can make amends by giving Uriah a night off and a basket of food."

"You don't understand, Atarah. I need Uriah to come home to me."

"Why? You should be used to him sleeping at the palace."

"It's complicated."

"What, you're not . . ." Her voice trailed off as she realized what her sister was implying.

"Yes, I'm pregnant, and if Uriah doesn't come home, I'm ruined."

Atarah sat staring at her with her mouth hanging open.

"Oh, close your mouth before you catch a fly," Bathsheba said, growing more and more annoyed with her sister.

"Does David know?"

"Yes, that's why he tried to send Uriah home. If only he would cooperate, everything would be fine. I just don't understand him. Why doesn't he want to be with me?" The familiar feelings of doubt and abandonment started to resurface. "You should have seen the meal I prepared for him, and my robe, and . . ." She knew it didn't matter. None of it mattered. Uriah was bound to his duty by something she would never understand. Perhaps David would try again. Perhaps tonight her husband would come home to her.

The next day came and went, and there was still no sign of Uriah. The following afternoon, Atarah came again to see her, eager to share the latest news. Once they were comfortably seated, Atarah began.

"My friend, Libi, is one of the girls who serves the king his meals. She came to me this morning with some information she thought I would be interested in since it pertained to my brother-in-law."

"Well, what is it?" Bathsheba urged her on.

"Last night, Uriah dined with the king and his family. In itself that would have been a great honor for any soldier, but then after everyone else had finished eating, David asked Uriah to stay. The two of them continued talking and drinking together until late into the night. Libi said she tried to count how many times she was told to fill Uriah's cup, but she lost track after a while. Anyway, David finally told Uriah to go home to his wife to enjoy some time away from the siege.

"When Libi took breakfast in to the king the next morning, she found him very upset. He had just been informed that Uriah had not gone home, so he sent a guard to bring him in. When Uriah arrived, David asked him why he insisted on staying at the palace. Uriah told him he couldn't in clear conscious sleep in the comfort of his home and lie with his wife while his fellow soldiers slept out in the field. Then David himself wrote a letter, without even calling a scribe. He sealed it and gave it to Uriah to deliver to his commander, Joab. Then David sent him back to the battle-front. Uriah just left a few hours ago—so much for David's great plan."

Bathsheba listened to the story with a sick feeling in the pit of her stomach. She had never felt so unloved and rejected in her life. Every measure was taken to make Uriah come home to her, and yet he still chose to stay away. How could he pretend to love her so much when he was with her, but then act as if she didn't matter to him at all when he was away? She wanted to be everything to him, but she felt like nothing. Well, it didn't matter anymore. It was just a matter of time, and everyone would know she had been unfaithful to him. Then Uriah really wouldn't want anything to do with her.

Once her sister left, Bathsheba sat for hours trying to mentally prepare herself for what could happen when her condition became obvious. Once Uriah declared her an adulteress, she would be taken to the elders of the city for judgment. She could picture their faces— old men who were friends of her father, the man who performed their marriage ceremony, even her grandfather. They would question her and try to find out the name of the baby's father. She swore to her-self she would never tell. It was bad enough to hurt Uriah; she couldn't bear to hurt the other man she cared about as well. They would find her guilty and sentence her to stoning outside the city walls. Because her parents protected her from such events, she had never seen a stoning, but she remembered hearing about a neighbor girl who had been caught in the act. She had been dragged out through the western gates of the city and stoned to death in the area called Hinnom. Though the girl's parents wept for her, they were the first to cast stones.

Bathsheba wondered whether David could find a way to save her without implicating himself. It didn't seem possible. Why would he jeopardize his crown, even his life, for a girl he barely knew? She was doomed. Too exhausted to agonize more about it, she surrendered herself to whatever fate would befall her. She was afraid of the humiliation, pain, and death that faced her, but she knew she deserved it all. She just hoped no one else would be hurt by what she had done.

Chapter 29

Several days later, Bathsheba was awakened by a knock at the door. She was still half asleep when she opened the door and saw a soldier standing outside. His head was bowed respectfully, and he did not make eye contact with her. He could have been there for any number of reasons—a problem with her family, a summons from the king, a report from the battle in Rabbah. Bathsheba was not at all prepared for what he told her.

"Are you the wife of Uriah the Hittite?"

"I am," she answered slowly.

"I regret to inform you that your husband was killed in battle near the walls of Rabbah. He died bravely with several other mighty soldiers while attacking the city. Services will be held for all of the men this afternoon at the tombs in the Kindron Valley. The king will provide the funeral meal this evening at the palace." The soldier bowed low to her and departed.

Bathsheba stood frozen in place for several minutes after he left, her mind spinning. *Uriah dead, how can this be? It was a siege, not a battle. Why was he sent in to attack a city as well protected as Rabbah? The army had been there for months; surely the city would have surrendered soon enough.* She couldn't think straight. Something wasn't right about all of this, but she couldn't figure it out. Her thoughts were interrupted by the sound of a woman wailing several houses away. Someone else must have just received similar news.

Bathsheba went inside to dress and prepare herself for the funeral. Some power other than her own moved her through the various tasks. She was surprised that her eyes were still dry. She felt too shocked and confused to cry; anyway, it was better to just keep moving.

Before she reached the palace gates, she heard the mourners wailing. There were so many people there. She wondered how many other men died with Uriah. Her sister and mother were there crying with the other women. She almost didn't recognize her mother. Was it possible that Shiran had aged so much in such a short time? Atarah came to Bathsheba's side as soon as she could get through the crowd.

"Oh, sister, I'm so sorry. Please come walk with Eema and me."

Without a word, Bathsheba followed her to the group of women. For the first time, she noticed Rivka standing in the crowd with her son on her hip. Both of them were crying. Bathsheba knew how much Uriah meant to her, so she went to try to offer comfort. But as she approached her friend, she was shaken by the look on Rivka's face. She knew Rivka was still angry with her, but she hoped they could reunite in their shared love of Uriah. When she looked into Rivka's swollen, red eyes, she saw it was not to be.

"Do you see now what you have done?" Rivka chided. "Do you see how many people you have destroyed?"

"Rivka, what do you mean? I had nothing to do with Uriah's death."

"Someday you will understand, and you will truly be sorry. May God forgive you when that day comes." Without another word, Rivka turned and walked away.

Bathsheba stood stunned until her sister spoke.

"Don't mind her," she said, "she is grieving too much to know what she is talking about."

"I know she loved her cousin very much, but I had no idea . . ."

"It's not just her cousin she mourns for. Rivka's husband, Zabad, died too."

A groan escaped Bathsheba's lips, and she felt faint. Her sister, being the only one who knew about her condition, tried to help keep her steady. The procession began moving along the familiar route she had taken for her father's funeral. Atarah stayed close to her sister, giving much-needed support to make the short journey. Once they reached the caves, she saw seven bodies wrapped tightly in grave clothes lying on the ground. Two men stood in front of the opening of the tomb. One was dressed in priestly garments and the other in royal robes. She blinked several times before she realized it was King David standing next to the Levite. The king stepped forward and began to talk about the bravery and valor of the men who died in his service. Bathsheba was too stunned to hear the words he was saying, but she did not miss the occasional glances he sent her way. When David finished speaking, he stepped aside, and the priest finished the burial services. The bodies were then carried into the large cave and placed on shelves chiseled into the walls. Once they were all inside, a group of soldiers pushed a rock in front of the opening. The mourners wailed and cried. Bathsheba could not make a sound, but she felt the hot tears slide slowly down her cheeks.

Chapter 30

That evening, the mourners were ushered into a large dining area in the palace for the funeral meal. Bathsheba sat at a table to the left of the head table, where the king and his family were seated. She looked at the women seated around her and realized they were the family members of the other men who died with Uriah. Rivka was seated there as well, but she avoided making eye contact with Bathsheba. The old woman next to her cried softly into a small piece of cloth that looked like it had been torn from a cloak. Bathsheba was moved by the woman's grief and asked her if there was anything she needed.

"No, dear, thank you," she said as she patted Bathsheba's hand. "Look at you, so brave. Which one was yours?"

"My husband is, I mean was Uriah, the Hittite."

"Oh, yes, I've heard of him. My Elhanan was recently transferred to his regiment."

"Was Elhanan your son?"

"Yes, my youngest. I have two older boys, but they both married Moabites and moved to Kir-hareseth. My Elhanan has been taking care of me since my husband died. Poor thing spent all his time fighting battles and taking care of his old mother. He never even had time to find a wife, and now . . ." She broke off in a sob.

Bathsheba put her arm around the woman and found herself crying right along with her.

"Now, now, dear, I'm sorry to get you upset. You were doing so well until I started blubbering." She used the edge of her robe to wipe Bathsheba's tears. "There now, that's better. So, tell me, did you and Uriah have any children?"

"No," Bathsheba said simply.

"Oh, I'm sorry." The old woman was quiet for a moment then continued more gently, "Do you have family in the city?"

"None that I can stay with. I'm really not sure what I'm going to do now."

"Well, I'm probably going to have to go to Moab. I wish my sons hadn't taken those foreign wives. It's too bad I can't take you with me. You're ten times prettier than either one of those heathens. Well, a girl like you isn't going to have any trouble finding another man." She smiled at Bathsheba and then dipped a piece of bread into her soup.

Bathsheba tried to eat some of the food placed before her, but she couldn't get it past the lump in her throat. With the older woman focused on her meal, Bathsheba was able to sneak a few glances at the king. He sat quietly while conversations swirled around him. He raised his eyes from the untouched food in front of him and looked over at her. Their eyes met and held for what seemed like hours but was probably just an instant. She saw the dull, sad look on his face clear when he looked at her, and she felt the heat that took its place. Was it possible she meant more to him than a one-night affair? She had thought about their evening together many times in the past few weeks. She wondered if he had too. He seemed to read the questions in her eyes, and for a moment, it looked as if he wanted to cross the room and pull her into his arms again. Her heart quickened, and she felt color race to her cheeks.

"Are you well, dear? You look flushed. Here, drink some water." The voice of the woman next to her jerked Bathsheba back to reality. Bathsheba took the water the woman offered her and drank it dutifully. She was thankful for the cooling effect it had on her. When she looked at David again, he was engaged in conversation with the man on his left. All she saw was the back of his full, dark hair, but she felt another set of eyes on her. When she turned, she saw Rivka watching her. Though everyone else in the room seemed oblivious to what had just transpired between the king and his mistress, Rivka had seen it all.

Chapter 31

The week of mourning passed slowly. Bathsheba received few visitors, so she had plenty of time to herself. Most of the time, she sat on the roof crying and thinking. She wept for Uriah, for the little time they had together, for never giving him a son, but mostly for never making him truly happy. In her solitude, she also shed tears for the loss of her friendship with Rivka. She wanted to help her through the deaths of her beloved cousin and husband, but Bathsheba knew her help wouldn't be appreciated. It was understandable that she was angry about the affair, but Bathsheba couldn't figure out why Rivka seemed to blame her for the deaths of all those soldiers. She replayed Rivka's last words over and over in her mind, but couldn't make sense of them. Well, she had enough to worry about without adding Rivka's condemnation. Bathsheba still didn't know what would become of her when her pregnancy became obvious.

When her tears were spent and the mourning period was over, Bathsheba washed the ashes from her hair and took off the sackcloth she had been wearing. She studied her abdomen before slipping her linen tunic over her head. It would be months before anyone would notice, perhaps she could think of something before then. Perhaps she could go to her grandfather for help. She wondered if he even knew about Uriah's death. He hadn't attended the funeral, and no one had seen him for several weeks. She decided she would go to the palace the next morning to see if she could find out where he was. He was her closest living male relative; surely he would take care of her. Having some kind of plan in place, she slept soundly through the night.

The next morning, Bathsheba dressed in one of her nicer robes. She knew her clothing was far inferior to what the women of the court wore, but she tried her best to look presentable so she wouldn't embarrass her grandfather. While she was eating breakfast, she saw four guards approach her house. She couldn't imagine what they could possibly want with her. But she rose from her mat to greet them.

"King David wishes to see you," the man in charge spoke briskly. "Please take a few moments to gather your belongings. I will escort you to the palace, and my men will follow with whatever items you would like to take."

"What items? Why would I take my things to the palace?" she asked, feeling confused.

"I don't know, ma'am. I was just told to bring you and your belongings to the king."

Not knowing what else to do, she began bundling some kitchen items.

"Uh, excuse me, ma'am, I don't think you'll be doing any cooking. You can leave your dishes here."

"Oh, yes, of course," she stammered. She went inside and gathered up her clothes and personal items. As she packed, she started to understand what was going on. Perhaps David intended to take her as a concubine. She and the baby could live at the palace! She remembered the beautiful gardens she walked through near the women's quarters. She never dreamed she would live there. She quickened her pace as the excitement coursed through her veins. Not only was she probably going to live at the palace, she would get to see David. She knew she had to share him with several other women, but just to see him again would make her feel so much better.

She stacked her few belongings in the corner and showed the men what needed to go with her. Then the leader of the group escorted her the short distance to the palace. The neighbors watched the procession, their mouths gaping. Bathsheba didn't care. Let them stare. She was going to see David; nothing else mattered.

Chapter 32

Once inside the palace walls, Bathsheba was led through the inner courtyard toward the staircase leading to David's quarters. The court was full of people who watched her curiously. When she reached the top of the stairs, David was standing there, apparently waiting for her. He instructed the guard to have her belongings taken to the women's quarters; then he escorted her to his bedchamber.

"Bathsheba, I have done nothing but think of you all these weeks. Please tell me you've thought of me too."

"I have," she said breathlessly.

The king seemed relieved to hear it. In one fluid motion, he pulled her into his arms and held her close.

"I've taken care of everything. Now that Uriah is gone, we can be together. You will be my wife now. We will have this child together."

It was too much for her to absorb. Bathsheba pulled away from the king's embrace and stood staring at him in shock. Finally, she started to understand the depths of what he had done.

"Tell me how my husband died," she said guardedly.

"Didn't you hear me? I want you to be my wife. You will be a queen."

For the first time, she was unimpressed by the man standing before her. He was no longer the great, godly king she had admired since her childhood. He was a desperate murderer.

"You killed him," Bathsheba whispered in horror. "You killed all of them."

"I didn't kill them. They died in battle," he retorted, looking a little shocked by her impertinence.

"How did they die? Why were they sent so close to the walls of the city? You ordered it, didn't you?"

"Bathsheba, please," he urged, "I need to be with you. When I got your letter, I didn't know what to do. I tried to get Uriah to go home. It made me sick to think of sending him to lie with you, but I did it to save your honor. If only he would have listened to me." He swore under his breath, then continued, "I tried, really I did. I didn't know what else to do. When he refused to go home, I sent him back to the battle with a note for his commander, Joab."

"What did the note say?" Bathsheba asked even though she didn't really want to know the answer.

"I told him to place Uriah's regiment near the wall and then start attacking the city. Once the battle was in full swing, I told him to pull all the other troops out—Bathsheba, I must have you. I'll do anything. You will have everything you've ever dreamed of—the finest clothes, jewels, anything, just name it and it's yours. Besides, you must think of our child, our little prince. He will have your beauty and my strength; what a king he will make someday. Please say you'll be my wife."

At that moment, Bathsheba finally understood what her mother meant when she warned her of the things women sometimes have to do for their children.

She swallowed her anger and bowed low before him. "Yes, David, I will be your wife."

David lifted her into his arms again and kissed her passionately.

"I have prepared a wedding and feast for you," he informed Bathsheba. When he saw the look of fear on her face, he quickly continued, "Don't worry, it's just family and a few close friends. We'll have the wedding ceremony on the roof so the people of the city can witness our union and have no doubt that you are mine. I'll keep the guest list to the meal small, but you do have to meet the rest of the family," he said with a slight smile.

He led her farther into the room where a beautiful gown had been prepared for her. She had never seen anything like it. The tunic was made of a soft blue silk that looked as if it had been pulled from the sky. The girdle and headdress were made from a darker blue material that had been embroidered with gold stitching.

David quietly slipped out of the room and sent a female servant in to help Bathsheba dress. The girl rubbed henna oil into her hands and feet and brushed her hair until it shimmered. She then arranged the garments so they most flattered Bathsheba's beautiful figure. When the servant sat down to tie her sandals, there was a knock at the door. The servant answered and returned with Atarah.

"Oh, sister," Atarah gasped.

"Atarah, what are you doing here?"

"Well, I heard you are getting married, and I didn't want to miss it again."

"I'm so glad you came. I just can't believe all of this is happening. I just finished the week of mourning for Uriah yesterday, and now I'm marrying the man who sent him to his death."

"What are you talking about?" Atarah questioned.

"I just found out Uriah's death was planned. David did it all so we could be together. It is my fault. Rivka was right," Bathsheba admitted and started to shake uncontrollably.

Atarah held Bathheba and let her cry for a moment. "You have to stop worrying about the past. David obviously loves you, or he wouldn't have gone through all this trouble. You are about to marry the most handsome, powerful man in the country. You are going to be a queen. Now you have to compose yourself. The townspeople are gathering in the streets outside of the palace. They've come to see a wedding. We can't have the bride crying." She dried her sister's eyes and helped to smooth her headdress. "There, you look so beautiful. If only Eema could see you now."

"Where is Eema?"

"She's at home with the children. She didn't think you would want to see her right now. She knew you would have a lot on your mind."

"Oh, I guess I haven't been very forgiving to her, have I? It really isn't her fault. I have to tell her I'm not angry with her. Will you please send the servant to fetch her? I would like to have you both with me when I get married."

"Better yet, I'll get her, and we'll meet you on the roof. You should see the canopy David is having erected. It's at the highest point of the palace where everyone can see it from below. He's really going all out for you."

Bathsheba was shocked that he would even bother with a wedding after everything that had happened. Perhaps he really did care about her. He was willing to make her a wife rather than a concubine and honor her with a ceremony and feast. She would try her best to be grateful and kind to him. She vowed to be a better wife to him than she had been to Uriah.

Chapter 33

When Bathsheba had finished dressing, the servant girl guided her to a staircase that led to the roof of the palace. Several people had already gathered there, including her mother and sister. She rushed to them and embraced her mother, kissing her on both cheeks. This simple act brought tears to Shiran's eyes.

"My daughter, you are more beautiful than even I could have ever imagined. King David is a lucky man to have such a wife."

"Oh, Eema, I'm so glad you're here. So much has happened; there's so much I want to say. . . ."

Just then, David approached the three women. He stared at Bathsheba, drinking in her beauty for a moment before turning his attention to the others.

"I hope you don't mind, I asked my sister and mother to attend the ceremony," Bathsheba spoke respectfully, keeping her eyes down.

"No, of course I don't mind. I'm delighted to have them. Please introduce me to these lovely women."

They all smiled at his charm; then Bathsheba told him their names. He nodded politely to Atarah then gave Shiran a slight bow.

"I knew your husband well, Shiran. He was a good man. Since he is not here, I would like to pay you the bride-price for your daughter." The king slipped a ring from the smallest finger on his left hand and gave it to Shiran. It was a thick band of gold with a large emerald in the center, surrounded by tiny rubies. Bathsheba didn't know much about jewelry, but she knew this ring was probably worth more than her father could have earned in a year. "You are welcome to live here at the palace as well. I will have a room prepared for you in the women's quarters, if you would like."

Shiran's face lit up, not just from the precious stones she held, but also at the thought of spending the rest of her days in comfort at the palace. It was the dream of her life, fulfilled at last. She bowed low to the king.

"You are too kind to an old woman. Thank you for your generosity. I pray my daughter makes you very happy. My blessings to you both."

David squeezed Bathsheba's hand. "A few more minutes, my love, and the ceremony will begin. Ladies, please stay for dinner. I will have the servants prepare a place for you. Atarah, I'll see to it that your husband has the rest of the evening off so he can join you. I'm sorry your grandfather, Ahithophel, is still away on business, but if you have other family you would like to invite, please do." With one more delightful smile, he turned and walked away.

All three of the women turned into giggling girls the minute the king was out of earshot.

"Look at this ring," Shiran squealed, holding it out for her daughters' inspection. "I've never seen anything so beautiful in my life. And can you believe the king invited me to stay here at the palace? I hope you don't mind my moving out, Atarah."

Atarah laughed without malice, "I don't know, Eema; it will be awfully lonely in our poor little house without you." She put her arms around her mother and hugged her. "How could I hold you back from your dream of being a lady of the court? We'll get by without you."

Bathsheba was proud to make her family so happy. Their joy was contagious, and she couldn't help but be swept up in the moment with them.

Chapter 34

The wedding ceremony was held under the large white canopy David had erected for the occasion. A very old, small man had a prayer for the couple, then blessed them. The people around cheered when the ceremony was over. David walked his new bride to the edge of the roof so the people gathered below could get a better look at them. Bathsheba felt light headed from the height, and she quickly closed her eyes. Taking a deep breath, she opened them again and tried to behave as she imagined a queen should. David motioned to the servants stationed in various places throughout the crowd, and they began to distribute cakes to the spectators. The faces of everyone around them showed nothing but happiness for the couple, but Bathsheba knew they would find out the truth eventually, and then they would not think so highly of her. She put the dreadful thoughts out of her mind and tried to enjoy the moment.

Keeping her gaze down, Bathsheba allowed David to lead her to the stairs and into the dining area. It was the same room she had been in just a week earlier for Uriah's funeral meal, but this time, she was seated at the head table next to her new husband. Her family was seated at a small table, and there were a few other people there she did not recognize. She was relieved that it was not a huge feast.

Servants brought drinks and platters of fruit for everyone to start on while David introduced his family to his new wife. First came his oldest son, Amnon, who walked arm in arm with his mother, Ahinoam. They stood before the head table and bowed respectfully to Bathsheba. Amnon was a handsome young man about her age. He looked her directly in the eyes, which made her uncomfortable. He seemed to have a dark, hungry look about him that she had seen in the eyes of other men. She knew immediately that he was not the kind of man she wanted to find herself alone with.

David's second oldest son, Chileab and his mother, Abigail, followed them. He was a small-boned young man with a high forehead and light brown eyes. There was nothing powerful or threatening about him. It was hard to imagine him ever sitting on a throne. Abigail was at least as old as Bathsheba's mother but was still a very beautiful woman. There was also a kindness and intelligence in her eyes that Bathsheba was instantly drawn to.

Bathsheba recognized the wife named Maacah—she was the awful woman Bathsheba had met in the garden with her nephew just a few years earlier. Her son, Absalom, and daughter, Tamar, had grown taller, but Maacah hadn't changed a bit. Maacah bowed dutifully, but did so with a smirk on her face.

Next came Adonijah and his mother, Haggith. He was a very intense boy of about ten, who seemed to keep his mother looking eternally tired. Then the wife named Abital followed with her son, Shephatiah. Then came the sixth son, Ithream with his mother, Eglah. The parade of concubines followed with their many children, whom Bathsheba could not keep track of.

By the time David called over his first wife, Michal, daughter of the late King Saul, Bathsheba's head was swimming with names. Michal was well past her prime, but it was obvious she had been a great beauty in her day. She stood before the head table and glared at her husband.

"I hope you don't expect me to bow to your whore, David," she said spitefully.

Everyone in the room stirred uncomfortably, but no one said a word. Angry color flooded David's face, but when he spoke, he was surprisingly calm.

"I've warned you before to hold your tongue, woman, and I will not tell you again." He rose from his chair and stood directly in front of her. "Barren daughter of Saul, not only will you bow to my new wife, you will surrender your title to her. Servants, please have Michal's belongings moved to a lesser house in the women's quarters. Bathsheba will take her house when our wedding week is over. Family, please make welcome my new first wife, Bathsheba, daughter of Ammiel."

At this, the small crowd broke out in excited whispers. Michal turned and ran from the room, completely humiliated. Bathsheba was afraid she had just made a new enemy but the encouraging looks on the faces of her family pushed her fears aside.

David calmly walked back to Bathsheba's side and sat down. With a nod to the servants, the dinner was served. David barely ate, but instead spent most of his time looking at his new wife. Despite the anger she had felt toward him earlier in the day, Bathsheba found herself drawn in by the dark eyes that were so attentive to her every move. She caught herself smiling at his boyish attempts to make her comfortable. He held her hand whenever he could and absentmindedly stroked her wrist with his thumb. His touch sent heat up her arm and through her entire body. Everyone else in the room seemed to disappear as the two sat with their fingers intertwined under the table.

At last David rose to leave. He placed his hand under his wife's elbow and gently lifted her to her feet. Everyone rose and bowed to the couple as they walked out of the room together. He led Bathsheba through unfamiliar corridors of the palace that were completely empty. When he was sure they were alone, he made an attempt to grab her, but she escaped coyly and pretended to run from him. He laughed and chased her playfully until she finally allowed herself to be captured. She fell into his arms giggling for the second time in one day. Never before had she felt so loved and so happy. The long weeks filled with worry and fear vanished with a single kiss from David. She knew at last everything would be all right.

Chapter 35

They spent an entire week together, never leaving David's bed-chamber. The servants brought food throughout the day and night. David and Bathsheba slept whenever they felt tired and when they awoke, there was always a fresh tub filled with scented water for them to bathe in. They learned much about each other during those days. They shared not only their bodies with one another, but also their minds and souls. David told her stories of his childhood—the long summer days spent tending his father's sheep, the relationships with his brothers, his dear friend, the prophet Samuel, who secretly anointed him king when he was just a boy. He sang songs to her, comparing her beauty to the flowers of the field. Bathsheba was shy with David at first, but he asked her questions and encouraged her to share her thoughts and memories with him. Eventually she opened up and told him things she had never even said out loud before. She talked about her mother and sister, her nephews, and even her friend Rivka. At one point, Bathsheba broke down and cried when Uriah's name came up, but David didn't become angry; he just held her and stroked her hair softly until her sobs subsided. She was embarrassed for behaving like an emotional woman in front of him, but she couldn't help but love him more for his tenderness toward her.

Sometimes when they slept, David tossed and turned and woke covered in sweat. She would find him sitting next to the bed with a blanket over his shoulders and his face in his hands. It reminded her of their first night together, and it filled her with guilt and sorrow. He never shared his nightmares with her, but he didn't have to.

The week came to an end all too soon, and David had to resume his royal duties. Their last morning together, he called for a servant girl to help Bathsheba dress and settle into her house in the women's quarters. Before he left, he kissed her softly and spoke tenderly in her ear, telling her they would be together again soon.

The servant brought with her a beautiful gown made of soft green linen. She helped Bathsheba dress and then led her through the palace gardens to her new quarters. She inhaled the late summer scents that surrounded them as they walked under the trees leading up to the entrance of the women's quarters. The servant spoke in a low voice to the eunuch who was standing guard. He bowed low to Bathsheba then hurried inside. A moment later, he returned with an older woman at his side.

"Shalom, Bathsheba. My name is Matana. I have been asked to serve you. Please follow me."

The woman seemed much too elegant to be a maid. Bathsheba suddenly felt intimidated by her new surroundings. If her servant was able to unnerve her so easily, what would she do around the other queens and princesses?

Bathsheba dutifully followed the woman into the most beautiful courtyard she had ever seen. The grassy area in the center was edged with lilies in full bloom. A few women reclined on cushions under a large shade tree in the center. Several small stone houses encircled the courtyard. Directly in front of the entrance was a much larger structure made of wood. This is the house she was led to. When she entered the front door, she was shocked by the size. The large open room was a richly furnished sitting room. A jar of water and a basin to the right of the door was used to wash the feet of guests. To the left of the door was a sleeping mat for the servant. In the center of the room was a table set low to the ground with several cushions placed around it. The walls were decorated with rich tapestries depicting golden birds flying over seas made of shimmering threads that sparkled when the light hit them. The large rug on the floor was even more beautiful than the one in the king's own bedroom.

When Bathsheba walked farther into the house, she found two sleeping rooms on either side of the sitting room. Both were equally beautiful and elegantly decorated.

"Who is to live here with me?" she asked the maid who was busy setting out a plate of food for her mistress.

"This is your home, Ma'am."

"It's much too large for just me. What am I to do with all of this?"

"I believe the king would like for you to fill it with children," she answered with a smile.

Bathsheba's hand reflexively went to her abdomen.

"Perhaps it won't be long?" the maid pried.

"Oh, I uh, I hope not," Bathsheba stammered. She silently scolded herself for her behavior. She was a queen now and she had to start acting like one. She couldn't let this servant get her so rattled. "Have you been here long?" she asked Matana, trying to turn the focus off of herself.

"Yes, I have been serving the kings' families since I was a child. My mother was one of King Saul's concubines, and I was given to Michal when I was old enough to attend her."

"So does that mean Saul was your father too?"

"That's right, and Michal is my half sister. If my mother had been in higher standing in the king's harem, I would have been a princess rather than a servant. But, you'll find out soon enough how unimportant women can be in a place like this."

Bathsheba was shocked by the woman's candor, but she took advantage of her willingness to talk. "Where is your sister now?"

"She's in the last house on the left. You probably won't see her for a while, but when you do, you'd better watch out."

"Why?"

Matana laughed out loud, "She's not exactly happy about her

change in position. She has been the head queen for a long time, and she won't take kindly to you stripping her of that position."

"Yes, but it wasn't my fault . . ." Bathsheba started then quickly changed the direction of the conversation. "Matana, this must be difficult for you as well. I don't want to separate you from your sister. If you would like to go to her, please don't let me stop you. I am quite accustomed to life without a servant."

"Oh, no, Ma'am. Please don't misunderstand. I'm happy to serve you." Matana bowed low, acting like a maid for the first time since they had met. "Let me stay here. Michal has never been an easy woman to live with, and it's not going to get any better now. Besides, you'll find I'm very useful to have around."

"Very well then. Perhaps you can start by telling me where my mother is?"

"Yes, of course. Shiran is in the home directly to our right. Would you like me to inform her of your arrival?"

"Oh, yes please," Bathsheba exclaimed, sounding more excited than she intended. "Could you ask her to come over to join me for breakfast? Did you make enough?"

"Certainly, Ma'am. I will return in a moment." Matana bowed again before leaving.

Bathsheba didn't have to wait long. Matana returned quickly with Shiran at her side.

"Your highness," Shiran said with a laugh as she bowed low to her daughter. "I believe I have someone here you may like to see." She tugged on a rope, and Adina waddled into the room.

"Oh, Eema, it's so good to see you, both of you." Bathsheba bent down to nuzzle her pet sheep. "I've missed you, my little friend, and I've missed you too, Eema. It's nice to have you so close. How is your house? Do you have everything you need?"

"It's wonderful, though not as nice as this," Eema said, looking away from her daughter and at her surroundings.

"Isn't it amazing? I still just can't believe it."

The women sat down at the table and allowed Adina to nibble on a few scraps of food while Matana finished preparing their meal. "I always knew you would be happy here," Shiran said. "Perhaps you will have better luck conceiving a child now."

"Oh, Eema, you don't know yet. I'm pregnant. It happened the first night David sent for me. It's been more than two moons already."

"Bathsheba! How wonderful. You may have the next king of Israel in your womb."

"David has plenty of sons already. I'm sure one of them will succeed him. But we will have a beautiful little prince or princess." Bathsheba's eyes grew dreamy as she spoke of her child.

"You have been honored as his first wife. It's very possible he will make your son the heir to his throne."

The reality of her mother's words set in, but was quickly followed by fear and doubt. "But what if people should find out about the affair and cover-up? He would have a great deal of difficulty gaining the crown under such circumstances."

"Don't worry, darling." Shiran patted her daughter's hand. "No one will ever find out."

As they spoke, Matana quietly served their meal, barely concealing the smile that was forming on her lips.

Chapter 36

As the days passed, Bathsheba grew more accustomed to her new life at the palace. She no longer spent her time fetching water, grinding barley, baking, and sweeping—now all of that was done for her. When she awoke in the morning, Matana had her breakfast ready for her. By late morning, she usually received word that the king would like to dine with her or have her come to him after dinner, depending on his evening responsibilities. A new gown was prepared for her every afternoon, and she spent several hours preparing herself for David. Matana had acquired a box of cosmetics, and she taught Bathsheba how to color her lips and cheeks. She also showed her different ways to arrange her hair using the jeweled combs that the king had given her as a gift. It was strange to have so much free time to spend on herself, but Bathsheba grew to like it more and more every day.

When she wasn't preening or spending time with her husband, Bathsheba enjoyed walking through the palace grounds with her pet. Adina loved the thick grass in the gardens and grew fatter with every passing day. She frequently saw most of David's other wives, but none of them spoke to her except for Abigail. On Bathsheba's second day in the women's quarters, Abigail came to visit, bringing gifts of sweet cakes and perfume. She didn't stay long, but promised to come again soon. Bathsheba liked her very much and hoped they could be friends.

Bathsheba noticed that the other women seemed to hate her. Perhaps they were angry that she had taken so much of David's attention. He spent every available night with her and completely stopped calling for his other wives. She lived in the most luxurious of the women's homes and wore the finest gowns; she understood why they resented her, so she tried to be as kind and friendly as possible.

One morning after breakfast, Bathsheba's sister came to visit. They met up with their mother and went for a walk together around the courtyard. The three women approached a small group of David's concubines, who stopped talking as soon as they were within earshot.

"Shalom," Bathsheba said as they drew near.

They pretended not to hear her and walked away as a group. One younger woman glanced over her shoulder once then quickly turned and left with the others.

"I don't understand why they treat me like that. I've done nothing to them," Bathsheba puzzled.

"I'm sure they're just jealous, dear," Shiran assured her daughter.

"You two really are sheltered here," Atarah said, sounding a bit smug and superior. "You have no idea what people are saying, do you?"

Bathsheba and Shiran were protected in their little world, so they really didn't know what Atarah was talking about.

"There is a rumor that David is very ill and that he may be dying from some kind of disease."

"That's ridiculous," Bathsheba interrupted. "I'm with him more than anyone else. If he's sick, surely I would know about it." She did have to admit to herself that he didn't look well lately. He had grown thinner and pale, and he woke often during the night shivering with a chill that made his entire body tremble. She was usually able to comfort him and warm him with her body, and he would fall asleep in her arms. When she tried to talk to him about what was wrong, he always said he was fine as long as she was near. She knew something was troubling him, but it wasn't a disease.

"That rumor was quickly chased away by a much more believable one," Atarah continued. "Now people are saying he suffers from a great sin he committed."

"And what do they say that sin is?" Bathsheba asked fearfully.

"They say he took another man's wife and got her pregnant. Then he killed the man so he could marry his mistress. The mistress is now the head queen of Israel."

"How would they know such things? No one knows of the baby except the three of us and David."

"Somehow it got out, and everyone is talking about it. The rumor spread through the palace like wildfire then out into the city, where it was quickly confirmed by people who saw you come to the palace several weeks before Uriah's death and the wedding."

"Who could have started this poison?"

"What do you know about your maid?" Shiran quickly asked.

"That's it! It has to be her. She is the half sister of Michal. Of course she would want to get back at me for taking her sister's title. She's made me uneasy ever since I came here. What should I do?"

"You must get rid of her," Shiran said.

"You can't throw out a daughter of Saul; that would only make everyone hate you more," Atarah added.

Bathsheba thought about the situation. She knew nothing of palace politics and didn't have a clue how to handle this. If only she had a friend in this place who could give her advice. Then she remembered Abigail's kind, intelligent eyes. Perhaps she could help.

"Never mind," she told her sister and mother. "I think I know who to talk to about this."

That afternoon, Bathsheba walked her sister home and stopped by the kitchen to ask her brother-in-law for a favor then headed home to prepare for her evening with David.

Chapter 37

As Bathsheba walked through the halls of the palace on her way to David's bedchamber, she spotted her grandfather talking to a small group of men. She hadn't seen him in weeks and wanted to run to him and tell him what had happened since he had left town, but it wasn't appropriate for a woman to approach a man in such a manner. So Bathsheba stood where he could see her and waited for him to finish his conversation. When he caught sight of her, he quickly excused himself from the group.

"Bathsheba, it is true. I've been hearing rumors since I arrived this morning, but I didn't think it was possible."

"Yes, Sav. David and I are married now."

Then Ahithophel did something that shocked his granddaughter— he spit on the ground and cursed David's name. "I have served that man loyally all these years, and this is how he repays my family? By disgracing my granddaughter and killing her husband, my friend!" Ahithophel was practically shouting now. "You think he honors you by giving you fine clothes and a title? Hah! He has ruined you. For eternity your name will be synonymous with adultery. Everyone is talking about you. They know about the child, and they know about its conception. I wondered why you were here so early that morning, but I didn't want to believe the talk. When I questioned David, he laughed and sent me to Hebron to take care of something any lesser servant could have handled. He just wanted to get rid of me. Well, I guess I should consider myself lucky he didn't get rid of me the way he did Uriah. This is what happens, child; this is what comes of giving men too much power. Well, I'll have no more of it!" Ahithophel raised his voice and addressed the people standing around the court, "I will no longer serve this king. I will not give my advice to a murderer and adulterer." He spit on the ground one more time then turned and walked away, leaving his granddaughter in the middle of the curious crowd.

As soon as Ahithophel left, everyone began talking at once. Now that the stories were publicly confirmed, the courtiers buzzed like bees. Bathsheba had never felt more exposed or vulnerable. She almost ran to the safety of David's bedroom. She longed for the warmth of his arms and his soothing words to chase away all the horrible things they had done, but when she entered his room, it was obvious he was in no state of mind to offer comfort. He sat huddled in the corner, wrapped in a blanket. He looked up at her when she entered, and his eyes were full of pain and grief.

"What's wrong, my love?" Bathsheba asked as she rushed to his side.

"I'm just so cold," David said trembling.

"Well, I'm warm enough for both of us. This baby keeps me toasty," she said, trying to make him smile as she pulled him into her arms.

She felt his body shake, but not from cold this time—he was crying. It frightened her to see such a brave, strong man break down in tears. She had never seen her father or Uriah cry. She didn't know what to do.

"Oh, David, what's bothering you? Please tell me. Perhaps I can help."

David composed himself and looked at her sadly. "My friend Mephibosheth circumcised his baby today. I joined him at the tent of the Lord for the ceremony. Once it was finished and the baby was calm, they asked me to sing a psalm for the occasion. I tried to sing and praise God's goodness, but no words would come out of my mouth." David swallowed hard a few times then continued. "You warm my flesh like no woman ever has before, but inside . . . I just can't . . . ," he broke off and could no longer speak.

The two sat in silence, huddled together under David's blanket. Bathsheba felt the weight of what she had done pushing down on her once again. Not only was she responsible for starting a chain of events that resulted the deaths of Uriah and the other soldiers, but she had also ruined this great man. She remembered how godly David had seemed standing in front of the congregation gathered in front of the tent of the ark. The man who once wrote songs and sang like an angel couldn't even make a sound in praise to God. If only she would have been more careful, more modest. If only she had said No that night. He would have let her go, and he probably would have thanked her for it later. Bathsheba did love him, more than she thought was possible, but surely God would have found a way to bring them together without destroying so many lives. If only they had left things in His hands.

She fell asleep in David's arms and woke up with sunlight peeking into the room. David kissed her tenderly on the forehead. He looked as though he hadn't slept at all. As they gazed into each other's eyes, a fluttering feeling low in her stomach startled her. She jumped noticeably, causing her husband to give her a questioning look.

"What happened?" David asked.

"I don't know. I just felt something strange. Oh, there it is again." Bathsheba put her hand on her belly and waited for it to happen again. "I think it was the baby. I just felt him move!"

David quickly put his hand on her stomach to see if he could feel anything. They stayed frozen in place for a few minutes, but nothing happened. David laughed and kissed his wife again.

"Oh well, I'm sure I'll feel him soon enough." Bathsheba looked into David's tired eyes and thought she saw a glimmer of hope.

Chapter 38

A few hours later Bathsheba was back at home, preparing to pay a visit to Abigail. A servant delivered a basket that she had asked Nadav the previous afternoon to prepare. Bathsheba smiled when she looked at the beautiful arrangement of sweet breads and cakes he prepared all covered with a delicate piece of yellow cloth. She would have to remember to do something nice for her brother-in-law to thank him for his help.

Matana gave her a curious look when she left, but Bathsheba ignored it. She was trying to distance herself from the maid to avoid inadvertently giving her information that could later be used against her. She spent too much time worrying about what she already said in front of this potential spy and decided that it was better to talk to her as little as possible.

When Bathsheba reached Abigail's house, she was greeted warmly. The older woman invited her in, and the two sat comfortably on cushions in the main room of the house. Abigail graciously accepted the basket and asked one of her maids to prepare a plate so she could share the delicacies with her guest.

After exchanging formal niceties, Bathsheba took the conversation in a more personal direction.

"May I ask you a question, Abigail?

"Yes, of course."

"Why is it that you are the only one of David's wives who treats me with any kindness?"

"Well, the main reason is that I know several of your family members. Your grandmother was very dear to me."

"You knew my Sava? How?"

"Yes, and your grandfather and father as well. You see, when David and I were first married, he was still in hiding from Saul. There were several hundred men with him, including your father and grandfather. Some of the men had their families with them. There were no walls to separate men and women out in the wilderness, so we all developed special friendships. In the evenings, we would sit around the fire and tell stories and sing songs. Your grandfather was very entertaining." Abigail smiled as she reminisced. "I don't know if I would have made it those first few years if it wasn't for your grandmother. David had recently married Ahinoam, and she was unkind to me from the moment I came into the camp. Your grandmother took me under her wing and treated me like her own daughter. I loved her very much. Unfortunately, the wilderness was difficult for her. Your grandfather had to bury her in a cave on the mountain of Hachilah."

"Were you with her when she died?"

"Yes, I was right by her side, taking care of her until the very end."

"Then I owe you even more appreciation. Not only were you kind to the Sava I never knew, but also you have treated me nicer than anyone else here. The others won't even speak to me."

"It's difficult to share a man with many women. Some of them may be jealous because David seems to really care for you. Others are angry because they've heard you are pregnant and our husband still sleeps only with you. Most of these girls don't care much about David, but they do want to have as many children for him as possible. If one woman keeps all of his seed for herself, the others tend to become angry."

"But I have no control over what David does."

"Don't you? I think you underestimate his feelings for you. I've known him for a long time. I've seen many women pass through his bedroom, but I've never seen him look at any of them the way he looks at you. I believe he really loves you, Bathsheba."

"Oh, and I love him too. I really do, but do you think I should try to convince him to spend more time with the other wives?"

"He has plenty of children. Any more would just cause competition for the throne. If he is happy with you, there's no need to bother him with the silliness of women. The other women will come around eventually. They just need some time to get used to the idea that there is a new beauty in the palace." She smiled kindly and served Bathsheba another helping of bread and honey.

"What about Michal?"

"Well now, that's another story. I don't think she'll ever accept the fact that David has given you her position. She hasn't given you any trouble, has she?"

"No, not at all. In fact, I haven't even seen her since I moved here. Her half sister is another matter, though. Matana was left in Michal's house, and she is now my maid. I believe she may be spreading rumors about me, and I'm not sure what to do about it."

"Matana is harmless enough. I would be careful what you say, though, because she may accidentally take information back to Michal, who wouldn't hesitate to slander you. Do you feel they are spreading lies about you?"

Bathsheba hesitated. She wanted to be honest with her new friend, but she wasn't sure whether she could completely trust her. "No, they aren't really lies, just information that I don't necessarily want people to know about me."

"Well, unfortunately, that is something you'll have to get used to living here. All of our stories have been told around the city wells for years."

"What do you mean 'our stories'?"

"You don't think we all came to this palace as spotless maidens, do you? You may see a bunch of pampered women sitting around in the shade, but many of us have pretty interesting pasts."

"Really?"

"Sure, take Michal for example. You may think she's just a wicked snob, but things haven't been easy for her. Of course, you know she is the youngest daughter of King Saul. Well, she was in love with David from the time she was a little girl. She used to follow David and her older brother, Jonathan, around like a shadow. When she found out her father planned to give her older sister to him in an attempt to keep his loyalty, Michal was devastated. She went to her father and begged to be given to David instead. Saul didn't really want to give his oldest, most beautiful daughter to his enemy, so Michal was a good second choice. David was just a poor man and couldn't pay the bride-price for a princess, so Saul asked him for the foreskins of one hundred dead Philistines for her dowry. He did this in the hopes that David would be killed, and then he wouldn't have to deal with him anymore, but our David came through.

"Michal was a good wife to him. She protected him from her father's murder attempts and did everything she could for him while he was running for his life. It was difficult for her to be torn between her husband and father, but she remained loyal to David even when he was in hiding and she remained in Saul's palace. Eventually, she was given to another man named Phaltiel, who lived in Gallim. She was told that David was dead, and because she lived so far out of the city she had no way of knowing it wasn't true. In time, she grew to love her new husband and was very happy with him. But several years later, after David was crowned in Hebron, he sent his man Abner to return Michal. It was strictly a political move for David. He needed to try to make peace with Saul's surviving sons, and by taking their sister back, he showed there was no animosity between their houses."

"That must have been horrible for her. Didn't her new husband fight for her?"

"No, but he did follow her for miles, weeping all the way until Abner sent him home."

"Wasn't she happy David was still alive?"

"She probably would have been, but a lot had changed."

"What do you mean?"

"David married Ahinoam and then me while he was hiding from Saul. Once he was King of Judah, he added four more women to his harem. When Michal returned, she was still the first wife, but in name only. Ahinoam had already given David an heir, and I was expecting a child as well. His heart no longer belonged to Michal, and she quickly grew bitter and angry toward him. Her sharp tongue has kept her out of David's bedroom for years. I don't think he's called for her once since we've been in Jerusalem. So now she has no children, and she's trapped in a loveless, political arrangement for the rest of her life while the man she longs to be with is miles away."

"And what about you, Abigail; do you have a story?"

"Yes, but mine isn't nearly as sad. I was also married before. My husand's name was Nabal, and he was a wealthy landowner in Carmel. My beloved parents died when I was young, and my grandparents were too tired and old to secure a love match for me. So they settled for the largest bride-price. Nabal was a violent-tempered man who drank too much, but I worked hard for him and managed to stay out of his way as much as possible. I learned quickly how to take care of the many shepherds and servants he had as well as run much of the household. At the time, David was hiding in the country to avoid King Saul's death threats. He had a large army of about six hundred men following him. I knew they were living on our property, but since they offered protection to our flocks, I allowed them to stay. During the shearing festival, David sent a man to ask Nabal if he and his men could participate in the feast. After all, they had been partly responsible for the successful year we had, and they deserved to be rewarded. As usual, my husband responded with anger; he insulted David's man and sent him away empty-handed. When David found out, he rallied his troops to attack us. Fortunately, a servant warned me. I quickly prepared gifts for David and his men and then personally went out to greet them. Bowing low to David, I begged his forgiveness for the mistake my husband made.

"Surprisingly, David not only listened to me, but also thanked me and told me I had saved my entire household."

"Was your husband angry with you for acting without his knowledge?"

"I couldn't tell him about it that night because he got too drunk at the feast. The next morning when he had sobered up, I told him the whole story. He had a heart attack right there and died ten days later."

"So how did you come to be David's wife?"

"When he found out Nabal was dead, he sent a messenger to ask me if I would marry him. I had known the moment I saw David that I would do anything for him. He was so handsome and strong, and I could tell the Lord was leading in his life. I gathered my maids and went to David as quickly as I could—and I've never regretted it. Don't get me wrong. It's not easy for me to see him with other women, but I know in his own way he loves me. When I see our son smile at me, it's David's smile. I'm so much happier here than I was with Nabal. I thank God every day for what He did for me."

"You think God arranged it so you and David could be together?"

"Of course. He may have created the sun and moon and stars, but He still takes time for someone even as insignificant as me."

Back at her own house, Bathsheba kept thinking about Abigail's statement. What if she would have waited for God? How different things would have been for her and David!

Chapter 39

After her visit with Abigail, Bathsheba saw the other women through new eyes. She tried to return their hateful glances with smiles. Whenever she could, she brought them treats from the kitchen and, in time, they warmed to her kindness. Michal still avoided her, so Bathsheba decided to try to reach out a hand of friendship. She gathered flowers from behind her house and arranged them into a beautiful bouquet then put them in a clay pot filled with water. Bathsheba's maid curiously watched her every move. Matana even followed at a distance when she walked over to Michal's small house. When Michal answered the door, Bathsheba held the gift out to her.

"I saw these flowers growing behind the houses, and I thought you might like them," she said with a smile.

Michal glared at her but took the flowers and didn't throw them to the ground as Bathsheba half expected her to.

"What do you really want, first wife of David?"

"Nothing. I just wanted to come over and tell you I'm sorry about the way things turned out. I didn't mean for any of this to happen to you."

"If you think flowers are going to fix everything, you're wrong."

"I'm afraid I don't have it in my power to fix anything, but we have to live within the same walls for the rest of our lives, and I don't want to be your enemy."

Michal looked at her steadily for a moment. "Perhaps I underestimated you, daughter of Ammiel." With that she returned to her house and closed the door.

Bathsheba went home feeling just a little lighter. Matana continued to watch her as she worked, but she didn't say a word.

"Do you have something to say, Matana?" Bathsheba finally asked her.

"I just don't understand why you would be so nice to Michal after what she has done to you."

"Why, what has she done to me?"

"Don't you know she spread the story about your pregnancy? I guess it was my fault for telling her what I heard, but she made sure the rumor reached the ears of the appropriate people."

"Why did you tell her, Matana? Did you intend to hurt me?"

"No, it's not that. It's just that I don't really have anyone to talk to here, and she is my sister."

"Are you sure you don't want to go back to her? You are welcome to go, if you would be happier there."

"I hate to say it, but she really isn't a very nice woman. Even though I can tell you are suspicious of me, you have still treated me kindly. May I stay with you, if I promise to be more careful about what I repeat to my sister?"

"Of course, Matana. You've taught me a great deal since I've been here. I would hate to lose you. Now, let me help you with that laundry. We can get it done much faster if we work together."

Matana gave her mistress a refreshingly honest smile. Bathsheba felt so good from her small acts of kindness that she decided she would try to do more for the women around her.

That night when she was with David, she spoke to him about it.

"Why don't you call for your other wives anymore? I'm getting too big to be of any use to you."

"I just can't imagine being with any of them. You're the only one I want."

"What about Abigail?" Bathsheba continued as if she didn't hear him. "She is such a wonderful woman."

"She really is, but she's past her childbearing years. It would do me no good to spend the night with her."

"Well then, what if you just invited her for dinner? She loves you so much. I'm sure it would make her very happy to spend a little time with you."

David seemed to consider it for a moment. "Bathsheba, I don't want to hurt you by spending time with other women. After all, I've already caused you so much pain. I just couldn't bear to make you unhappy."

"Oh, my love, you could never make me unhappy. In fact, it would please me very much if you spent time with Abigail."

"I see. You're tired of me already. You just can't stand the thought of another night with an old man," David teased. "Very well, if it will make you happy, I will dine with Abigail tomorrow evening."

"Thank you, my lord," Bathsheba said, bowing playfully to him. When she had trouble getting to her feet, he helped her up and then held her and her growing belly in his arms.

Chapter 40

As the season changed, so did Bathsheba's body. Her once-tiny waist had expanded to twice its original size, leaving her feeling huge and awkward. Rather than pouting about her discomfort, she delighted in the miracles that were taking place within her. The women closest to her seemed to enjoy her pregnancy too. Her mother and sister came to visit her every day, offering to do whatever they could to keep her comfortable. Abigail sat with her in the mornings, telling her stories and keeping her company. But her maid, Matana, was the biggest help of all. She seemed to sense Bathsheba's needs and met them before she was even asked. Her beautiful gowns mysteriously grew bigger to fit her new shape, her bed was made softer, and her food tasted better every day. She knew it was all because of Matana. She wasn't able to do much to help her servant, but she tried to lighten her load whenever she could.

Bathsheba was unable to go to David as often, so she had more evenings to herself. She missed his body next to hers at night, but she didn't mind the time alone. Matana taught her how to use her loom more efficiently, and the two of them spent their evenings making a beautiful little cloak for the baby to wear when he or she got bigger.

One afternoon, while she was walking through the gardens with Adina, Bathsheba felt a sharp pain across her abdomen. She tried to ignore it, but a few minutes later, it was followed by another more intense pain. She remembered when her friend, Rivka, went into labor while walking home from the well. For a moment, Bathsheba considered returning to her house and sending Matana for the midwife, but then she recalled the long day she had spent with her friend while the labor went on and on. Bathsheba decided to finish her leisurely stroll but had to stop periodically to catch her breath. When she returned home, she still kept the pain to herself. After a few hours, it became impossible to hide the fact that she was in labor.

"Are you all right, Bathsheba? You don't look well," Matana asked her while the two sat together at the loom.

"I think the baby is coming," Bathsheba responded calmly.

"Oh, I'll get the midwife—and your mother, and I'll send word to David, and . . ."

"No, Matana, not yet. I think it will be a while."

"Well, at least let me get your mother. She will want to spend this time with you."

"Very well, but please tell her it's still early and she doesn't need to panic."

Moments later, Matana returned with Shiran by her side. Both women looked flushed as they scurried around Bathsheba, who sat calmly on her mat wincing in pain every few minutes. Shiran tried to push herbal drinks on her daughter, and for the first time, Bathsheba understood her sister's moodiness. After a few more hours, Bathsheba didn't care what her mother did or said. She drank the brew offered to her and soon fell asleep on her mat. She slept fitfully and woke periodically to see the faces of her mother and maid hovering over her. Sometimes there were other familiar voices in the distance, but she couldn't place them. Bathsheba's uneasy rest ended suddenly as a huge wave of pain made her scream in agony. A look passed between her mother and Matana, and the maid dashed from the room to retrieve the midwife. Bathsheba didn't know how much time passed, but eventually the two women returned. She recognized the midwife as the one who had attended her sister. The woman was old and gray, but she moved with a dexterity and confidence that eased Bathsheba's worries. She felt herself being hoisted onto a small three-legged birthing stool. She tried to convince the midwife that she was more comfortable lying down, but everyone was too busy to listen to her whimpers.

"It's almost time, dear. The next time you feel the pain, I want you to push as hard as you can."

Bathsheba heard the words through a cloud of pain but did as she was told. The intense contractions went on for several more minutes until she finally felt the child passing through the birth canal. She heard the wails of the baby mingled with the cries of her mother and Matana, and probably hers as well.

"It's a boy!" the midwife exclaimed. "You have given the king a son."

She watched the old woman clean the baby then rub him with salt and wrap him in clean cloths. He was then placed in her arms. She was surprised to see that his eyes were open and looking directly at her. He turned his face toward her body and opened his mouth. She instinctively gave him her breast, and after a little fumbling, the child was able to nurse. The most incredible warmth and love flooded her when she held her tiny son and watched his little mouth suck rhythmically.

Like every mother before her and since, Bathsheba inspected her child with a sense of awe and wonder. He had ten perfect fingers and toes, beautiful little ears, and thick dark curls, just like his father. She couldn't wait for her husband to see the little miracle they had made together. Surely this child would thaw his cold soul. God must approve of their union if He gave them this wonderful little boy.

Her son fell asleep against her breast. She kissed his soft hair and whispered in his ear. "My little prince, I will call you Oded, meaning 'God's salvation and deliverance.' " With tears streaming down her face, she offered a prayer to the Lord. *My God and Creator, thank You for this child. Please use him to bring David back to Your heart. He's so lost without You, and I don't know what to do to help him. Please let this child be the answer.*

Chapter 41

Oded was a perfect baby. He only cried when he was hungry or wet, and he was happy the moment his needs were met. His father adored him and came to Bathsheba's house often to spend time with his wife and new son. It was unusual for the king to enter the women's quarters, but he couldn't stay away from her for an entire month while she went through her time of purification. The other women respected their privacy and gave them plenty of space while David was visiting.

When the baby was eight days old, David came early in the morning to take him to the tent of the Lord for his circumcision. With tears in her eyes, Bathsheba reluctantly handed the baby to David. When the ceremony was over, David did not bring the child to her, but sent him with a servant instead.

"The king sends his apologies for not returning your son to you himself, but he had a guest he did not want to keep waiting," the servant said as she bowed low to Bathsheba.

"Who is this important visitor?" she asked.

"It's Nathan, the prophet."

Bathsheba had heard of Nathan, but she had not seen him around the palace since her arrival. She knew he and David had been close at one time, and she wondered why he had suddenly reappeared. She dismissed the servant and took her sleeping child into the house and laid him on his bed.

Oded healed quickly from the circumcision and spent more of his days awake. He looked at everything with wonder, which made Bathsheba take a new look at the familiar things around her. The baby was the joy of her life, so she was not immediately aware of the fact that David had not come to see her in several days. When Bathsheba finally counted the days since his last visit, she grew concerned. She remembered Nathan's visit and wondered if it had anything to do with David's absence. No one could give her information about her husband other than to tell her he had locked himself alone in his room since the prophet had left.

She had to put her concerns about David aside when her baby woke in the night with a fever. The usually peaceful baby cried and wailed and would not be quieted. He refused to eat and slept only for short periods of time. After two days with no improvement in the baby's condition, she sent word to David, but he did not respond. The midwife came every day to check on Oded, but she was unable to do anything for him. Shiran stayed with her daughter, and with the help of Matana, the women tended the suffering baby night and day.

Bathsheba's fear and fatigue turned to anger toward her husband. She finally sent Matana to find out firsthand what David was doing while they all suffered with his dying child. Matana returned looking very somber.

"Your husband is fasting and petitioning the Lord for the life of his son."

"So he does know that the baby is very ill?" Bathsheba probed, feeling some relief.

"Yes, apparently Nathan told David that the baby would die as a result of his sin."

"No," Bathsheba wailed. "Oded doesn't deserve to suffer and die because of us. It should be me, not my son! Why, why!" she screamed, tearing her robes. Her frail baby stirred on his bed and whimpered. She rushed to him and held him in her arms. "Oh, my baby, my baby," she crooned in his ear. "What have I done? God, please take me instead, please! Why should this innocent boy have to pay the price for me? Let it be me." In the midst of her grief, she felt rather than heard a still, small Voice in her ear. Though she couldn't make out exact words, her mind suddenly became full of the image of a lamb on an altar. Her heart seemed to be breaking as her son struggled to breathe, but she also felt a sense of peace wash over her.

That night, Oded died in his mother's arms.

Chapter 42

When David finally came to her, he looked more like a man returning victorious from battle than a man who just buried his son. When he saw his broken wife sitting on her mat staring at nothing, he rushed to her side and held her.

"Oh Bathsheba, I'm so sorry. I never meant for you to suffer like this."

She knew she should have felt anger, but she had none, only grief and regret. She began to weep against his chest as his tears dampened her hair.

"It's going to be all right now, my love," he whispered in her ear.

"How can you say that?" she sobbed.

"God spoke to me through Nathan."

She stopped crying and looked up to him with tear-filled eyes. "What did he say?"

"Well, he started by telling me a story of a poor man who owned nothing of value except a little lamb. The animal was very precious to him, and he treated it like one of his own children. There was also a rich man who lived nearby. He had large flocks of sheep and cattle, but when a visitor came to his house one day, he took the poor man's lamb rather than killing one of his own to serve his guest.

"I was furious when I heard this, and I demanded to know who this rich man is so he could be punished for his cruelty. That's when Nathan told me that I am that man."

"What do you mean?"

"Don't you see, my love? You are the poor man's lamb. The Lord gave me everything—and still I wanted more. I had no right to take you from Uriah."

"Yes, but I . . ."

"No, Bathsheba. This was not your fault. I have been given great power, and with that comes responsibility. This is my sin. I am the one the Lord is displeased with."

"And God took Oded to punish you?"

"Not exactly. When a sin is committed, there must be restitution. It should have been me, but God chose to take my son instead. I begged and pleaded with God to take me, but the decision was His to make."

"But why! Why would such a loving God kill my baby?"

"Everyone knows what I did. If God turned a blind eye to my sin, all of Israel would have lost respect for His laws."

"But David, my baby, my precious little Oded . . ." Bathsheba broke down in tears again.

"Shhh, my love, it's going to be all right. We will see him again someday."

That's when Bathsheba took a good look at David for the first time since he arrived. "What has happened to you? You've been a hollow shell of a man all these months, and now that our son is dead, you are at peace. Have you no heart?"

"Oh Bathsheba, of course I mourn the loss of our baby. Believe me, if there was anything I could do to save him, I would have done it. But now, I have finally released the burden of guilt I have been carrying all this time. I know there will be difficult times ahead. I know I will have to spend the rest of my life suffering the consequences of my actions, but at least I have the assurance that the Lord has forgiven me. He will still allow my son to succeed me and build the temple I've dreamed of. He won't remove His hand of protection from our people because of my mistakes. Don't you see His mercy through all of this?"

"I want to David, I really do, but I don't have your faith. I don't know if I'm strong enough to survive this."

"You will survive, and you will have more children. Someday your son will wear the crown and build a magnificent house for the Lord. Just put your trust in God and wait and see what He will do through you."

Bathsheba felt a spark of hope ignite deep within her as David held her and whispered words of encouragement. He stayed with her for the rest of the day, allowing her to sleep in his arms while he softly sang songs of God's love that filled her dreams with peace and comfort.

Chapter 43

Bathsheba was surprised by the outpouring of love and support she received from some of David's other women. The senior wives, except Abigail, stayed away, but the younger members of the harem were very kind to her. Not a day went by that she didn't receive a visitor bringing a small gift of some kind. While the late winter rains fell outside, the women sat together in Bathsheba's home sharing their stories. She was amazed how many of them had lost children, either during their pregnancies or shortly after birth. They bonded in their shared grief and developed friendships they never would have had otherwise.

One sunny morning, Matana announced a visitor. Bathsheba rose from the table, where she was just finishing her breakfast, and was shocked to see her old friend, Rivka, enter the house holding her son Ronen's hand. The child had changed considerably since Bathsheba had last seen him. His hair had darkened, and he looked like a little boy instead of a baby. It was obvious that Ronen had no memory of her; she was now just a stranger in fine robes. Rivka, too, seemed somehow different; perhaps it was the new lines that had formed on her brow or her slightly stooped posture. But her eyes were the same kind eyes that Bathsheba had grown to love when she was a girl.

Bathsheba remembered how much fun Ronen used to have chasing her pet sheep, so she asked her maid to take him outside to the grassy area between her house and Shiran's. Without a word to her guest, Bathsheba went to her and washed the dust from her feet. When she rose from her task, she saw tears in Rivka's eyes. The two women embraced for a moment; then Bathsheba offered her friend a seat.

"I heard about your son, and I'm very sorry," Rivka said kindly.

"Thank you. It has been a very difficult time. But I'm the one who is sorry. You were right about everything. I had no idea my sin would hurt so many people. It is my fault Uriah and Zabad are dead. There is nothing I can do to bring them back, but please know how very sorry I am."

"You've suffered enough. I'm not here to bring you more pain. I want you to know I forgive you."

"Oh, Rivka, you don't know what that means to me," Bathsheba said with tears dampening her cheeks.

"I've also come to tell you Ronen and I are leaving Jerusalem."

"Where will you go?"

"Zabad's parents have asked me to live with them. They have a small herd of sheep and goats that they keep on their land just outside of Jezreel. His mother has been very ill since she received the news of her son's death. She has two other sons, but Zabad was her oldest and favorite. My father-in-law sent me a message asking me to come help them. Her other sons are unmarried, so she has no daughters to care for her, except me. I think seeing Ronen will help her recover too. He looks more and more like his father every day, don't you think?"

"He does. I just can't believe how much he's grown. I'm sure you both will be a great comfort to Zabad's family."

"We are leaving the day after tomorrow with a caravan headed north to Tyre. My neighbor's son is leading the group. She promised he will take good care of us during the journey."

"Is there anything you need, anything at all?"

"Well, there is one thing," Rivka said hesitantly. "I would like to take Zabad's remains home to his family. I don't even know if it's possible, but I thought . . ."

"It is done. I will see that they are brought to you first thing tomorrow morning."

"Oh, Bathsheba, thank you." Without any thought, she bowed low to the queen.

Bathsheba lifted her by the shoulders and laughed. "You never have to bow to me, my friend." She then took from her hair one of the beautiful combs David had given her and put it in Rivka's hand. "I'll miss you so much. Please don't forget me."

"I will never forget you, cousin," Rivka said as she kissed Bathsheba on both cheeks.

The two women went outside arm in arm to watch Adina and Ronen play. The child sat in the grass squealing with laughter while Adina nuzzled his head and tried to nibble on his ears and hair.

"You said Zabad's parents keep sheep?"

"Yes, why?"

"I was just wondering if your son would like a pet."

"Oh, I couldn't take Adina from you," Rivka protested.

"Nonsense, she would be much happier out in the open with other animals to play with. Here I have to keep her tied up so she doesn't destroy the gardens. Just look how much fun they have together."

Rivka agreed and called her son to her side. Ronen came obediently.

"Yes, Eema."

"Bathsheba would like to give you her pet ewe. But you must promise to look after her and take good care of her."

"Really?" he asked with excitement lighting up his face. "Adina can come with us?"

"That's right."

"Oh, thank you, thank you!" he exclaimed, hugging Bathsheba's legs.

"You are very welcome, Ronen." Bathsheba knelt down to his level and hugged him back. She held him for a moment, smelling the sunshine in his hair, and it made her grieve again for her lost son.

When it was time for her friends to leave, Bathsheba untied Adina and handed the rope to Ronen, who took it proudly. After a tearful goodbye, she went to the head eunuch and asked him to make sure Zabad's remains were taken to Rivka's home.

For the first time in many weeks, Bathsheba's heart felt light. She looked up at the sun that had long been hidden behind the winter clouds. She felt the warmth on her face and thanked God for the feeling of peace and forgiveness that washed over her.

Chapter 44

The new moon brought Bathsheba's time of purification to an end. David sent word that he would like to dine with her in his bedchamber that evening. Her body had changed since the birth of her son, so she spent several hours with Matana trying to find something to wear that would flatter her new figure. David had visited her many times during the past month, but this was the first time she was able to go to him. Bathsheba was excited and nervous, but couldn't explain why. Matana teased her throughout the day, telling her she was like a new bride on her way to meet her groom for the first time. When the maid brought out the cosmetics, she found none were needed because Bathsheba's cheeks were already flushed, and the sparkle in her eyes couldn't be improved upon.

When the sun was low in the sky, Bathsheba made her way to David's rooms. She found him sitting at a table with quill and scroll writing a new song, his ten-stringed harp on his lap. It occurred to her that she had never heard him play other than in public.

When David saw her, he immediately stopped what he was doing and rushed to her side.

"Oh my love, I'm so glad you're here. Would you like to hear my new psalm?"

"Yes, I would," Bathsheba said sincerely.

"It's not finished yet, but here's what I have so far:

"How blessed is he whose transgression is forgiven,
   Whose sin is covered! . . .
When I kept silent about my sin, my body wasted away
   Through my groaning all day long.

For day and night Your hand was heavy upon me; . . .
I acknowledged my sin to You, . . .
    And You forgave my guilt. . . .
You are my hiding place; You preserve me from trouble;
    You surround me with songs of deliverance."*

David's deep baritone voice filled the room and made Bathsheba fall in love with him again.

"I still have more work to do on it, but the words are just flowing from my pen."

"Oh, David, it's beautiful," Bathsheba encouraged.

Just then, a servant brought in a large tray of food. They ate together in the privacy of his room, talking as though they hadn't seen each other in years. Bathsheba watched David closely as he told her of his recent visits with Nathan. He seemed happier than she had ever seen him. She had caught glimpses of this man over the last several months, but he had been hiding so deep within himself she never really got to know him without the shadow of guilt hanging over their heads. Now with his sins forgiven and his relationship with God renewed, the real David was sitting before her.

After dinner, David held his wife as if for the first time.

"I would like a fresh start with you, Bathsheba. Will you stay with me this week so we can celebrate our union the right way?"

Bathsheba remembered how happy she had been with David that first week after they were married, but she also remembered the painful tears she had shed over Uriah and the nights David woke up shivering from the sin consuming his heart. She was happy to try again. She knew the sad memories would still be there and now the grief of her lost son was added to them, but the time together could help them both recover.

"I would like that very much," she said, kissing him softly.

David and Bathsheba got to know each other in a much deeper way during their second full week together. The fiery passion had cooled, making way for a much sweeter connection between them. Every morning, David left before the sun came up to go to the tent of the Lord to offer sacrifices and prayers. He returned to his wife still sleepy and warm in her bed. He read to her from scrolls, sharing stories with her that she had never heard or had somehow forgotten. They prayed and sang songs together, and Bathsheba was pleased to find that their voices harmonized beautifully. When the priest's horn signaled the upcoming Sabbath, a servant left a large basket of food and enough water to get them through the next day. Bathsheba set the table for dinner and lit the candles while her husband offered the blessing. She no longer felt like a queen who had to share her king with several other women—she was his wife and he was her husband.

The week came to an end, and Bathsheba knew that David had to resume the duties of the king. She also felt much closer to God and looked forward to deepening that relationship on her own. This time she didn't leave David feeling anxious about the future, but completely at peace.

---

*Psalm 32:1, 3, 4, 5, 7, NASB.

Chapter 45

The following weeks were busy with preparations for the approaching Passover. Every corner of the palace was scrubbed and every garment washed. Each man, woman, and child did his or her part to get ready for the celebration.

David called together his family and friends for the evening feast on the first night of Passover. The large dining area was crowded with women and children on the left, men on the right, and David sitting at the head table with his older sons and close friends by his side. Bathsheba was given a place of honor at the women's table with Abigail and Ahinoam seated on either side of her. From where she sat, she had a clear view of David. She hadn't seen his sons together since her wedding feast, and she enjoyed trying to figure out who was who. Bathsheba recognized Abigail's eyes in her son Chileab, who was seated to the left of his father, so she immediately knew who he was. She didn't recognize the other men right away so she asked Abigail for help. It became a bit of a guess-who game that both women enjoyed. Once the sons were all accounted for, they moved on to the other guests.

"The small crippled man at the end is Mephibosheth," Abigail explained while they ate their flat bread and bitter-herb-seasoned lamb.

"Oh, yes, I've heard of him. He's Saul's grandson and Jonathan's son, right?"

"That's right. David and Jonathan were loyal friends, and when David learned that one of Jonathan's sons had survived, he invited him to live here at the palace. He also gave him all the land his grandfather once owned. It's good land and produces a healthy income for him. He seems very grateful and loyal to David, and I think the two have developed a close friendship over the years."

"Who is that older man at the other end?" Bathsheba asked.

"That's Nathan, the prophet."

Bathsheba stared at him in wonder. That was the man God used to deliver messages to David? He didn't look at all the way she had expected. Judging from his long gray beard and slightly hunched shoulders, he had seen many Passovers. Nathan's clothing was much plainer than those seated around him, which surprised her. If anyone had cause to boast, it was the mouthpiece of the Lord, but Nathan didn't wear a high turban or an ornate cloak. The tassels hanging from his clothing were much shorter than those of the priests. Shouldn't they drag on the ground behind him so everyone could tell he was God's messenger? As Bathsheba studied him, Nathan looked up from his meal and held her gaze. For a moment she was sure he was reading her mind, and she began to squirm uncomfortably in her seat, but then Nathan gave her the kindest smile she had ever seen. She couldn't help but smile back at him.

David's second wife, Ahinoam, interrupted her thoughts.

"My son Amnon looks very handsome tonight, don't you think? I made his cloak myself and gave it to him as a gift for the Passover celebrations."

"It is flattering; you have always been talented at the loom," Abigail responded.

"Perhaps you would like me to make something for Chileab. His robes are looking a bit old," Ahinoam offered Abigail.

"They aren't old, just well used. My son is very active, unlike some of the other brooding young men around here." Both women glared at each other for a moment before returning to their meals.

The tension was thick between the two. Though they had been together longer than any of David's other wives, they would never be friends. Their sons were born only a year apart, so they were natural rivals. Abigail was kind and forgiving of any wrong done to her, but if it involved her Chileab, she was a force to be reckoned with. Amnon had always been close to his cousin Jonadab, and the two boys ganged up on Chileab from the time they could walk. Abigail did everything she could to keep them separated as boys, but now that they were men, they were all out of her reach. She still counseled her son to keep his distance from his moody brother, and she took her own advice when it came to Ahinoam.

After the feast ended and the dishes were cleared, a servant came to Bathsheba and quietly informed her that David would like her company. A few of the women seated near her gave her resentful stares, but she ignored them and excused herself from the table. She knew David would be delayed talking to people for a while, so she decided to take a little walk before going to his rooms.

Bathsheba strolled under the moonlight in the main palace garden. The almond and apricot trees were showing off their beautiful blossoms, and Bathsheba breathed in their fragrance. A few other people were walking in the garden, so she wasn't startled when a man approached her and fell into step next to her.

"Shalom," he said kindly. "You must be Bathsheba."

"I am, and you are Nathan. I've heard a lot about you."

"Yes, and I've heard a lot about you as well. You are the apple of your husband's eye," Nathan said, smiling that wonderful smile. "And even more beautiful than he described—if that's possible."

"You flatter me, Nathan. It's just the moonlight playing tricks on your eyes," she teased, feeling surprisingly comfortable around this stranger.

"Ah, it's true; the moonlight does complement your beauty."

Bathsheba froze in place, unable to speak or move, stunned by the realization that this man knew everything about her. He knew about her bath on the roof under the full moon. He knew about the sense of power and pride she felt when David wanted her over all the women in Israel. He knew the secrets she kept hidden even from herself.

"I'm not here to judge you, Bathsheba," Nathan said as if reading her thoughts. "The Lord has heard your prayers of repentance, and

He has forgiven you. It's you who can't let go of your guilt, not Him. God will use you for great things, if you will let Him."

"What things?" she asked hesitantly.

"You and David will have another son. He will be greatly loved by the Lord. He is the one who will usher in a time of peace in Israel. It is your responsibility to protect him from the evil that lurks in this palace. You must teach him God's ways and laws."

"But I don't know if I can."

"You can't do it by yourself. You must ask God to help you."

Bathsheba nodded in agreement.

"There's more, Bathsheba." Nathan looked her straight in the eye. "Not only will you be the mother of a great ruler, but the King of kings will also come through your lineage."

"The King of kings?" she asked not understanding his meaning.

"Yes, the Redeemer and Ruler of the entire world will be born of you."

"Why me?" she asked, barely keeping her emotions under control. "I'm an adulteress, a liar, a murderer. I don't deserve to wash the feet of God's Redeemer, let alone carry His Seed."

"Was our father Jacob a perfect man? Was Israel a great nation when God lead her out of captivity? Was Moses an eloquent speaker? No! God takes the weak and makes them strong. He takes the sinful and makes them pure. The sins you and David committed will be a warning to future generations, but they will also be a promise."

Bathsheba was so absorbed in the conversation that she didn't realize they had reached the staircase leading to David's bedroom.

"Now, go to your husband, Bathsheba. I'll be seeing you again, I'm sure." Nathan gave her another smile then turned and walked away.

The first of Nathan's prophecies came true several months later. Almost exactly one year after Oded died, Bathsheba gave birth to another healthy son. When David found out the midwife was with Bathsheba, he left his throne and went to the women's quarters, where he paced outside her house for hours. Bathsheba was told he was outside so she did her best not to cry out when the pains took her, so she wouldn't alarm him. When David heard the baby wailing, it was all Shiran and Matana could do to keep him from barging in the house before Bathsheba had been cleaned up. At last, he was allowed to enter his wife's sleeping room, where she sat propped against the wall on her sleeping mat. The child was fighting off sleep as he lay against his mother's breast. Bathsheba handed the little bundle to David when he approached.

David inspected his curly black hair and high forehead, his perfect little nose and cupid bow lips. Unlike his wife, he did not find it necessary to count fingers and toes but knew without looking that the child was flawless.

"Have you thought of a name for him yet?" he asked.

"No, not yet, I thought something would come to me when I saw him, but I just can't decide."

The baby let out a long sigh that made both his parents smile. Then he fell into a quiet sleep in his father's arms.

"He looks so peaceful in your arms, David."

"I hope this child's life is more peaceful than mine has been."

"It will be, my love. God has promised rest from war during his reign."

"Then let's call him Solomon, meaning 'peaceful,' " David suggested.

"Yes, I like it. Bathsheba tried the name on her tongue. "Solomon."

"Solomon, king of Israel," David added proudly.

Chapter 46

The winter rains were unusually heavy, keeping Bathsheba indoors with the baby during her entire month of purification. Matana worked hard to keep the house warm so Solomon would not get sick. She fretted over every whimper he made and frequently touched his forehead to see whether he had a fever. In contrast, Bathsheba was surprisingly calm. Although she appreciated her maid's efforts, she knew they were not necessary. This child belonged to the Lord; there was nothing to fear.

When spring finally did arrive, Bathsheba took Solomon for walks around the palace. Even when his eyes were closed, she would point out different trees and flowers that were starting to bloom. She whispered stories in his ears and prayed with him several times every day. When David called her to his rooms, Bathsheba usually brought the baby with her. David loved his other children a great deal, but he took a special interest in this son. The baby loved to hear his father sing and play the harp. Solomon showed his appreciation by honoring David with his first gummy smile.

His son's affection made it difficult for David to leave when Joab sent word that the king should join his troops at Rabbah. The city was about to surrender, and it wouldn't be proper for a mere general to lead the victorious army through the gates. David knew Joab was right, so he reluctantly left his wife and newborn son to deal the last blow to the Ammonites.

One lazy afternoon shortly after David and the remaining troops left Jerusalem, Bathsheba sat under a tree with Solomon next to her on a blanket. He had just discovered his toes and seemed to get endless enjoyment from grabbing them and pulling them into his mouth. She was so interested in her son that she didn't notice a girl approach.

"Is that my new brother?" she asked without introduction.

Bathsheba had seen the girl around and knew she was Tamar, the daughter of Maacah. She did her best to avoid Maacah ever since their run-in several years earlier, so she had never spoken to Tamar before. Her mother was nowhere in sight, so Bathsheba decided it would be safe enough to talk to the girl.

"Yes, his name is Solomon."

"He's cute. May I hold him?"

"Sure. Here, sit on the blanket and I'll help you." Bathsheba placed her wriggly son into Tamar's arms. "Be careful now, he wiggles around a lot."

Solomon looked up at his big sister and gave her a huge smile. This delighted Tamar, who tried to get him to smile again. She stuck her tongue out, crossed her eyes, and made all kinds of silly noises to humor the baby. He rewarded her by pulling a strand of her long brown hair and sticking it into his mouth. When he was tired of being held, Bathsheba placed Solomon on the blanket so he could wiggle safely. Tamar was amused with every move Solomon made until he finally got tired and laid his head down. Tamar stayed by Bathsheba's side, turning her attention to Bathsheba instead of the baby.

"You're really pretty," the girl said candidly.

"Thank you. You're really pretty too," Bathsheba replied. When she looked closely at the girl, she realized she really was a stunning child. Though she was at the age that most children become gangly and awkward, Tamar carried herself with the grace fitting a princess.

"Really? Do you think so?"

"Sure I do. I bet the boys are already looking at you."

"I don't like boys," Tamar said adamantly. "They're mean and stupid. My brothers and cousins are always picking on me, and I don't like it. I don't think Solomon will be mean and stupid, though. He looks like he'll be a nice boy."

Bathsheba laughed at the girl's candor. "Well, I certainly hope so."

Just then, Maacah appeared out of nowhere. She hoisted her daughter onto her feet and nearly dragged her away from Bathsheba.

"Come along, Tamar. You mustn't bother the queen," she said sarcastically.

"It's all right, Maacah. We were just talking. She wanted to see her little brother." Bathsheba rose to her feet and quickly tried to defend her new friend.

"Tamar, run along and play with your *real* brother. I'll be there shortly," Maacah said to her daughter then turned to face her rival. "You stay away from my daughter, you whore," she hissed. "She is a very beautiful girl, and the last thing she needs is to have influences like you in her life."

Bathsheba rose to her full height and looked down at the arrogant woman before her. "How dare you speak to me in such a manner? You may have been able to do that when I was just the wife of a soldier, but I am no longer subject to you."

"Just because you climbed your way out of a soldier's bed and into a king's doesn't mean I owe you an ounce of respect."

Bathsheba swallowed the bile that was rising in her throat. She had every right to slap the woman across the face, but something inside calmed her. She could imagine Tamar's future filled with heartache and pain. Her anger was replaced with pity, and for some reason she suddenly felt fearful for Tamar.

"Very well, Maacah. I will stay away from your daughter, but I suggest that you keep her close to you." With that, Bathsheba scooped up her sleeping baby and returned to her house.

Chapter 47

The years passed, and Bathsheba gave birth to two more sons, naming them Shammua and Shobad. They were darling little boys who filled her house with noise and happiness. Solomon grew to be a strong, healthy young man and was now old enough to leave the women's quarters and move into one of the small houses David had prepared for his unmarried sons in the palace. Bathsheba also grew, but her growth was spiritual, not physical. From time to time she could be found in the garden talking to Nathan. He told her stories about a boy named Joseph, who had many troubles with his older half brothers. He told her about the Israelites wandering in the desert for years while learning how to obey and trust God. She had heard many of the stories before, but for some reason, when Nathan told them, she paid special attention. Somehow she knew they would be important to her later.

Bathsheba's wasn't the only family that was growing; in fact, everything around the palace was increasing. The wealth from conquered countries poured into Israel. David was given more concubines as gifts from neighboring kings, making the women's quarters more crowded every day. There were now eight wives and ten concubines, plus their servants, children, and other family members. David's holding of land had also grown considerably during his reign, so he gave large parcels of property to each of his sons. Chileab, Absalom, Adonijah, and Ithream all took wives and moved to homes outside of the palace walls. However, David's oldest son, Amnon, refused to leave. Bathsheba often saw him lurking outside the women's quarters with his cousin, trying to peek in when the guards were distracted. At first she thought one of the young concubines had caught his eye, but then she realized it was his half sister, Tamar. She had grown lovelier with the passing years, but she was completely unaware of the effect she seemed to have on her brother. Unfortunately, the girl's mother also seemed oblivious to the potential danger.

One evening, while Bathsheba was dining with her husband, she tried to broach the subject.

"Don't you think it's time Amnon found a wife?" she asked cautiously.

"He doesn't want one. I've tried to talk to him about it before, and he just isn't ready to get married. Besides, I'm more worried about his health than his marital status."

"What do you mean?" Bathsheba asked. "He seems healthy enough."

"Have you seen him?" David retorted, sounding annoyed. "He's becoming thinner every day. He doesn't eat, and he doesn't go out with his brothers anymore. All he does is roam around the palace like a ghost. I think I'll have a doctor take a look at him."

"David, it's not a doctor he needs; it's a wife."

"That's enough!" he snapped at her. "Amnon is my son, and I know what's best for him."

Bathsheba dropped the subject. She had never seen her husband get so upset with her before. Of course, she had never tried to tell him how to deal with one of his children before either.

"Solomon is doing very well in his studies," she said, trying to change the subject to something safer. "All of his teachers tell me how intelligent he is."

"He'll be a wonderful king," David replied, relaxing slightly.

"If he's half the king you are, Israel will be very fortunate." Bathsheba rubbed David's shoulders and caressed his neck, feeling the tension slowly leave him.

"I don't know how you do it, woman," David said, smiling as he grabbed his wife and pulled her onto his lap.

"Do what?" she asked coyly.

"After all these years, you still know how to reduce me to a lump of clay in your hands," he said as he kissed her and carried her to bed.

Several nights later, Bathsheba was on her way through the gardens to David's quarters. The sun had already set, and the twilight was deepening. Fortunately, she had walked this way many times before, so she had no trouble finding her way. Because the weather was cold and windy, she assumed she was alone in the garden until she heard the sound of someone crying. She followed the sound until she found Tamar huddled on the ground under a large tree. The beautiful gown she wore showing her status as an unmarried daughter of the king had been torn, and her head was bare. When Bathsheba drew closer, she saw the ashes on Tamar's hair and face.

"What has happened, Tamar?" she asked, startling the poor girl. "Has someone died?"

"I wish I were dead," Tamar wailed.

"Tamar, you have to get control of yourself. Please tell me what happened," Bathsheba said more forcefully, taking hold of the trembling girl's shoulders.

"My half brother Amnon . . . He told our father he was sick, so I was sent to make dinner for him in his rooms. Then he sent everyone away and he . . ." She began sobbing again.

"What did he do to you, Tamar?"

"He raped me," she whispered.

Bathsheba scooped the distraught girl into her arms and rocked her like a child until she calmed down enough to continue with the story.

"When he was finished, he looked at me with so much hatred and anger in his eyes. He told me to leave, but I wouldn't. I begged him to marry me so I wouldn't be ruined forever, but he threw me out of his house and barred the door. How could he do this to me? My own brother. I'm ruined forever." Tamar started wailing again.

Although horrified, Bathsheba finally composed herself enough to try to take care of the girl.

"Come, Tamar. Let me take you to your mother. She'll know what to do."

She practically carried Tamar back to the women's quarters. When she reached Maacah's door, she took a deep breath and knocked. A familiar servant answered, took one look at her mistress, and ushered the two women inside without any questions. Maacah was in the main sitting room and rose instantly to her feet.

"Daughter, what has happened to you?"

The girl's tears started again and she was unable to speak, so Bathsheba told her the entire story. Maacah listened to every word, growing more and more irate as the details spilled out before her.

"That man must be punished!" she practically screamed. "His father should have him stoned for this."

At the mention of David, Bathsheba remembered she was supposed to meet him in his room.

"I'm sorry, Maacah, but I must go. I will tell David, if you like."

"Yes, tell him. He must take care of this immediately." Maacah's face softened as she looked at her former enemy standing before her. "Bathsheba, thank you for bringing Tamar to me and for being so kind to her."

"You are welcome. I will do whatever I can to make this right," she promised as she turned to leave.

Once in David's rooms, she found him sitting at his writing table working on a new psalm.

"Where have you been?" he asked, sounding concerned.

"David, something terrible has happened. I found Tamar in the garden . . ." Bathsheba wasn't sure how to tell him, so she just blurted it out. "She was raped by her half brother, Amnon."

"Oh, no," he moaned. "Where is she now?"

"She is with her mother. Something must be done to Amnon. Tamar said he threw her out and barred his door. David, please do something." Bathsheba was starting to lose the control that she had so carefully held together in front of the other women.

"Yes, I'll go take care of it right now. You stay here."

When David returned a few hours later, Bathsheba was eager to hear what had happened; however, he was reluctant to talk about it. David simply undressed and climbed into bed. "Are you coming?" he asked Bathsheba who looked at him in shock.

"You're just going to go to sleep? Aren't you going to tell me what happened?"

"It's taken care of."

"Has he been thrown in prison? Will he be stoned? Will you force him to marry Tamar?"

"Enough questions, woman! Come to bed."

"No! You must tell me what happened!"

David flushed with anger but then calmed before replying. "I talked to Amnon about it. He's going to leave the palace for a little while and go work his land. I'm going to find him a wife, and it will never happen again. I've sent Tamar to live with her brother, Absalom, on his land in Baalhazor."

Bathsheba stared at David, speechless. She couldn't believe that the strong, decisive king who conquered nations was unable to deal with his own son.

"Stop looking at me like that. What was I supposed to do? You know perfectly well I'm guilty of much more than Amnon. How can I condemn him? He's my son. Now come to bed before I send for one of my young concubines." The attempt at humor did not work on Bathsheba. She was furious with her husband, but she knew there was nothing she could do. Somehow she felt like it was partially her fault that he was unable to discipline his son.

"When will our sin go away?" she whispered more to herself than anyone else as she climbed into bed next to her husband.

Chapter 48

The mood in the women's quarters was very dismal when Bathsheba returned the next morning. Everyone felt the loss of the princess, and they mourned for her as if she had died. In a way she had. As the daughter of the most powerful king in the area, Tamar should have spent her life as the first wife of a neighboring ally. Because she was beautiful and her mother was also a daughter of a king, she could have had her choice of handsome young princes; but instead, she would spend the rest of her days hidden away in her brother's country home.

Maacah was given permission to leave the city to spend some time with her children. When she returned, all the women of the palace treated her kindly. Bathsheba especially went out of her way to make sure she was well cared for. Maacah wasn't a young woman, but the recent events had aged her considerably. She rarely left her house, and when she did, it was for short walks with her maid. All the fire and fight that Bathsheba had seen in her eyes on more than one occasion had completely vanished. Her former rival was now a sad, aging woman.

Life did eventually get back to normal. The seasons went on without any regard for the trials humans faced. Bathsheba found herself growing large with child again. David was pleased that his favorite wife was so fruitful, and it made her happy to add to her little flock. Her sons Shammua and Shobad were rowdy, carefree boys who spent their time chasing each other around the house, which seemed to get smaller every day. She wondered how she would raise another child amid so much chaos.

One summer afternoon, Bathsheba took her sons to the gardens to escape the heat of the house. They immediately joined a group of boys and began playing with them. She found a bench under a tree and lowered herself carefully onto it. Her sons were old enough to take care of themselves, but she seldom let them out of her sight. She usually allowed them to fight their own battles, but there were times that she had to step in when things got out of hand. Nathan had stressed the importance of protecting her children, and she had been diligent since Solomon was a baby.

She sat quietly watching the boys act out the famous battle their father had fought against the Philistine giant Goliath many years earlier. They took turns playing the hero, David, and also took turns thudding to the ground as they imagined Goliath had done. She smiled to herself and wondered if her husband knew how much his children admired him—at least the younger ones. She couldn't help but think back to his reluctance to handle the situation with Amnon. It bothered her that he had been so weak. Just then, her thoughts were interrupted by her friend Nathan, who sat down on the bench next to her.

"Shalom, Bathsheba. How goes the great battle with the giant today?" he asked, referring to the children's game.

"I think David has him beat again," she replied with a smile.

"Ah, I don't know how they have so much energy in this heat. I'm tired just looking at them," he said as he wiped his forehead with his sleeve. "I must be getting old."

Bathsheba had to smile. Nathan wasn't getting old; he already was old. She remembered thinking that he was ancient when she met him all those years before, and here he was still shuffling around complaining good-naturedly about the weather.

"How's our boy Jedidiah?" Nathan asked. Even though Bathsheba and David had named their son Solomon, Nathan insisted on calling him Jedidiah.

"I should ask you. You probably see him more than I do now that he's moved into his own house."

"Yes, I guess I do," Nathan admitted. "Well, the last time I saw him, he was doing quite well. He's been doing some traveling, but

I'm sure you knew that. Did you know he's been writing poetry? I'd say he has his father's gift."

"And how do you know he didn't get it from me?" she asked teasingly.

"He got a much better gift from you. He got your gentle spirit. He really is a peaceful boy, our Jedidiah."

"How wonderful that you care so much for our children, Nathan."

"I do, I really do. I couldn't love them more if they were my own flesh and blood."

"Why didn't you have children of your own?" Bathsheba had the courage to ask.

"Well, I guess I was always too busy, and before I knew it, I was an old man with no wife and no sons. It must just be what the Lord intended for me. I can't complain though. I've had a good life."

"Don't make it sound like it's over, Nathan."

"No, it's not over. Bathsheba, I have a feeling there's still plenty for me to do around here."

"What do you mean?"

"I don't know exactly. I haven't received any visions or dreams; maybe it's just a feeling. I just know we haven't seen the end of the Amnon situation."

Chapter 49

Late in the night, Bathsheba was awakened by a terrible pain in her abdomen. Having already experienced four uncomplicated deliveries, she expected this child's birth to be problem free as well, so she was worried when the pains felt different. Matana heard her cry out, and she immediately left the house to get the midwife. Moments later she returned with the midwife and Shiran. Bathsheba's mother had developed a friendship with the midwife, and she had even started working as her apprentice. Shiran had been present at most of the deliveries in the palace over the last several years, even delivering a few babies on her own. Her specialty, of course, was herbal remedies. The two women learned a great deal from each other and obviously liked working together.

When the midwife took a look at Bathsheba's face, she knew something was wrong. Shiran immediately got to work making a drink to ease the pain, and the midwife checked the baby.

"We have a little problem, Bathsheba, but I don't want you to worry. The baby is ready to come, but his feet, not his head, are down. I'm going to try to turn him around. Now, drink your mother's medicine; it will help ease the pain."

Bathsheba had heard of women dying while trying to deliver a baby feetfirst. She started to panic, but then relaxed as soon as the warm liquid her mother gave her reached the back of her throat. She felt the midwife trying to turn the baby, and she screamed out in pain.

"There now," the older woman soothed. "Let's just give it a little bit of time; then we'll try again. Just try to relax and have another drink."

Bathsheba felt a warm thickness move over her. The pain was still there, reminding her not to fall too far into the darkness that she so desperately wanted to escape into. Every time she drifted away, she was pulled back to reality by the stabbing heat spreading across the middle of her body. Bathsheba didn't know how much time had passed or what had happened during that time, but after a while she felt herself being hoisted onto the familiar three-legged birthing stool. She thought she was dreaming, but the ripping pain was too real. She heard voices that sounded like they were deep in a cave. They were telling her what to do, but she couldn't concentrate. Finally she heard a piercing scream and realized it came from her mouth. With all her strength, she focused on the child—David's child, whom she did not want to lose. She worked with the midwife and after a few pushes and with the midwife's assistance, she was able to deliver another healthy son. Everyone in the room began crying with relief, including Bathsheba herself.

"You almost didn't make it this time, darling," her mother said to her with tears running down her cheeks. "This will be your last child."

Bathsheba smiled at the bundle in her arms and did not feel a bit of remorse that she couldn't have more.

"God has given me much. I will call him Nathan meaning 'God gives.' I think my friend, the prophet, will like it."

With that, Bathsheba let the warm sleep take her, and she dozed peacefully for hours.

Chapter 50

The following spring, Solomon came to his mother's house to visit. She held little Nathan on her lap while he slept; the two older boys were outside, playing in the garden. Bathsheba sat with her oldest son at the table while Matana served them soft breads and grape juice. Bathsheba couldn't help but admire how handsome Solomon had become. His cheeks were still smooth, but he had already grown taller than his mother and was well on his way to surpassing his father. He had the same thick dark hair that his father had in his younger days. But instead of David's muscular build, Solomon was slim and elegant. His hands were those of an artist. With pride Bathsheba noticed the graceful way he held his glass.

"Eema, stop staring at me. You're making me nervous," Solomon protested with a playful smile on his face.

"I can't help it. It seems like I was just holding you in my arms, and now you're a young man." Little Nathan stirred slightly, and Bathsheba smiled down at the bundle, trying to remember to savor the moments with him before he, too, was gone.

"Yes, Eema, I am a man now; and Shammua and Shobad are getting older too. They'll soon be old enough to move into their own houses, you know."

"I know. Is that why you've come today? Does your father want the boys to move out?"

"No, not just yet, but he does want them to go to Baalhazor with me."

"Baalhazor, why?"

"Our brother Absalom is having a feast to celebrate the sheep shearing. He has invited all of his brothers."

"Even Amnon?" Bathsheba asked suspiciously.

"Of course. You don't think there are still hard feelings over what happened with Tamar, do you? It's been two years. I'm sure the incident is long forgotten."

"I just find it hard to believe that he would invite the man who raped his sister to a party, regardless of how much time has passed. Something doesn't seem right, Solomon. I don't want you to go."

"Eema, you've always been overprotective. I'll be fine and I'll take good care of my brothers."

"No, Solomon. I know you're a man, and I can't stop you from going, even if I don't approve—but I will not allow Shammua and Shobad to attend. They are still mine to protect."

"But all of the brothers will be there. How will I explain their absence?"

"I don't care. They're not going. That's final."

Solomon sulked for a few moments, but he knew his mother well enough to know there was no point in arguing.

"Fine then. I'll be leaving in a few hours," he said as he rose to leave.

"Solomon," she called after him, "please be careful."

He turned to her and gave her the smile she remembered from his childhood. "Don't worry, Eema. I'll be fine."

* * *

That night while Bathsheba slept in her husband's arms, they were both awakened by a knock at the door and a servant calling out that he had urgent news. They dressed quickly, and David told the servant to meet them in his sitting room. When they entered the room, the servant bowed low before them.

"I bring you the worst possible news," the man said to David. "Absalom has killed all of your sons. Not one of them is left."

David tore his robe and began to wail. Immediately the servant followed the king's example. But Bathsheba stood frozen in place. She was sure her heart would forget to beat. Her son Solomon! What about God's promise to make him a great king? How could this happen? She should have tried harder to stop him? Feeling faint, Bathsheba fell on the floor and began to sob.

"Oh Solomon, Solomon!" she wailed.

Soon a great lament echoed through the halls of the palace. All of the servants cried out pitifully when they heard the news. Then a young man ran into the sitting room, trying to catch his breath. It was the sneaky cousin, Jonadab, she had always seen lurking around with Amnon.

"Uncle, the first information you received is incorrect. Not all of your sons have been killed—only your son Amnon. Absalom has been planning his revenge for what was done to his sister Tamar ever since it happened."

David stopped weeping and stood staring at his nephew in shock. Bathsheba expected him to accuse Jonadab of prior knowledge of the murder plans, but he didn't. Just then, they heard more footsteps. Another servant ran in the room and informed David that some of his sons had been seen entering the palace. Bathsheba's head was spinning. *Is Solomon all right? What about the others?* Bathsheba followed David out of the king's chambers and into the hall to see what was happening. So many people milled about in the darkness in so much confusion that she didn't know what was going on. Her head cleared when she heard the unmistakable sound of Solomon's voice. She pushed her way through the people who congregated outside of David's rooms. All of the princes, except Amnon and Absalom, were crying and talking at once. David finally silenced them and asked his son Chileab to explain what happened.

"Abba, it was awful. I'm not exactly sure how it all happened because Absalom had served so much wine. We were all having a good time, but then he gave a signal to his servants, and they surrounded Amnon and killed him. As soon as we saw what happened, we got on our mules and fled for home."

"Where is your brother Absalom?" David asked.

"I don't know. We left quickly before he could kill any more of us," Chileab answered.

David sent two of his trusted guards, who were in the crowd, to find out what had happened to Absalom. Once everyone else was sent away from his rooms, David returned to his bed and sat weeping.

"My son, my firstborn son, Amnon, is dead, and now Absalom is missing. This is more than I can bear," he wept.

Bathsheba was so shaken she had no words to offer him, so she held him in her arms while he sobbed. It took hours for David to exhaust his tears and fall asleep. While he tossed and turned next to her, she lay awake thinking. She thought of her three sons tucked safely in their beds at home. She was so glad she hadn't allowed Shammua and Shobad to go with Solomon. With all the drinking and confusion, anything could have happened to her young boys. Bathsheba offered up a silent prayer to God, thanking Him for protecting Solomon and for giving her the wisdom to take care of the others. If only David would ask God for help and guidance with his other children, but she knew he was afraid he would look like a hypocrite to his sons. How could he, a man who committed adultery and murder, ever earn back the respect of his adult children? Bathsheba would never forget the sins she and David had committed, but she did feel the fullness of God's forgiveness. She knew David had repented of his transgressions to the Lord, as well, but for some reason, he was not able to completely let go and move on. He would never be able to be an effective king or parent if he didn't forgive himself.

Chapter 51

An uneasy tension filled the palace in the days following Amnon's murder. David's guards reported back to him that Absalom had fled Jerusalem and was hiding with his grandfather, the king of Geshur. Bathsheba was disappointed but not surprised that David did not send soldiers to retrieve his son so he could be punished.

When the funeral and mourning period passed uneventfully, the entire community seemed to collectively breathe a sigh of relief. Bathsheba was isolated from the general population, but her mother's new midwife duties introduced her to many women around the palace, so she always knew what was going on. According to Shiran, most of the Israelites thought Amnon was properly punished for raping his sister (even though the punishment should have been from his father), and Absalom's exile to Geshur was sufficient retribution for his part in his brother's murder. Everyone started to feel at ease again—everyone except Bathsheba. She still went to her husband's rooms night after night and saw firsthand the effects of grief on the king. At first she thought his tears were for the death of his son Amnon, and they may have been for a while, but his mourning continued long after Amnon's death. Bathsheba finally mustered up the courage to talk to him about it.

"David, why do you still weep for your dead son?"

"It is not for Amnon that I mourn. Yes, I miss him, but he is at peace. It is for Absalom that I weep. I just don't know what to do. I know he should be punished for murdering his brother, but how can I condemn my own son?" David didn't say it, but Bathsheba knew he wanted to add, "after what I've done."

"You have every right to punish Absalom for what he did. You are the king and his father. I'm not saying he should be put to death, but something should be done to show the country that you are still in charge."

"I just miss him so much," David continued as if he hadn't even heard Bathsheba. "If only he would come home; maybe everything would be all right. Oh, it's no use. He'll never come back. He's probably terrified of what would happen to him. I just wish there were something I could do."

Bathsheba knew it was pointless to talk to him in this state, so she just sat by and listened as David vented his frustrations and grief.

Fortunately, she could talk to Nathan the prophet about her concerns. Their friendship had deepened considerably over the years, and she knew she could always find godly advice and comfort in him. When Bathsheba looked for him in his usual place in the garden, she found him talking to a man she had never seen before. When she approached, both men rose from their bench to greet her. Little Nathan toddled off on unsteady legs to chase a butterfly.

"Shalom, Bathsheba. I'd like you to meet my friend Gad."

Bathsheba felt a strange sense of jealousy as she visually inspected the younger man standing next to her friend. He was short and round with cheeks that were red from the heat. He was dressed in a simple robe similar to Nathan's. Gad greeted her with a warm, friendly smile that she tried to return even though she was disappointed that she had to share her friend with this newcomer.

"Gad will be staying here at the palace while I go to Jezreel to take care of some business," Nathan explained.

"How long will you be away?" Bathsheba asked, trying to conceal the apprehension that rose in her mind.

As always, Nathan seemed to know what she was thinking. He took her hand and gave it a squeeze. "I'm not sure. I just received word that my nephew is ill. His parents are both dead and I'm his only living relative, so I must go to him."

"But what about David? Who will give him godly counsel? Who will help him get over what has happened to his sons?"

"No one can help him with that, Bathsheba. He will have to seek the Lord for himself. But Gad will be here to help him whenever he can. He is also a prophet and seer."

"I'm sorry, Nathan. I'm such a selfish woman. I understand that you have to take care of your family right now. I hope your nephew will be all right." Bathsheba then addressed the new man, "Gad, welcome. If there is anything I can do to help you get settled, please let me know."

Just then, little Nathan fell and scraped his knee. He let out a howl that sent Bathsheba rushing to his side. She returned to the men a moment later with the sniffling child in her arms.

"Come here, little Nathan," the old prophet said, holding his arms out to the child. Nathan immediately went to him and buried his tear-streaked face against the old man's shoulder. "There now, little one. You're going to be just fine," he cooed into his ear. His long beard must have tickled the child because he started to giggle and squirm. Bathsheba couldn't help but smile. She knew she would miss her friend, but he had helped her to develop a close relationship with God so she knew that she would be all right on her own, no matter what was to come.

Chapter 52

The years passed quickly, and Bathsheba had to send her sons Shammua and Shobad off to live in the world of men. She was thankful to still have little Nathan at home to keep her company in the quiet that remained. Nathan was a thoughtful child and reminded her much of Solomon when he was young. Perhaps it was because she knew she wouldn't have any more children, but Bathsheba cherished every moment she had with her growing son.

Even though Shiran lived next door, Bathsheba saw very little of her. While Bathsheba was consumed with raising her youngest child, her mother's days and nights were filled with the new midwife duties she had taken on. The previous midwife was much too old to handle the increasing workload, so Shiran had taken over most of the deliveries and all of the daily medical care of the women and babies. Even though Shiran was no longer a young woman, Bathsheba thought she somehow looked more alive than ever; perhaps there was something to all those herbal potions after all.

On quiet evenings when David did not call for his favorite wife, she would sit in the courtyard visiting with the other women. When Shiran was available, she stopped by to give them the latest news and gossip. It seemed that the recurring topic was David's second-oldest remaining son, Absalom. For three years he remained in exile in his grandfather's kingdom. Finally, David allowed him to come back to Jerusalem, but Absalom was never to set foot in the palace. During his time in the city, Absalom was very busy convincing the citizens that he had been wronged. Many of the men supported him for taking action against his brother when his father appeared too weak to do so.

Being an incredibly handsome man, it didn't take long for the women to fall in line behind him as well. Absalom had his father's charm as well as his strong physique and handsome features, which were framed with a beautiful head of long dark hair that he was very proud of. Bathsheba hadn't seen Absalom in years, but there were plenty of detailed descriptions from the women who had been lucky enough to catch a glimpse of him as he passed by in his royal chariot.

David seemed to be the only person in Israel who was blind to Absalom's political ambitions. With every year that passed, David grew more and more depressed about the rift in his family. Those closest to the king knew something had to be done. Finally, Joab, David's nephew and the commander of his army, arranged for the estranged father and son to meet.

The day Absalom returned to the palace, everyone waited anxiously to find out what would happen. Would David pardon him, or would he have him thrown into prison? Was Absalom going to try to take the throne from his weak and aging father? Crowds of servants and courtiers stood around the palace waiting to find out what was happening in the throne room. The women bustled about restlessly, waiting for any news to trickle into the women's quarters. When Absalom left his father that day, the entire palace seemed to breathe a sigh of relief. Though the result wasn't as exciting as some had hoped, the news finally made its way throughout the kingdom that David had forgiven his son and all was well.

Having his father's blessing to move freely through the kingdom and palace, Absalom continued his political maneuvering with even more intensity. He acquired a larger chariot and hired fifty men to run before it, announcing his arrival every time he entered the city. He also stood near the city gate, intercepting anyone who was on their way to take a case to the king. He managed to convince the people that he was more interested in their problems than the king was. Once he had gained the love of the people and planted spies throughout the country, he went to his father and asked permission to go to Hebron to worship. David didn't suspect a thing, so he sent his son with his blessing. Little did David know his ambitious son had bigger plans.

Chapter 53

The day Absalom arrived in Hebron, word reached David that his son planned to declare himself the new king of Israel. David's strength and resolve returned, and he made an immediate decision to get his family and palace officials out of the city before Absalom had a chance to attack them.

The eunuch in charge of the women's quarters made an announcement late in the afternoon that everyone should be prepared to leave the next morning at dawn. The women scurried about trying to decide what to take on the journey. Because they didn't know when, if ever, they would return to the palace, it was difficult to know what to take. Everyone was frightened, but no one shed a tear—except Absalom's mother, Maacah. She feared for her husband and her son; it was certain one of them would have to die before this attempt to seize the throne was over.

After a sleepless night, the women and children were prepared to leave. David personally came to the women's quarters to speak to ten of his concubines whom he had decided to leave behind to take care of the palace. He then ushered the rest of his family to a well-guarded position in the procession leaving the city. Bathsheba, her son Nathan, and her mother, Shiran, got in line with the other women and young children as the crowd began to move out. Bathsheba had never before seen so many people moving in one direction. There were priests, soldiers, advisors, and servants, all headed east out of the palace toward the Kindron Valley. Bathsheba couldn't help but think of the stories Nathan had told her about the Israelites leaving Egypt to wander in the wilderness. She prayed it wouldn't take them forty years to reach their destination this time.

They hadn't traveled far when Bathsheba saw a tall soldier and two young men approaching her. She didn't recognize them as her sons until they got closer, and even then, it took her a bit longer to realize that the man in battle gear was Solomon. Of course, she knew all of David's sons were given extensive military training, but she had never seen her son carrying a sword before. She was surprised how natural it looked on him. The women nearby whispered and stared, but Bathsheba was filled with pride that her children were concerned enough about her to break rank and stay by her side through the journey. Shammua lifted his little brother Nathan onto his shoulders and Shobad offered an arm to his grandmother. Solomon walked protectively by his mother's side.

When they reached the outskirts of Jerusalem, just before crossing the Kindron Valley, the large group stopped.

"I'm going to find Abba and see if I can get some information. I'll be back in a little while," Solomon said. "Shammua and Shobad will stay with you," he added, giving his younger brothers instructions with his eyes.

Bathsheba watched him walk away and noticed again how much he looked like a king. She reminded herself again that God had promised to put him on the throne, and she felt peace in her heart even though she was walking in the midst of chaos.

There were too many people crowded around Bathsheba for her to see much around her. David had purposely placed his wives in the center of a large group so they would be safer if Absalom decided to attack. The group slowly began to move again, and after they crossed the small valley, the ground beneath their feet began to grow steeper. Bathsheba felt relieved when Solomon returned with news.

"After we climb the Mount of Olives," he began, "we will continue east toward the Jordan River. Once we cross it, Abba plans to lead us north toward Mahanaim to the forest of Ephraim, where we will have protection in the wilderness."

"Why were we stopped for so long? Did something happen?"

"The Levites were offering sacrifices. Abba has now sent four of them back to the city with the ark of the Lord. He said if God wants him to continue leading His people, then God will bring him safely back to Jerusalem to worship. It will also be good to have the priests inside the city so they can report any information about Absalom's rebellion."

A sound began at the front of the crowd and spread all the way to the back. It was the sound of people crying. "What has happened?" Bathsheba asked, feeling suddenly frightened.

"They are crying for their king. When I left him, he had taken off his sandals and was ascending the mountain with his head covered, while in prayer and supplication," Solomon answered.

Solemn sadness swept over every one of them, and even Bathsheba found herself weeping. David was loved by his people. He had led them through countless battles, he had brought them wealth and prosperity, but now he was sent fleeing from his palace, barefoot and humbled, by his own son.

"Eema, there's something else," Solomon said cautiously.

"What is it?"

"Abba received word that your grandfather, Ahithophel, is helping Absalom."

A moan escaped Bathsheba's lips. "I should have known he would do something like this," she cried. "All these years he has been hiding away in Hebron, nursing his anger toward David."

"Is it because . . . ?" Solomon seemed unable to even talk about what happened between his mother and father.

"Yes, son. Even after all this time has passed, we still see the consequences of our sins." She was quiet for a moment as she thought about the dangers of having her grandfather advising their enemy. "He will be a great help to Absalom," Bathsheba continued, unable to keep the concern out of her voice.

"Abba has prayed that God will turn Ahithophel's advice into foolishness. Perhaps he will be the downfall of Absalom."

Bathsheba remembered Nathan's telling her how God took the weak and made them strong; perhaps He could also turn a wise man into a fool. She had no choice but to trust.

Chapter 54

The group descended the Mount of Olives and traveled slowly toward the wilderness that lay ahead. As the sun crawled higher in the sky, the young children whined, and the women grew noticeably tired. The procession had grown quiet as they walked on in the growing heat. Sometime after noon, David met the servant of his friend Mephibosheth. He had with him several donkeys loaded with two hundred loaves of bread, a hundred clusters of raisins and figs, and a huge container full of new wine. The gifts were brought to David's wives. Once the food was unloaded and distributed—first to the women and children, then to the others—the donkeys were given to the women to ride. Bathsheba gratefully accepted a stocky spotted animal that was brought to her. Solomon helped her onto the donkey and then placed his exhausted brother Nathan in front of her. She looked over at her mother and Abigail, who were also seated comfortably on donkeys. She was so thankful to have the gifts, not just for herself, but also for the older women who were struggling with the long walk.

News traveled slower than donkeys, so it took a while for her to find out more about the giver of the gifts. The man's name was Ziba, and he was the servant in charge of the land David had given to Jonathan's crippled son, Mephibosheth. According to Ziba, his master had stayed in Jerusalem, hoping the Israelites would eventually turn against Absalom and restore the kingdom to Saul's grandson.

When Bathsheba heard this story, her heart broke for her husband. It seemed as if the people closest to David were betraying him on every side. First his own son, then his trusted advisor, now one of his closest friends. She desperately wanted to go to him to offer comfort, but she knew it was impossible.

Just when she thought it couldn't get any worse, she heard a man shouting. Solomon firmly held on to her donkey so he wouldn't become excited by the commotion. This time, her son Shammua went to find out what was going on. By the time he returned, everything had quieted down, but no one was really sure what had happened.

"It was just an angry Benjamite," Shammua explained when he rejoined his family. "He was standing by the road shouting curses at Abba and throwing stones at the crowd."

"Did your father have him killed?" Bathsheba asked.

"No, he just left him there. I guess after being betrayed by his own son, Abba is not going to get upset over a stranger yelling at him," Shammua replied.

"When Abba takes his crown back, that man will pay for humiliating him like that," Bathsheba's more aggressive son, Shobad, interjected.

"Let God handle it, brother. Abba has bigger things to worry about than Saul's bitter relatives standing beside the road and cursing him," Solomon said in his usual diplomatic manner.

Bathsheba smiled to herself as she watched the interaction between her sons. As difficult as the situation was, she was glad to have them by her side.

At last they reached the Jordan River. David decided to let the exhausted, hungry group stop and rest. After everyone had a light meal, they began making preparations to set up tents so they could spend the night by the river. Before the fist pole was in the ground, messengers rode through the crowds, telling everyone to pack their belongings and prepare to cross the river immediately. Word had reached David through the Levite spies in the city that Ahithophel had advised Absalom to attack them that night. This information was enough to make everyone forget their sore feet and sunburned faces.

It took all night, but by daybreak, everyone was safely across the Jordan River. They knew Absalom was close behind, so they continued on their way to the wilderness without stopping to rest. Though the second day's journey was longer than the first day's and everyone had gotten very little rest the previous night, somehow they made it to Mahanaim by nightfall. There three men bearing gifts greeted them. They brought bedding, blankets, bowls, and pots for David and his people. They also brought enough lentils, beans, cheese, and even sheep to feed the entire crowd. Again, Bathsheba was overcome with gratitude. Though at times it seemed as if enemies surrounded them, they still had many friends along the way.

David and his followers entered the city gates and were greeted warmly by the people there. The women and children were housed in a large stone building that looked as if it had been built for soldiers. Beds had already been prepared for them, and a group of women had prepared soup for anyone who wanted to eat. Bathsheba hadn't seen her husband since they left Jerusalem, so she asked Solomon to take her to him. She knew she wouldn't be able to stay with David, but she at least wanted to see his face to make sure he was surviving the journey and its tribulations.

The soldiers had set up camp near the city gates. Her son led Bathsheba to a large tent in the center of the cluster, where her husband was organizing his soldiers. There were several men inside sitting on mats discussing plans for the upcoming battle. When a servant informed David that his wife was outside, the other men respectfully left the tent.

"Oh, Bathsheba, you're a breath of fresh air right now," David said, embracing his wife as if hadn't seen her in years. "How are you handling the journey? Did you get a donkey? Is young Nathan all right?"

"Yes, love, please don't worry about us. Our sons are taking very good care of me. And little Nathan has been brave and obedient."

"I'm so glad," David responded. "You and the other women will be able to rest here for a while. I am sending my best men out to fight Absalom in the morning."

"You are not going with them?" Bathsheba asked hopefully.

"I want to, but my generals think it would be better if I stay here. They fear Absalom's men will come after me and take me down at all costs. I hate to say it, but I know they are right. If I die, it will be almost impossible to take the throne from Absalom."

"Oh, David, I'm so glad you've made such a wise decision. You will be so much more useful to the troops here."

"Yes, yes, you got your way, and you didn't even have to work at it," he teased.

Bathsheba took advantage of the light mood to bring up a painful subject. "Have you received any news about my grandfather?" she asked carefully.

David sighed deeply before answering. "Yes," he said, "Ahithophel's first advice to Absalom was to take my concubines to the roof and claim them publicly. He erected a tent in the very place that you and I were married, and he raped them in front of the entire city."

"Oh, no," Bathsheba gasped.

"I knew Ahithophel was angry about what I did to you, but I had no idea he would be so vengeful."

"David, I'm so sorry. I . . ."

"No, it's not your fault. Nathan predicted all of this years ago. When he confronted me with my sin, he told me what the consequences would be. He told me that because I took another man's wife in private, my wives would be taken publicly for everyone to see. He even told me someone close to me would do it. I had no idea it would be my own son."

"Oh, David," she cried.

"There is some better news," David continued. "That is the only advice Absalom has taken from your grandfather," he said trying to cheer her up. "Ahithophel recommended that Absalom attack us at the Jordan River, but my friend Hushai was there to offer another plan. Fortunately, Absalom took Hushai's advice, and he is in the process of assembling every fighting man left in the area. It was enough of a distraction to buy us the time we needed to get to safety. We also have the advantage now of fighting them in the wilderness rather than out in the open. My men are much more experienced than Absalom's and with God on our side, I'm sure we will have victory."

Bathsheba couldn't help but feel encouraged as she listened to her husband's plan. Beneath his now gray hair and aging bones still beat the heart of a great king and warrior. She was suddenly filled with a sense of awe standing before him.

"You will have victory, my king," Bathsheba said, kissing his hand and bowing to him.

He smiled at her act of reverence and seemed strengthened by her faith in him. "You must go now, my love. I have a lot of work left to do tonight. I'll see you soon."

Chapter 55

The next morning at dawn, Bathsheba went to the soldier's camp to find her sons. She saw the units lining up behind the three commanders David had selected to lead the men into battle. She looked into the faces of the soldiers who had been with David for years—hard, experienced men who had fought and won many battles for their king. She felt confident that they would be victorious again.

Eventually she found Solomon organizing the reserve troops who would stay in the city and wait to be called in if reinforcements were needed. She knew David would not send Solomon into battle unless it was absolutely necessary to do so. Her other sons Shammua and Shobad were still too young to fight, but she saw them bustling about preparing weapons and armor for the soldiers in case they were needed.

She didn't want to distract Solomon from his duties, so she kept her distance from the reserves, watching to see how her son handled the responsibility given to him by his father. Again, she was amazed at his kingly bearing and confidence. Even though he was younger than most of the soldiers he was commanding, they seemed to respect him.

When the three units of David's best soldiers left Mahanaim, the inhabitants of the city, as well as the exiles from Jerusalem, saw them off with cheers of encouragement. David stood by the gates giving last-minute instructions as well. As they marched away, David shouted to his commanders, "Be kind to Absalom for my sake!"

When the troops were out of sight, everyone returned to the city. Bathsheba saw Solomon sitting in front of his tent by a fire, so she went to sit with him.

"Shalom, my son. How are you this morning?"

"I'm well, Eema. Were you and the other women comfortable last night?"

"Yes, very. Two days of walking was enough to keep even that group quiet," Bathsheba said jokingly. "I see your father put you in charge of the reserves."

"Yes, he left a few of his senior officers here to make sure I can handle it, but so far I haven't had to call on them. I am glad to know they're here in the event we are called to join the battle. I've never even fought an actual battle, let alone led troops in one," Solomon admitted quietly so no one else could hear him.

"You'll be fine, Solomon. These men look as if they would follow you anywhere."

Just then two young women approached the fire carrying a basket of food. They both wore fine robes, indicating that they were the maiden daughters of a prosperous family. When they drew nearer, Bathsheba saw they were both very pretty, though one was still quite young. They bowed low before the queen; then the older girl spoke to Solomon.

"Shalom. Are you the king's son Solomon who is also called Jedidiah?" she asked respectfully.

"I am."

"My name is Ayala, and this is my sister, Donora. We are daughters of Rachamim, from the tribe of Levi. Please accept these gifts on behalf of our father."

"Thank you, Ayala," Solomon said as he took the basket from the attractive girl.

Bathsheba watched her son carefully and noticed a new shade of pink rising to his cheeks. She tried to conceal her smile.

"Won't you girls join us for breakfast?" Bathsheba invited. She noticed that Solomon looked uncomfortable, so she called him over to help her find plates.

"What sweet girls," Bathsheba said quietly so only Solomon could hear her.

"Uh, yeah," he replied, unable to resume his usual composure.

"Here we are," Bathsheba said as she sat down next to the girls and opened the basket of food they brought. "Oh, what lovely bread. Did you bake it yourselves?"

"Yes, well, our mother helped us a little," the younger girl, Donora, said.

Solomon passed around a bowl of water so everyone could wash their hands, and then he offered a blessing for the food. It was much shorter and simpler than his usual prayers, but he managed to get it done properly.

"So, Ayala, is your father a priest?" Bathsheba asked even though she knew the girl had said they were the daughters of a Levite.

"Yes, he is the lead musician."

"Oh, Solomon loves music. Don't you, son?" When he was able only to nod, Bathsheba continued for him, "He plays the harp like his father, and he has also started writing his own songs. He's quite talented."

"I play the lyre," Ayala replied. "My Abba doesn't have any sons, so he taught me to play. Donora doesn't really play, but she has a beautiful singing voice." She tried to include her shy younger sister in the conversation.

Solomon sat silently eating his food while the women talked. Every time Bathsheba tried to include him in the conversation, he would only nod and smile. At last a young soldier came to him and told him his father requested his presence in the guard tower. He looked grateful and quickly rose to his feet, saying goodbye to the women over his shoulder. As he walked away, the two girls began to giggle.

"I'm afraid my son doesn't have much experience with young women," Bathsheba said apologetically.

"Oh, I think he's wonderful," Ayala said quickly. Her face immediately turned red, and she lowered her eyes so Bathsheba wouldn't see her embarrassment.

Bathsheba smiled kindly at the girl. "Does your family spend much time in Jerusalem?" she asked casually.

"Yes, Abba tries to take the family at least once a year so we can participate in one of the festivals. I think he would move to the city if he could find work there."

"Well, perhaps when this war is over, we could find something for him. My son is working with his father on plans to build a magnificent temple to house God's ark. Many Levites will be needed to help with the project."

Bathsheba saw both girls' faces light up.

"It must be so exciting to live in Jerusalem," Donora said eagerly.

"I think it would be exciting to live in the palace," Ayala said shyly. "The outside of it is very beautiful. Much more impressive than anything we have here in Mahanaim."

"Yes, it is very nice. The next time your family is in Jerusalem, I would love to have you come visit me. Please tell your mother I said that, OK?"

The girls were too young to appreciate Bathsheba's meaning, but she hoped their mother would understand her intentions.

Ayala and Donora helped her clean up; then they returned to their home. Bathsheba decided she too should go back to the barracks to rejoin the other women. As she walked back, she allowed her mind to paint a picture of her handsome son Solomon dressed in the robe of a bridegroom standing next to one of those beautiful young Levites. She smiled all the way to the barracks.

Chapter 56

The battle against Absalom and his inexperienced fighters did not last long. David's troops met them in the forest of Ephraim, where they slaughtered more than twenty thousand of the rebel soldiers. David saw the runners approaching the city from his place in the guardroom between the city gates. He went out to meet them to hear the news. When he learned about the victory, he was pleased, but his questions always went back to his son Absalom. Finally David was told that Absalom had been killed. When David heard the news, he didn't rejoice for Israel's victory, but instead he returned to his room, mourning and weeping for his dead son. The returning soldiers could hear their king crying out in a loud voice, "O my son, my son! Absalom, my son."

David's commander Joab was angry to hear the king grieving for his son rather than praising the victorious troops who had risked their lives to keep him on the throne. Joab entered the guard tower and scolded the king for discouraging his troops. When the two men came down to meet the victorious soldiers, David wiped his eyes and did his best to congratulate his men.

A few days later, the large group of soldiers and refugees moved out of the city and headed west to the Jordan River. This time, David had his wives and children ride in the front of the procession with him and his generals because they were no longer in danger. Bathsheba was glad to be near him again and out of the dust and chaos of the crowd. Though the king was still mourning the loss of his son, the rest of the group was cheerful as they journeyed closer to their home.

When they reached the eastern bank of the river, they were greeted by a group of Benjamites. One of the men threw himself at David's feet and begged forgiveness.

"That's the man who cursed us on our way out of Jerusalem," Shammua whispered to Bathsheba. "I can't wait to see what Abba does to him now."

David's generals watched for the command to kill the man, but it did not come. Instead, David showed him mercy and took an oath that he would not execute Saul's relative for cursing him. Shammua was obviously disappointed, but Bathsheba was relived that there would be no more bloodshed.

Also in the group of Benjamites was Jonathan's son Mephibosheth, who had reportedly stayed in Jerusalem in the hopes of getting his grandfather's crown. He rode on a donkey and approached David looking very ragged and unkempt.

David was hurt deeply by the betrayal of this man who he had called friend, and the pain showed in his eyes when he spoke to him. "Mephibosheth, why didn't you come with me when I left Jerusalem? Did you think you would be made king if you stayed?"

"Oh, King David, may you life forever," Mephibosheth exclaimed almost in tears. "It was a mistake, a terrible mistake. . . . Because I can't walk, I told my servant Ziba to bring me my donkey so I could go with you, but he left without me. I heard he lied to you and told you I stayed in the city in the hopes of taking the throne. I want you to know it isn't true. Every one of my grandfather's descendents deserves to die because of the way you were treated, but out of love for my father, Jonathan, you gave me a place with your family at your own table. I have no right to ask you to show me mercy again, but I want you to know I . . ."

"Don't say another word, my friend," David interrupted. "You are always welcome at my table. I am disappointed that your servant lied to me, but he also showed us kindness when he brought food and donkeys for my family. For that, I will forgive him as well."

Then the Benjamites, who were all relatives of the former King Saul, escorted the group across the Jordan River, showing their respect and acceptance of King David. On the other side of the river, even more people were waiting to welcome them home. There were thousands of people from the tribe of Judah all cheering for the king. The crowd only grew larger as they got closer to Jerusalem.

David himself led his family back into the palace. His first order of business was to see his wives safely to their homes. When they reached the women's quarters, he called together the ten concubines who had been raped by his son. They all came out to him wearing torn robes and ashes in their hair. The other wives wept when they saw them.

David addressed the concubines who stood before him, "You must all get your belongings together and move out of this area immediately. From this day on, you will live in the servant's quarters on the east side of the compound, and you will wear the robes of widows."

All of the women began sobbing, but they did what they had been commanded. When their personal items had been gathered, they were escorted through the courtyard and out of the women's quarters, never to be seen again by the respectable wives of David.

The remaining women cried as their friends departed. They cried not only for the poor girls who had suffered pain and humiliation at the hands of Absalom, then the chastisement of their husband, but they also cried for themselves. Every one of them realized that if they had been ordered to stay at the palace while David fled, they would be suffering the same fate. As women, they had very little control over their lives. They all knew deep down inside how vulnerable they were, but seeing the poor discarded concubines just brought their reality to the surface.

Chapter 57

Just when life at the palace seemed to settle down, war broke out again. It seemed there would be no rest for the aged King David. His old enemies the Philistines rose up to challenge the Israelites once more. David went with his troops but found that he had become too old to be effective on the battlefield. David returned home uninjured, but morally defeated. When Bathsheba heard her husband had returned, she expected to receive word that he wanted to see her. When none came, she sent her trusted maid Matana to find out what was wrong.

"He just wants to be alone," Matana reported back to her.

"It doesn't make sense," Bathsheba replied. "David always sends for me when he returns from battle. Something must be wrong, and I have to find out what it is." She then proceeded to send a message to her husband, asking if he would join her for dinner in her home. The messenger returned and told her that the king was too tired to dine with her.

Several more days passed with still no word from David. Matana kept her eyes open to find out if he was sending for his other wives, but he wasn't. Growing more and more concerned for her husband, Bathsheba decided to go to Solomon to see if he could help. When she arrived at his house, she found him sitting at a table reading a letter. He quickly set it aside as if he didn't want her to see it. He respectfully rose to greet her then offered her a seat. When the two were comfortably seated, she began her request. "Solomon, I want you to talk to your father for me. I haven't seen him in weeks, and I'm worried about his health."

"He wasn't injured in battle. The doctors have all checked him, and they say he is fine," Solomon tried to reassure her.

"I know he's physically fine, but I'm worried about him emotionally. It must have been very difficult for him to be bested by a

Philistine. After all, his first great victory was over their champion Goliath all those years ago, and now he's unable to defeat a common Philistine soldier."

Solomon thought about what his mother said. "You're right, Eema. He must be very depressed. Do you think you could cheer him up?"

"I don't know, but I'd like to try. Sometimes a woman's touch can do great things for a man."

She noticed color rising in Solomon's cheeks, and he glanced nervously at the table on which the letter lay.

"What is it, son?" she asked suspiciously. "Are *you* feeling all right?"

"Yes, its just, well," he stammered, "I got a letter from the father of that Levite girl, Ayala."

"He wrote to you?" Bathsheba asked, trying to keep the surprise out of her voice.

"Yes, he is requesting a job here in Jerusalem."

"What are you going to tell him?" she asked.

"I've done some checking, and I've found out he's a talented musician. It might be nice to have him here."

"And what about his daughters?" Bathsheba asked, trying to sound casual.

"I only met them the one time, but I found Ayala very nice."

"She would be a lovely bride."

"Eema, I don't even know her," Solomon protested.

"Yes, but if her family comes to the city, you could get to know her."

"Perhaps we should talk to Abba about it before we make any decisions."

"I think that's a good idea. You can send word to him that we want to discuss wedding plans with him. Then he's sure to see us. Maybe it will even cheer him up a bit."

"All right, I'll send a servant to request an audience with him tonight. If you don't hear otherwise from me, I'll meet you at his rooms at sundown. Now, don't go planning any weddings yet," Solomon teased as he kissed his mother goodbye.

Chapter 58

When Solomon and Bathsheba arrived at David's rooms that evening, they found him sitting on a couch looking old and dejected. He tried to put on his best face for his visitors, but the struggle was obvious.

"Shalom, please come in," David said without getting up to greet them. "Bathsheba, you look stunning tonight. Is it possible that I had almost forgotten how beautiful you are?"

Bathsheba appreciated the compliment. She had taken extra time to prepare herself so she would look her best. She knew she was no longer the youngest, most beautiful woman in the palace, so it was good to know her husband still found her attractive.

The three sat together on cushions in David's sitting room while a servant served them fruit.

"How are you feeling, Abba?" Solomon asked, obviously concerned about his father's health.

"The doctors tell me I'm fine."

"Yes, but how do you *feel*?" Bathsheba jumped in.

"Oh, I don't know. I guess I just feel old. But it doesn't matter. My servant said you have something to discuss with me. What is it?"

"I think I'm ready to start looking for a wife," Solomon answered simply.

"Do you have anyone in mind?"

"Well, there was this one girl I met in Mahanaim. She is the daughter of a Levite priest."

"A Levite?" David said sounding disappointed. "I'm sure she's very nice, but son, you should really try to think of your political future.

How is marriage to the daughter of a priest going to strengthen our kingdom? A future king must make his choices carefully. I've already received word from both the king of Tyre and the king of Ammon suggesting that we join families in order to reinforce our alliances."

"David, this Ayala is a wonderful girl from a very godly family. It would be good for our son to have a wife who loves the Lord," Bathsheba interjected.

"There will be plenty of time for love matches later, but Solomon must choose his first wife carefully," David continued. "I believe the Ammonite princess would be a better choice. Perhaps you can take the Levite girl as a concubine or even a lesser wife."

Bathsheba had always hoped her son would take only one wife. She knew how much trouble David had with all his women and children, and she didn't want that for Solomon.

"Yes, Abba, I suppose you're right. It would be better for the country if I marry a princess," Solomon responded after some thought.

"But what about Ayala? What about her family?" Bathsheba asked, feeling her emotions rise.

"I will take her as a concubine. After all, she is just a Levite," Solomon responded.

"Just a Levite? Those are God's anointed priests! You are going to choose a heathen foreigner over a daughter of Israel?" Bathsheba protested.

"Don't worry, Bathsheba," David spoke calmly. "We'll give her father a good job, and the girl will be happy in the harem."

Bathsheba wanted to tell them no woman is truly happy in a harem, but she managed to hold her tongue.

"If you are ready to take a bride, I will ask the king of Ammon to send his daughter Naamah to Jerusalem. What do you think of a spring wedding?" David asked, smiling sincerely for the first time since they arrived.

Bathsheba had dreamed of a spring wedding in the garden for Solomon—but not to a heathen princess. She was disappointed, but tried not to let it show. If Solomon accepted the fact that his first wife would be a stranger from another country, then she would try to be supportive.

"I think the garden would be lovely," she replied.

"Fine, my love, you go ahead and start planning. You have my permission to do whatever you like," David said with a familiar spark returning to his eyes. "But, you can't start until tomorrow. I would like you to stay with me tonight. All this talk of weddings has made me feel a bit younger."

It was not how Bathsheba had envisioned the evening, but she was pleased that her husband seemed to be regaining some of his vigor. Solomon quickly left his father's room so his parents could be alone.

Chapter 59

Bathsheba put her feelings aside and tried to plan the nicest wedding she could. Her brother-in-law, Nadav, had become well known for the delicacies he prepared for the king's table. She was sure he would make a feast beyond compare for her son's wedding. She spent much of her time with her sister and mother making arrangements for the big day. Every detail—from the food for the banquet to the garments her son would wear—was planned. If only the winter rains would come and refresh the garden, everything would be perfect. Israel had suffered two years of drought, but because Bathsheba was so far removed from farmers and crops, the dry weather was merely an inconvenience to her. Though the rest of the area was suffering, the tables at the palace were still laden with the best foods available.

One warm winter afternoon, Bathsheba sat with her mother and sister under a withered tree, trying to take advantage of the sparse shade. Now that her children and nephews were old enough to live on their own, she was able to enjoy her sister's company without the duties of motherhood pulling at them. It was strange for them to sit together without being interrupted by someone crying for their attention.

"Has Solomon heard from the king of Ammon yet? Do you know when his bride will arrive?" Atarah asked.

"It should be any time now. I'm sure the princess has to get her things in order before she leaves. It's just as well; it gives Solomon the time he needs to finish the building project he has going on in the women's quarters."

"What is he building?" Atarah asked.

"He's putting in a new home for his wives. It looks like it will be a large wooden structure with several rooms. It seems awfully big for one woman, but I'm sure princess Naamah won't be alone long."

"What do you mean?"

"Well, the Levite family we met in Mahanaim has already arrived in Jerusalem. They are currently living in a comfortable house near the tent of the Lord, but Solomon intends to take the girl Ayala as a concubine as soon as he is able. I don't know how wise it is for him to put the women together, but no one seems interested in my opinion."

"At least he plans to stay here at the palace rather than moving out to the country the way his brothers did," Atarah said.

"I think Solomon would like to spend some time away from the city, but his father is keeping him close so he can groom him for the throne," Bathsheba replied. "I'm glad, though. At least here he is protected from his brothers. Until David makes his intentions of giving the crown to Solomon known to everyone, none of us are truly safe."

"You don't think one of his brothers would rise up against Solomon, do you?" Shiran asked, joining the conversation.

"Why not? If we've learned anything in this place, it's that even family can't always be trusted. Just look at what Absalom did to his father and what Grandfather did to me."

At the mention of Ahithophel, Bathsheba noticed an uncomfortable look pass between her mother and sister.

"What is it?" she asked suspiciously.

"You haven't heard, have you?" Atarah asked.

"Heard what?"

"Our grandfather is dead," her sister replied.

"Dead? How? I thought he fled before we returned to Jerusalem. Who killed him?" Bathsheba asked.

"He killed himself."

Bathsheba took a moment to absorb the information. Though her grandfather Ahithophel had humiliated her and betrayed her husband, she couldn't help but remember him in his younger days. He had always been kind to her when she was a child, giving her special gifts and praising her every accomplishment. She remembered the funny stories he brought from the palace when he came to visit their home. As a child she used to feel such love and admiration for him.

"Oh, Sav," she sighed to herself, "why did you have to hold on to your anger? If only you could have forgiven David and me."

Shiran put her arm around Bathsheba, and her sister took her hand. She looked into the eyes of her remaining family and felt much love for them. Through the years they had made her cry, but they had also been there to wipe away her tears. She knew that despite the problems they had had in the past, these women would be by her side no matter what happened.

Chapter 60

Solomon's bride arrived in Jerusalem early in the spring, riding in a chariot pulled by two matching white horses. Her father, the king of the Ammonite city Rabbah, received a handsome bride-price for her and reciprocated with gifts to be presented to the future king of Israel as a dowry for his daughter. The Ammonites who had been lifelong enemies of Israel now honored the Hebrew prince by sending their princess Naamah.

A crowd gathered around the palace when they saw the royal procession enter the city. Notified that her daughter-in-law had at last arrived, Bathsheba hurried to meet her. Naamah was adorned with such beautiful clothing and jewels that it was not immediately apparent that she did not possess much in the way of natural beauty.

The princess stepped down from the chariot, assisted by two male servants, and walked to where David and Solomon stood waiting for her. She bowed low before her future husband and father-in-law, showing them the proper respect. Bathsheba watched her son's face closely to see if she could read his reaction on first seeing his new wife. Solomon's expression revealed nothing.

When it was appropriate, Bathsheba went over to greet the young woman.

"Welcome, daughter," Bathsheba said after they had bowed politely to one another. "Please allow me to escort you to the home my son has prepared for you."

"Thank you, mother," the girl replied in her strange accent.

As they walked toward the newly expanded women's quarters, a line of servants followed closely behind, carrying Naamah's belongings. The girl seemed unimpressed by the beautiful new house Solomon had built for her. She stepped inside and began snapping orders at her people without giving any further attention to her mother-in-law. When Bathsheba saw she was not needed, she quietly slipped out and returned to her home.

Bathsheba couldn't help feeling disappointed in their first meeting. The aloof princess was very different from the sweet Levite she had wanted for her son. She hoped that Naamah just needed time to adjust to her new surroundings and would warm with time.

The next day, the palace buzzed with preparations for Solomon's wedding. The ongoing drought had ruined Bathsheba's dreams for a garden wedding. It was much too hot and dry to have the ceremony outside, so David made plans to move the event indoors.

Bathsheba went to her daughter-in-law's house to see if she could help her get ready for the wedding. A servant led her into the main room where several others were scurrying around performing various tasks for their mistress. Naamah entered the room half-dressed and looking unhappy. She seemed annoyed to have Bathsheba there.

"Is there something you need, mother?" she asked curtly.

"No, I just came by to see if I could be of assistance to you," Bathsheba replied.

"As you can see, I have plenty of servants. Your help is not needed."

"Oh, well, I'll just be going then," Bathsheba managed to stammer as she turned to leave. If she disliked the girl at their first meeting, she liked her even less now.

Not knowing what to do with her time while she waited for the wedding, Bathsheba walked over to Solomon's house to see if she could be of assistance there. She was greeted at the door by a young man who was more of a friend to her son than a servant. He smiled warmly at her and led her into the house. Solomon had been seated, but rose to greet her when she walked into the room.

"Oh, Eema, it's nice to see you," he said sincerely.

When Bathsheba saw him, her heart skipped a beat, and for a reason she couldn't explain, she felt her eyes fill with tears. Solomon looked so handsome in his wedding clothes it took her breath away. It was hard to believe this man standing before her was the child she cradled in her arms so many years before.

He wore a calf-length linen tunic made of a deep purple embroidered with gold thread. His cloak was a rich red trimmed with the same purple. Solomon went to her and gave her a huge, warm hug. She breathed in the fragrance of the musky perfume his robe had been treated with.

"Solomon, you look so handsome," Bathsheba said almost unable to speak.

"Thank you, Eema. And you look so lovely that I only hope you don't outshine my bride," he responded.

Solomon sat down to put on his sandals, but Bathsheba quickly knelt at his feet so she could do it for him. When she had the last strap tied, she stood up and put his jeweled crown on his head. Again, she had to hold back her tears.

"Well, I guess I'm ready," Solomon said calmly.

He offered Bathsheba his arm and led her to the palace. Once inside, he escorted her to where the women were starting to congregate; then he went to find his father. Bathsheba found her mother standing with Abigail and Atarah near the front of the large open room where the ceremony was to be held. She joined them, and they waited patiently until the sound of trumpets outside announced the arrival of the bride.

The large doors swung open, and Naamah entered the room draped in light yellow fabric that shimmered in the sunlight behind her. She was followed by a string of beautiful young maidens all dressed in fine pale-colored gowns. She joined Solomon and stood at his right side. David stood at his left. It had been a long time since Bathsheba had seen her husband looking so regal and strong. David began the ceremony with a psalm that he had written for the occasion. In it, he praised God for His goodness, and then he celebrated his son and daughter-in-law and their union. When the song was over, the prophet Gad offered a prayer for the couple's future.

After the ceremony, the congregation moved to the dining area, where a banquet was ready to be served. The famine, which had been going on almost three years, was impossible to ignore, even in the king's palace. The feast was not as elaborate as Bathsheba would have liked, but her brother-in-law had done a wonderful job with the available resources. Bathsheba watched her son closely throughout the evening to see how he interacted with his new wife. Though Solomon had a smile on his face throughout the festivities, she couldn't really tell whether he was happy. When the couple rose to leave, everyone cheered. Solomon looked relaxed and confident as he led his bride out of the room, but Bathsheba thought she saw a flicker of anxiety in his eyes.

Chapter 61

That year the drought in Israel ended. Along with the rains came Solomon's second wife, Ayala the Levite. There was no ceremony or feast to welcome her, but Bathsheba did all she could to make the girl feel comfortable. Unfortunately, Solomon's first wife, Naamah, was not as friendly to the newcomer—or to anyone else. She kept herself secluded in her miniature palace within the women's quarters. Whenever she went outside, an entourage of maids always followed her. Ayala, on the other hand, spent most of her days outside in the courtyard to avoid her temperamental housemate. When the weather was too wet, Bathsheba brought her into her own home. She offered to give the girl her extra bedroom that her sons had filled for so many years, but Ayala insisted on living in the place her husband had prepared for her. She obviously adored Solomon and did all she could to please him, but the demanding first wife took most of his time and attention.

Despite the constant turmoil in the nation around her, Bathsheba's days were peaceful and comfortable. As the years went by, she worried less and less about the frivolous things of youth. Her days were no longer spent at the dressing table preparing herself for her husband. She knew her beauty had faded some, but when she looked into David's eyes, she saw reflected there a real beauty that time and age would never spoil.

The years had not been as kind to David. While Bathsheba grew stronger and more confident every day, it was obvious David's days were coming to an end. The many battles he had fought, both with God and men, had taken a toll on him. He no longer had the strength to enjoy the company of his wives, so most of them lived as widows in the comfortable houses they had known most of their lives. However, he still longed for the companionship of his friend and confidant, Bathsheba. She spent many of her evenings preparing the soft foods she had fed her babies so many years earlier. David had no appetite, but she was always able to get him to eat something. At night, she used her body to keep him warm when the blankets were inadequate. She was glad to be able to offer him some comfort even when the doctors were unable to.

Late one evening, she held her husband in her arms while he slept fitfully. Bathsheba sang softly in his ear to soothe him, but he seemed unable to find peace. Suddenly, his body trembled violently, and she felt warm liquid cover both of their legs. Some women may have felt disgust or even pity to see the once great king reduced to a frail old man beneath the soiled sheets, but Bathsheba felt neither. She called for a servant and the doctor and immediately began to take care of her husband's needs. When David's eyes fluttered open and he recognized her standing there, she saw a look of fear wash over his face.

"David, it's going to be all right. The doctor will be here soon." Bathsheba spoke softly as she gently brushed his thin hair from his forehead.

He tried to speak, but could only moan. Then David attempted to get up from the bed, but he was only able to lift his head. Realizing he had lost all control of his body, David's fear quickly turned to embarrassment and then anger. He looked at his beloved wife with an expression of unexplainable hatred that she had never seen in his eyes before. His moans became louder and more intense, and his face flooded with color. At that moment several doctors and servants burst into the room. Bathsheba was brushed aside while the flurry of activity surrounded David's limp body. The shouts continued to pour out of his mouth, and from the direction of his gaze, they all seemed aimed at his wife. She was sure he was hurling insults at her, but she didn't understand why. Finally, a doctor took Bathsheba's arm and ushered her out of the room.

"What happened?" he asked briskly.

"I don't know. David was sleeping restlessly; then suddenly his body started shaking and he . . ." She caught the sob in her throat before it could escape. "He can't talk and he can't move; what's wrong with him?" Bathsheba was almost yelling now.

"I don't know. We'll have to examine him before we can determine what happened. But, for now, you should go back to your house. For some reason, he seems very upset by your presence. It would be better for both of you if you were not here right now."

"I'm not leaving my husband," Bathsheba said adamantly.

"You may not go back into David's bedchamber," the doctor insisted.

"Fine, then I'll stay out here."

"I don't think that's a good idea."

"Then you will have to call a guard to physically remove me from the area." Bathsheba stood to her full height and gave the doctor a look that confirmed her threat.

"But, you're the queen, no guard will want to . . ." After pondering for a moment, the doctor walked over to a young servant standing nearby and whispered something in his ear. The servant left immediately, and with one more look at the strong-willed queen, the doctor stepped back into David's bedroom and closed the door behind him.

Left alone in the hall, Bathsheba collapsed to the floor and began weeping. A few minutes later, the doctor's servant returned with Solomon by his side. When she looked up at her son, she saw his sleepy eyes were filled with concern, not just for his father, but for her as well.

"Oh, Eema," he sighed as he sat on the floor next to her. He had thoughtfully brought her a blanket and used it to cover her soiled sleeping gown. "The doctor's assistant told me what happened. I would like to go in and see Abba, but there seems to be a lot going on right now. I would hate to get in the way."

"David is dying," Bathsheba said plainly, "and he hates me."

"He doesn't hate you!" Solomon tried to reassure her.

"Yes, he does. You should have seen the anger in his eyes."

"Did you stop to think how humiliated he must be? No man wants the woman he loves to see him in such a state. Besides, he's probably terrified, and you are the only one with whom he has ever been able to share his true thoughts and fears. Now he can't even do that."

"Oh, Solomon, how did you get to be so wise?" Bathsheba said gratefully.

He smiled sheepishly and gave his mother's hand a squeeze. "You really should go home and get some rest."

"I don't want to leave him. I want to be close if he needs me. I'll just sleep here on the floor if I get tired."

"The last thing we need right now is for you to get sick too. If you don't take care of yourself, you'll be no help to Abba. Now please, go home. Here, I have something that will cheer you up," Solomon said as he put a letter in her hand.

"What is this?"

"It's a letter from the prophet Nathan. I think he's ready to come back to Jerusalem. When Abba's condition is more stable, perhaps I will go to Jezreel and escort our friend home."

For the first time in hours, Bathsheba felt a glimmer of hope. With the precious letter in hand, she walked to her house without further argument.

Chapter 62

For the next several days, Bathsheba stayed close to her husband's rooms but was not permitted to enter. She was able to pick up bits of information from the servants and doctors who buzzed in and out of the bedchamber. Her sons also came every day to check on their father, bringing with them updates on his condition and words of comfort and hope. They all made sure their mother was properly cared for in the little nest she had prepared for herself in an out-of-the-way corner of the hallway. One of them personally escorted her back to her room every evening so she could get a proper night's sleep. Every morning, she returned to her corner to wait for word that her husband wanted to see her. Finally, one afternoon Solomon came out of his father's room, and with a large smile lighting his face, he walked over to Bathsheba.

"Eema, he's doing much better today. He's going to make an appearance on the roof so the people of the city can see he is still alive and well," Solomon announced.

There had been rumors trickling through the palace and into the streets below that the king was dead. The townspeople said his advisors were hiding the fact until his successor was secured. Apparently, David thought it was more important to please his kingdom than his wife, Bathsheba thought bitterly to herself. Solomon saw the dark look cross his mother's face and quickly continued.

"David would like to see you first," he said smiling. "You must try to go easy on him, though; he has to reserve his strength."

"He wants to see me?" she asked hesitantly, feeling a little guilty.

"Yes, he'll be ready for you soon, but Eema, please, don't grieve him for not sending for you sooner. He has been very weak, and he didn't want you to see him in such a condition." Solomon squeezed her hand and looked seriously at her for a moment. "You don't understand how hard it is for a man like Abba . . ."

Just then a servant stuck his head out of David's room and spoke to her. "The king will see you now."

Bathsheba quickly got to her feet and tried to straighten her wrinkled gown. She smoothed her hair and adjusted her head-dress.

"Eema," Solomon said before she walked into the room. "I'm leaving for Jezreel in a few hours. The doctor is sending one of his assistants along to search for herbs and medicines in the northern hills. I'll bring the prophet Nathan with me when I return."

Bathsheba stopped and embraced her son. "Travel safely, son. I will look in on your wives to make sure they are getting along all right while you're gone."

"Yes, please do. I'm afraid of what they'll do to each other if left alone too long." Solomon smiled sadly, "Now go on. Abba is waiting for you."

Bathsheba quickly walked into David's bedroom but stopped abruptly when she saw the man propped up in the bed. He looked as though he had aged ten years since she had last seen him. Never before had the difference in their ages been so noticeable. She tried to conceal her shock and smiled as she approached her husband's side, but it didn't fool him. He turned his head from her as silent tears slid down his cheeks.

"Oh, David," she whispered as she sat next to his bed and took his frail white hand in hers. "You look . . . better." Bathsheba tried to sound convincing.

He turned his head to face her. His once strong dark eyes were now gray and cloudy, but he could still see clearly enough to know what he must look like to his beloved wife. "You don't have to stay here with me, Bathsheba," David said in a hoarse, unfamiliar voice.

"You are still young and beautiful and full of life. You should not spend your days surrounded by death. Change your robes and live as a widow. I am no longer your husband. You are released from me."

As much as she wanted to control her emotions, Bathsheba couldn't. Tears sprang from her eyes as she kissed his hands. "Please don't say such things. You are not dead! You are still my husband. I will never leave your side. I love you more today than I did the day we were married. Don't you understand, David? Nothing will ever change that."

David sobbed openly now, and she sat on the bed next to him. "You didn't think you could get rid of me that easily, did you?" Bathsheba said between tears and laughter.

He smiled and held her close. "I don't want to get rid of you, my love. I heard that you have been sitting outside in the hall all this time. Is that true?"

"Well, the boys insisted that I go home at night, but yes, I've been out there every day just waiting for you to call for me. I knew you couldn't stay away from me forever," Bathsheba teased as she kissed David's forehead.

"Now that you know I'm recovering, I want you to go back to your home."

"Can't I stay here with you?" Bathsheba coaxed. "I could help serve you and take care of you until you're completely recovered. Besides, I know exactly how to make you feel better," she added with a playful sparkle in her eyes.

"You're a queen, the head queen of Israel and the mother of my sons. I can not have you acting like a servant, even to me." David hesitated, looking embarrassed and sad. "Besides, having you in my bed reminds me of what I used to be—and I'm not that man anymore. In fact, I'm hardly a man at all." David's voice trailed off, and Bathsheba could barely hear his last words.

"I will do whatever you want me to do. If you want me here, I'll be here in a moment. If you need to be alone, I understand and give you as much time and space as you need to recover. But, David, please know that I love you and I always will."

The two held each other in silence until a servant entered the room to prepare David for his appearance on the roof. Bathsheba was led outside, where she waited to catch a glimpse of the king as he passed by.

Several others started to gather in the hallways. It seemed everyone wanted to see whether the rumors about the king were true. When the door to his rooms finally opened, she saw a group of servants carrying David on a small throne. It was done in an attempt to make the frail man seem more regal, but Bathsheba knew he was actually too weak to make the journey to the roof.

The small crowd around her erupted with cheers for David. She saw tears in the eyes of some of the women standing next to her. She wondered if they cried because they were happy to see him alive or because they saw through the royal adornment and wept for the loss of the man they once exulted in having as king of Israel.

David played his part well and held his hand up in response to the people who loved him. Bathsheba hoped no one else noticed how weak and unsteady the hand looked. The servants did not linger in the hallway, but continued up the stairs, carrying the king and small throne on their shoulders as if he weighed nothing at all. The crowd continued up to the roof, following as closely as they were allowed, but Bathsheba just turned and walked back to her house. She suddenly felt very tired.

Chapter 63

The next morning, Bathsheba was in no hurry to get out of bed. She didn't expect to be called to see her husband, and she wasn't sure what to do with herself. Her maid, Matana, quietly stuck her head into Bathsheba's room to see if she was awake. Seeing her eyes open, Matana entered the room carrying a bowl of water for her mistress to wash in.

"Your breakfast is ready," the servant announced as she bustled around Bathsheba's room.

"I don't really feel like eating anything this morning, thank you."

"Is everything all right? You don't look yourself today."

"I don't know. I just feel . . . I can't explain it," Bathsheba stammered.

"I hear your husband is doing much better," Matana said, sounding hopeful.

"Yes, but for how long? You should see him; he looks so frail. I just don't know what I'll do if . . . when . . ." Bathsheba's voice broke.

"He's not going to die, Bathsheba."

"Yes, he is. Maybe not today, but I can tell it will be soon."

"Even if he does, you have nothing to fear. Didn't David tell you that Solomon will be the next king? You should be happy for your son."

Even after all these years, it still surprised Bathsheba a little when her maid took such an authoritative tone with her. It didn't upset her, though, because she considered Matana a friend more than a servant, and she had come to respect the woman a great deal.

"It's strange. I really do look forward to seeing Solomon sit on the throne, but I just can't bear the thought of losing his father. How do I deal with such conflicting emotions?"

"You should go to him."

"Who, Solomon? He's on his way to Jezreel."

"No, David. Just go sit with him for a while. Perhaps it will make both of you feel better."

"Has he sent for me?"

"No, I haven't received word, but I think under the circumstances, you may just have to take matters into your own hands. If he doesn't feel up to seeing you, you can always just come home, but I have a feeling, he may like your company."

"Maybe you're right, Matana. He thinks he's nothing more than a sick old man whom I don't want to be around. David will probably never call for me on his own. I don't have to serve him or lie with him; I'll just sit there." Bathsheba was now out of bed and washing her face and hands in the bowl Matana had brought her.

Matana served her a light breakfast then helped her get dressed and arrange her hair. As Bathsheba walked toward David's rooms, she felt light and hopeful. Of course she was aware that she had never gone to him uninvited and that he could send her away, but she was prepared for that. It just felt good to do something when just an hour earlier she had felt useless and depressed.

When she approached David's room, the usual guards were standing on either side of his door.

"Shalom," she said as she approached them. "I would like one of you to ask David if I could sit with him for a while."

The two men looked a little surprised at her boldness, but without hesitation, the man on the right bowed to her and walked into the room. A moment later, he reappeared.

"The king will see you," he said without making eye contact.

When Bathsheba entered, she saw two young servants bustling around the bed. One of the doctor's assistants was sitting at a table in the corner writing on a scroll. David sat propped up in his bed, arguing with the doctor who stood next to him. They stopped in the middle of their conversation when Bathsheba entered the room.

The doctor looked at her with an irritated expression. "You really should not bother the king right now; he needs his rest."

"How much rest am I getting with you and your servants pestering me?" David spat.

"I didn't mean to disturb you, David, I just wanted to see how you are feeling today," Bathsheba said innocently.

"I'm much better now that you're here. Now, I'd like all of you to leave so I can be alone with my wife," David said to the doctor and his assistants.

"I don't think that's a good—"

"I'll be fine," David interrupted the doctor. "Besides, if I need anything, I'll have Bathsheba call for you. Now please, just leave us alone."

When the door closed behind the four men, David sighed with relief. "I'm sure he's a good doctor, but sometimes I think the man is trying to kill me with his badgering."

"Now, David, he's only trying to take care of you, and I'd say he's doing a wonderful job. You look great today. How are you feeling?"

"Oh, I don't know. I guess I'm just tired of sitting in this bed all the time. Here, help me get up so I can stretch my legs."

Bathsheba was frightened to do anything that could endanger her husband, but he seemed insistent on getting out of bed. She decided he would do better with her help than without it, so she went to his side and let him put an arm over her shoulder. Once he was on his feet, he stood still for a moment testing his legs.

"There now, see? I'm just fine. Let's go out on the balcony to get some air," David said shakily.

Bathsheba led him through the door and onto the balcony, where they had a bird's-eye view of the city. It occurred to her that she had never been on his balcony before even though it had played such a major role in her life. She scanned the roofs to see if she recognized the house she had once shared with Uriah, but they all looked the same.

"It's that one there," David said, pointing to the left.

"How do you always know what I'm thinking?" she asked teasingly.

"Just a guess. It's what I think about almost every time I come out here." David took his arm off of her shoulder and turned to face her directly. "You do know how very sorry I am for everything that happened to you?"

"Of course I do," Bathsheba reassured him. "Besides, it was a lifetime ago. It's so hard to believe I'm even the same person. I guess in a way I'm not."

"What do you mean?" David asked.

"Well, I know I've made a lot of mistakes in my life, but I also know that God is merciful and forgiving. I just feel as if I've been reborn in a way. That girl you saw on the roof so many years ago has died, and God has given me a new life. I'm so thankful for the second chance He's given me." As she spoke, she absentmindedly twisted the thin gold bracelet on her wrist. It was the bracelet Uriah had given her. She had promised Uriah she would never remove it—and she hadn't. It was always there as a reminder of where she had been and the people she had hurt along the way.

She saw her husband shiver and without giving him a choice, she took his arm and led him back inside. He didn't argue, but allowed her to put him back in his bed and pull the warm blankets over him. His eyelids looked heavy, and it was obvious that even the slightest activity took a toll on him.

"Bathsheba, I . . ." David began.

"Shhh, just rest. The doctor won't let me come back if you get too tired."

"Will you come back tomorrow?" he asked wearily.

"Yes. And the day after, and the day after."

Once David was asleep, she quietly let herself out. She was surprised to see the doctor in the hallway talking to David's fourth son,

Adonijah. He was the only son of David's wife Haggith, who had died a few years after Bathsheba came to live at the palace. Haggith had been a perpetually tired, sick woman who seldom left her house, so Bathsheba didn't know much about her. She knew even less about her son. Adonijah and his wife had been living in the country for years. She saw him briefly while traveling with the families during Absalom's rebellion, but since then, he rarely came to the palace.

When Adonijah saw her, he quickly ended his conversation with the doctor and bowed respectfully to her. The doctor saw his chance to sneak back into David's room, so he excused himself from the queen and her stepson.

"Shalom, Bathsheba. I was just getting a report on my father's condition. I only recently heard he is not well."

Bathsheba found that very hard to believe. Everyone in the kingdom knew David was sick and had been for many days. How could the king's own son not know? She wondered what Adonijah was really up to.

"He seems to be feeling much better. He's resting right now, but I'm sure he would be pleased to see you. It's been a while, hasn't it?" Bathsheba responded politely.

"Oh, I don't want to bother him. I just wanted to see how serious it was."

"It appears it was not serious at all," she lied. The expression that flashed across Adonijah's face looked a lot like disappointment.

"Good. And how is my brother Solomon?" Adonijah asked, trying to sound casual.

"He is very well. His father sent him out of town on business, but he should return soon. I'll tell him you asked about him."

"Yes, please do. Now, if you'll excuse me, I have other business to attend to while I'm here." Adonijah gave Bathsheba another slight bow then turned and walked away. Something about his manner made Bathsheba feel very uncomfortable.

Chapter 64

As the days and weeks passed, Bathsheba felt a dark cloud of grief looming over her. She tried to push it away by keeping herself busy. If she didn't allow herself time to think about her fears, she thought they might just go away. She rose early every morning and tried to find things around the house that needed to be done. Matana, her maid, became increasingly annoyed when she began her day at the usual time and found that her mistress had already prepared breakfast and had started on the other morning chores.

Knowing that her daughter-in-law Naamah liked to sleep in, Bathsheba tried to wait until later in the morning to check in on the young women, as she had promised Solomon she would. She was always greeted warmly by Solomon's second wife, Ayala, and the two women would sit and visit until Naamah breezed into the room and demanded breakfast. Bathsheba usually took that as her cue to leave.

David had stopped sending a messenger to the women's quarters because he knew Bathsheba would come see him with or without an invitation. She usually tried to bring a happy little tidbit of information or some trinket to keep him amused. It was easier to pretend to be cheerful than to face the fact that her husband was dying.

Late one afternoon, she sat next to David's bed while he slept peacefully. Her eyes grew heavier and heavier, and she found herself nodding off occasionally. She knew a servant would bring dinner soon, so she tried to keep herself awake, but she found it very difficult in the warm, quiet room. A knock at the door brought her immediately out of her sleepiness, and she rose to see who it was.

"Who's here?" David asked in a confused voice as he, too, shook off sleep.

"I'm not sure, but I'll find out. You just relax."

When Bathsheba opened the door, she was thrilled to see her son Solomon standing before her. A group of people stood behind him, but her eyes didn't leave his beautifully suntanned face long enough to recognize them.

"Shalom, Eema!" he said as he scooped up his mother in a warm embrace.

She was surprised at how much he had changed during his absence. His chest and arms had grown thicker, and he seemed more like a man than she had ever seen him. It almost made her weep to see how much he looked like his father had in his prime.

After Solomon released her and strode across the room to greet his father, she finally saw the group of people in the hallway. There was the familiar doctor whom she had seen several times a day for so many weeks that she really didn't pay any more attention to him than she did a picture on the wall. He was reunited with his servant who had joined Solomon on his journey north. Behind them, she saw what she thought was a young girl until she got a better look. The veiled figure was very slight, but she had the obvious build of a shapely woman. She walked in slowly behind the men.

The doctor's servant bowed low before the king and spoke nervously. "My lord, we have brought you many things from the country around Jezreel. I have the finest herbs to help you in your recovery—"

"And let us not forget your greatest find," interrupted the doctor as he pushed the girl forward.

"Who is this?" David asked, looking confused.

"This is Abishag. My assistant assures me she is the most beautiful maiden in the country. She is sure to make you feel like your old self in no time," the doctor said with a snicker that Bathsheba found repulsive.

"She has some experience as a midwife's assistant," Solomon quickly interjected. "With a little more medical training from the doctor, she will make a fine nurse for you."

"Just take a look at her, my lord. A girl like this could make any man feel alive," the doctor said as he removed the veil that covered Abishag's head and face.

She really was a stunning girl. Her hair was thick and black, like Bathsheba's, but that is where the similarities ended. While Bathsheba's skin was fair, this girl's complexion was dark and smooth. She was also much shorter than Bathsheba with features so delicate she looked like a child. Her eyes were downcast, but Bathsheba could see that they were large and dark and held a great deal of wisdom and fire. Bathsheba would have felt humiliated by the open appraisal of the men in the room, but the girl handled it with a quiet dignity that made her seem much older than she appeared.

The room was silent for a moment as everyone drank in Abishag's beauty. Finally, the girl broke the spell by bowing low next to David's bed and speaking to him in a soft, even voice. "My king, it is an honor to serve you in any way I can." She then took his hand and kissed it.

David smiled at her and touched her soft cheek with his hand as if he wasn't sure she was real.

Bathsheba felt an unfamiliar burning feeling rise up in the pit of her stomach. *Is it jealousy?* she wondered. How could it be? She had shared her husband with many beautiful women over the years. Why should this Shunammite be any different? She had no reason to envy the girl. The poor thing had been taken from her home to tend to a dying old man whom she had never even seen before. But did she have to be so beautiful and graceful?

"Abishag, this is my mother, Bathsheba," Solomon said interrupting Bathsheba's dark thoughts. The girl rose from David's side and bowed politely before her.

"Your son has told me a great deal about you during our journey. He didn't tell me you were so beautiful, though," Abishag said, seeming suddenly shy. "I've been so excited to meet you. Solomon tells me you like music. I would love to sing with you sometime." Her dark eyes sparkled as she spoke, and Bathsheba found herself actually liking the girl.

She looked at her son and saw something on his face that she had never seen before. He couldn't keep his eyes off of her. It's true, all the men in the room were staring at the Shunammite, but Solomon looked at her almost reverently. She had never seen him look at either of his wives the way he looked at Abishag. Perhaps she had really been brought only as a nurse for her husband. Surely if David knew his son was in love with her, he would never spoil her. Bathsheba realized she had nothing to fear from this girl. Abishag had no intention of stealing David's love from her.

"Welcome, Abishag. If there is anything I can do to assist you with my husband's care, or anything else, please let me know," Bathsheba said kindly.

The girl smiled brilliantly at her, and Bathsheba couldn't help but smile back. Solomon stood between them looking as if he might burst with joy.

"If you'll excuse us for a while, Eema, we really need to show Abishag around. Why don't you go outside and enjoy the sunshine? It's a beautiful day. Besides, there's someone in the garden who would like to see you."

Bathsheba quickly went to her husband's side to see if he needed her. She took his hand in hers and knelt next to him.

"Abishag is really lovely, isn't she?" she whispered to him.

"Yes, I suppose she is. Do you think our son would like to have her as a wife once her duties to me are finished?"

Tears sprang to Bathsheba's eyes when she realized what David was implying. She was relieved that he recognized their son's feelings for the girl and that he had no intentions of taking her as a wife. But, at the same time, she knew just by looking at him that his days were short and Abishag's nursing care would not be needed much longer.

"Oh, David," she cried, "you're going to be fine. Everything is going to be all right." Bathsheba tried to convince herself. "I just found out our dear friend is back. He'll make everything OK again. I just know he will."

"Oh my beauty, please don't weep for me," David said as he stroked her soft hair. "I'm an old man, and I've had a full life. I'm ready to finally have peace."

"But, David . . ."

"Shhhh. Go now. Go see Nathan. He will help you bear this burden." He kissed her hand gently then wiped away her tears with his trembling hand.

Bathsheba turned to leave, looking over her shoulder once to see the girl Abishag take her place at the king's bedside.

Chapter 65

While her mind wandered, Bathsheba's feet led her down the familiar path to the palace gardens. The olive and fig trees were heavy with their fruit, but Bathsheba was blind to all the living things around her. Her mind was completely absorbed with thoughts of death. Of course many people she had loved throughout the years had gone to their rest; her father, Uriah, and several of the women she had befriended at the palace, but watching her beloved David wither away before her very eyes was almost too painful to bear.

Without realizing how she got there, Bathsheba found herself in her favorite part of the garden, the place she always had brought the children when they were little. She noticed that it was unusually quiet then realized everyone was probably eating dinner. The garden wasn't completely deserted, though. On the bench she usually occupied, she saw the figure of a hunched old man. She immediately knew who it was.

"Nathan, my friend!" she said as she approached him.

He rose from his seat and embraced her. "Ah, the beautiful Bathsheba. The years have been very kind to you."

"They've been kind to you too. It's amazing, but you don't look a day older than when I saw you last." She was shocked to find Nathan so well preserved, and again she found herself wondering how old he really was.

"Tell me, how is our king?" Nathan asked as they both sat down.

"He is not well. I'm afraid he doesn't have much longer . . ." The lump rising in her throat made it impossible for her to finish.

Bathsheba was surprised that Nathan did not get emotional when she told him David was dying. Instead, he sat there smiling, lost in some memory that she was not privy to.

"Don't you want to go see him?" she asked, feeling a little annoyed with her old friend.

"Yes, I just wanted to give him time to get settled in with the new nurse. Did you meet her?"

"Abishag? Yes, I met her. She's a very lovely girl."

"You do know your son is in love with her, don't you?"

"It was obvious the moment I looked at him."

"She is a very sweet girl, and I'm sure she'll keep David comfortable and happy until the end," Nathan continued.

"How can you be so unfeeling? The king is dying!" Bathsheba almost yelled at him.

Nathan's face softened, and he took her hand in his. "Now, now, I didn't mean to upset you. It's just that I don't really feel sad about David's impending death."

"What?" she was shocked that this man she loved like a father could be so cruel.

"I know it's hard for you, but you must understand David has been fighting battles his entire life. As a boy he had to fight to keep the beasts from his father's flocks. As a young man, he had to fight to preserve his own life when King Saul wanted nothing less than David's head displayed on a spear. And as the king, he has had nothing but war and turmoil, both in his country and in his family. Don't you think the poor man deserves a little peace?"

"Of course, but what about . . . ?"

"What? What about the nation? Solomon has been well trained. He is a wise, godly man now, and he will be a great leader if he continues to follow the Lord. God has promised a time of peace and prosperity for David's successor. Israel will have everything they've ever wanted and more." That explanation didn't seem to satisfy Bathsheba, so the prophet continued, "Are you concerned about the family? I'm sure Solomon will be able to take the reins and get things under control. David has been so ridden with guilt that he has let his family run amok for years. I'm sure your son will put an end to all of that."

"What about me!" Bathsheba burst out. "What will I do without him?" Tears flowed freely down her checks as the wall she had carefully built to protect herself finally came crashing down.

"Ah now, that's another matter altogether." Nathan continued to hold her hand and pat it gently. "You will mourn him for a long time, but then you will take off the sackcloth and put on your royal gowns, and life will continue for you. You will watch as your son is crowned king. You will be there when he builds the temple for the Lord. You will hold grandchildren in your arms and watch as they grow up before your eyes. Your life will go on, dear Bathsheba."

Nathan's words soothed her, and she felt comforted for the first time in months. Bathsheba knew in her heart that he was right; after all, he was a prophet.

Chapter 66

David's room felt crowded to Bathsheba, and she knew she really wasn't needed there, so she spent more of her time walking around the grounds and visiting with Nathan in the garden. One morning Bathsheba sat on the bench waiting for her friend to arrive. Nathan was later than usual, and she had started to feel apprehensive before she finally caught sight of him. When he was close enough for her to see his expression, she really began to worry. Nathan's wrinkles seemed deeper, and his hunched shoulders seemed to carry even more weight than usual.

"What's wrong, my friend?" Bathsheba asked.

"Trouble, trouble, always trouble with those sons of David," Nathan muttered, more to himself than to her.

Her heart sank. She remembered vividly the exodus caused by David's son Absalom when he had rebelled years before. Now who was creating problems?

"It's Adonijah, the son of Haggith. He's been riding through the streets of town in a chariot with hired men running before him. He's really caused quite a stir."

"Well, that's not a big deal," Bathsheba said, feeling relieved. "The princes are always making spectacles of themselves."

"This is different, Bathsheba. He has David's trusted general Joab and Abiathar the priest with him. He has invited his brothers to a feast this afternoon by the stone of Zoheleth."

"Oh, no . . . Solomon!" Bathsheba exclaimed, remembering the feast Absalom held during which he had his brother Amnon killed. "He's going to kill Solomon!"

"No, he hasn't even invited Solomon. All of the others were

invited, but not Solomon. I believe Adonijah is going to declare himself king today."

"But everyone knows David wants Solomon to succeed him."

"It hasn't been publicly declared, and Adonijah probably thinks his father is too weak to stand up to him."

"So that's why he's been lurking around. I wondered what he was up to," Bathsheba said, thinking back to all the times she had seen Adonijah around the palace recently. "What will he do to Solomon and me?"

"He will have you both killed unless we do something."

"What can we do?"

"You must talk to your husband."

"You know he doesn't listen to me when it concerns his children. I've tried countless times before, and he always gets angry."

"Bathsheba, you have no choice! You must tell him what's happening. Go into his room and ask him why he has allowed Adonijah to declare himself king when he promised you that your son Solomon would succeed him. While you are talking to him, I'll come in and confirm what you are saying. There's no time to argue about this; you must go now." Nathan gently guided her along through the gardens and into the hallway outside of David's room.

When she entered, she found David propped up on his bed with Abishag sitting next to him on the floor. She was singing an unfamiliar song to him, but she stopped immediately when she saw the queen enter the room.

"Shalom, Bathsheba. Is there anything I can do for you?"

"I am here to speak to my husband."

Abishag respectfully moved out of the way so Bathsheba could sit next to David. She then quietly excused herself from the room to give them privacy.

"My love, what brings you here today?" he asked calmly, oblivious to her nervousness.

"David, may I ask you something?" she began carefully. When he nodded, she continued, "Why is it that your son Adonijah is in Zoheleth right now declaring himself king over Israel when you yourself promised me before God that Solomon would be the next king?" The words she spoke seemed to flow freely without any thought. She wondered how she was able to speak so confidently when she was feeling so frightened. "Surely you know that Solomon and I will be executed as soon as you die. All of Israel is watching you right now to see what you will do."

Before David was able to absorb the information and respond, there was a knock at the door. Abishag entered looking very concerned.

"I'm sorry to interrupt you, but the prophet Nathan would like to speak with the king."

Bathsheba stepped out of the room with Abishag while Nathan entered to finish the job. The women stood in the hallway silently for a few moments knowing that both of their lives were about to change drastically. While Bathsheba had been speaking with David, Nathan had given Abishag a brief explanation of the day's events. Soon, Nathan opened the door and asked the women to join them.

When they entered the room, David was sitting up in his bed. His face was full of color, and he looked ready for action.

"Bathsheba, come here," David said, sounding more like a king than he had in years.

She obediently went to his bedside and bowed to him.

"I made a promise to you and to God. Your son Solomon will sit on my throne in my place, and I will make it happen today."

She trembled at the power in his voice and was reminded of what a great man she was married to. Overcome with emotion, she bowed low before him and kissed his hand. "May my lord, King David, live forever," she whispered.

"Now, we must find a priest who is loyal to me. Nathan, I want you to get the priest named Zadok. Have a servant ready my mule. I want Solomon to ride it to Gihon, where Nathan and Zadok will anoint him king over all of Israel. Have his mother place this crown upon his head; then lead him back to the palace and have him sit upon my throne." He gestured toward the table where his jewel-encrusted crown sat.

Bathsheba picked up the crown and was surprised by its weight. Everyone in the room was in awe of David's regained strength and decisiveness. They all seemed afraid to move until David barked authoritatively, "Now go! Find all who are loyal to me and stop this uprising before it's too late."

Chapter 67

Within hours, a crowd had gathered just inside the southern gate of the palace. Bathsheba watched in a daze as soldiers and priests bustled about trying to organize their groups. Lost in her own thoughts, she didn't even notice when her mother and sister approached.

"Oh, Bathsheba!" her mother exclaimed. "The day has finally come! Our Solomon will become king today."

The years at the palace had been good to Shiran. Bathsheba looked at the spry old woman with wonder. Until recently, she had worked tirelessly as a midwife, but the young women she had trained throughout the years had gradually started taking over until Shiran was needed only occasionally for very complicated deliveries.

"My daughter, the head wife of King David and now the queen mother—I always knew you were special!"

"Eema, I have done nothing to deserve the blessings God has given me," Bathsheba gently scolded her mother.

"Yes, I know, my flower. I'm just so thankful that He has done so much for our family—despite all the mistakes I have made. Our Lord truly is merciful."

It made Bathsheba so happy to see how the years had softened her mother. She wasn't sure what had brought about the slow changes in Shiran's attitude, but she thought it must have had something to do with her work as a midwife. It was impossible to see so many children born and not believe in a loving Creator.

Bathsheba's sister Atarah gently squeezed her hand and gave her a kiss on the cheek. Atarah, too, had changed a great deal over the years. Her once dark hair was now streaked with gray, and her slim figure had filled in from all the good food her husband prepared for her. With her sons grown and out of the house, the joy of her life was now her two beautiful granddaughters. It was hard to believe so much time had passed. Sometimes it seemed to Bathsheba that only a moment before she had been sharing her father's lap with her older sister, listening to his stories of faraway places.

As the crowd grew, more women came over to speak with Bathsheba. Her sister-wives had all long since overcome their jealousy and bitterness toward her and now treated her with respect and kindness, but none seemed as happy for her as her dear friend Abigail. When the aging woman finally made her way through the group to speak to Bathsheba, she looked exhausted from the effort, but still wore a smile that lit her entire face.

"What a day this is for you, my friend!" Abigail said as she embraced Bathsheba. "I only wish I could make the journey to Gihon. I know it isn't far, but these old legs of mine just won't make it. Please tell me all about it when you get back."

"Oh, Abigail, you know I will. I'm sure I'll bore you to tears with the details."

Just then, Bathsheba's maid Matana rushed toward her.

"There you are! I've been looking everywhere for you," she exclaimed a bit out of breath. "Your son would like you to walk in the front of the procession. Hurry now; they're about to open the gates!"

Matana pressed her mistress through the crowd until they could see Solomon sitting on his father's mule. He was looking around nervously but seemed to relax as soon as he saw his mother. His two wives were standing nearby, and they joined Bathsheba when the crowd started to move. It seemed as if the soldiers surrounding them were numberless, as if every one of David's military men had remained loyal and were now pledging their allegiance to Solomon. She saw Nathan, the prophet, and Zadok, the priest, standing on either side of the mule. It seemed everyone was there—except, of course, David's other sons, who were all with Adonijah just a few miles outside of the city. She wondered what they would do when they found out what they were missing.

The priests who were standing directly behind Bathsheba and her two daughters-in-law began to blow their horns. The sudden noise startled the women and caused them to jump. Ayala and Bathsheba giggled, but the regal-looking first wife Naamah just looked at the two of them as if they were silly children. The blast must have been a signal to the guards at the gate because the large wooden doors immediately swung open. Seeing the size of the crowd outside of the gates made Bathsheba gasp. As soon as the townspeople saw their new king, they began to cheer and shout, "Long live King Solomon!"

Many in the crowd carried palm branches that they waved as Solomon rode through the path they made for him. Some even laid their cloaks down on the ground before him so not even the feet of the king's mule would get dirty.

As the crowd headed south through the city, the numbers and volume grew until at last they reached Gihon. Then the priest, Zadok, raised his hand in the air, and everyone fell silent. Solomon stepped forward and knelt in front of the priest and the prophet Nathan. Solomon bowed his head while Zadok held out an alabaster jar in his hand. He opened the jar and poured the expensive oil over Solomon's head, anointing him as the new king of Israel. Bathsheba was standing so close she could smell the myrrh within moments after it was poured on her son. Then a servant brought her a richly embroidered cushion holding the crown. Without a word, she took the crown and walked over to where her son still knelt before the congregation, his dark hair glistening in the sunlight as the oil dripped from his head and down into his beard, and gently placed the crown on his head. Bathsheba was blind and deaf to the cheers of the crowd around her. She saw nothing but her son's dark eyes looking up at her. They were the same eyes she had looked into so many times when she held him in her arms as a baby. The same eyes she wiped tears from as a child. They were now the eyes of the king.

When Solomon rose to his feet, the earth shook from the music and the shouts of the people.

Nathan sidled over to Bathsheba's side and whispered loudly in her ear, "I imagine this noise won't be music to Adonijah's little party. It should be interesting to see what the thwarted prince does now."

The noisy crowd made its way back to the palace, where Solomon was seated on his father's throne. The Israelites continued to celebrate the peaceful crowning of the new king, but Solomon was not able to enjoy the festivities for long. His duties began almost immediately after he was seated. Bathsheba's other sons, Shammua, Shobad, and Nathan, entered the court, dragging their half brother Adonijah between them. The man who had so proudly paraded himself through town and tried to crown himself king now looked half crazed with fear as he threw himself on the floor in front of his brother Solomon.

"My lord the king, please have mercy on me," he begged pitifully. "I did not know our father's intentions of handing the crown over to you, or I would never have tried to declare myself king. Please spare me, brother!"

Solomon looked closely at Adonijah. It was obvious he was lying, but Solomon didn't want to start his reign with bloodshed. "Rise, brother," Solomon said calmly. "You should know here and now that I am not my father. We all know how it pained him to discipline his sons, but it will cause me no such pain. If you will be a worthy man, not one of the hairs on your head will fall to the ground, but if wickedness is found in you, you will die. Now go to your home and cause no more trouble here at the palace."

Adonijah bowed humbly before his brother then quickly scrambled out of the throne room. Bathsheba, who stood nearby, was delighted to see how well her son was conducting himself as king. She just hoped that he really had the courage to handle his family better than his father had.

Chapter 68

Before sunrise the next morning, Bathsheba felt a sudden urgency to go see David. She quickly washed and dressed without waking her maid, then slipped out the door. When she reached David's rooms, she was surprised to see a number of people lingering around in the hallway. The doctor was there with several servants, many of them were sitting on the floor looking as if they might nod off to sleep at any moment. Abishag was also there, sitting in a corner by herself. Bathsheba immediately knew something was wrong.

"What's happening?" she asked Abishag, trying to keep the panic out of her voice.

"David called for Solomon in the middle of the night. They've been in there talking for hours."

"It can't be good for David; shouldn't he be resting?"

"The doctor goes in periodically to try to talk David into going to bed, but he keeps getting thrown out."

Bathsheba paced back and forth for a while then finally gave up and sat down next to Abishag.

"How was David when you last saw him?" she asked the young nurse.

"He seemed very agitated last night. He was having difficulty breathing, and when I asked him if he wanted the doctor, he told me to send for Solomon instead. I don't think he has much time left."

Surprisingly, Bathsheba didn't cry at this frank statement. Deep down, she knew the end was near, and she was starting to feel as if she might be prepared for it.

Just then, Solomon opened the door.

"Please go get my mother," he said to a servant standing nearby.

"I'm here," Bathsheba said as she scrambled to her feet.

"Oh, Eema, I'm so glad. Abba is asking for you."

Bathsheba stepped into the familiar room and walked over to her husband's bed. She heard him gasp for every breath and watched as his chest heaved. Then she knelt next to his bed and took his hand. "David, I'm here, my love."

It seemed to take him a moment, but when he recognized her, he gazed up at her with his expression full of love.

"Bathsheba," he whispered as he moved his hand to touch her hair.

She rested her head on his chest and felt his fingers softly stroke the back of her head. She stayed there for what seemed like hours, remembering all the years she had with this man. There had been many trials, but through it all, there was love. She didn't speak or even open her eyes until she felt a hand on her shoulder. Only then did she realize that the chest her head rested on no longer fought for air but was completely still. When she looked at David's face, all signs of struggle had vanished. He was finally at peace.

"Eema," Solomon said softly, his hand still on her shoulder. "He's gone."

"Yes, I know."

The doctor and servants had returned to the room and all stood frozen in place. Abishag was next to Solomon, silent tears streaming down her face.

"Tomorrow is the Sabbath, so we will need to have the funeral today. Go home and rest while his body is prepared, and I will send someone for you when we are ready to leave," Solomon said calmly to Bathsheba.

Bathsheba nodded and was about to leave when she thought of Abishag. "Do you have any use for the girl right now?" she asked.

"No."

"Would you like to come to my house now that your duties to the king have ended?" she asked the Shunammite.

The girl seemed relieved. "Yes, thank you," she whispered.

Bathsheba kissed her husband's cold cheek one last time then left the room with Abishag by her side. As they walked through the courtyard toward the women's quarters, she noticed Abishag trying to stifle her sobs.

Bathsheba stopped walking and put her arm around the girl. "There, now. I know it's hard to see David go, but he is at peace now. You have no idea how difficult his life has been. Now he can finally rest." Bathsheba could hardly believe the comforting words were coming out of her own mouth.

"Yes, but he was such a great man, and now there is nothing," the girl cried.

"He is sleeping with his fathers, Abishag. Take comfort; we will see him again."

"How? He will turn into dust then disappear. How can we see him again?"

"The Lord has promised us that He will come and sound the trumpet, calling us all to be together with Him. Even death will not permanently separate us."

"Really?"

"Believe me. I've seen firsthand what God can do for those who love Him."

Abishag wiped her eyes on the back of her sleeve and sniffed softly. "I'm such a stupid, selfish girl. Here you just lost your beloved husband, and I'm the one who's sobbing. I'm so sorry, Bathsheba."

Bathsheba hugged the girl then continued on the way to her house.

"I wish I had faith like yours," Abishag said after a moment.

"If you want it, you can have the same kind of faith. I just hope you don't have to suffer the way I did in order to finally put your trust in God."

"I will try to be faithful—no matter what happens," she said shyly.

"What do you mean?"

"Well, it's just . . . I don't know what's going to happen to me now. I mean, it's assumed that I was given to the king for, well, you know, even though I never . . . I mean, I'm still a virgin, and now what?" Abishag seemed very uncomfortable with the subject but pushed on anyway. "Am I a widow, even though I wasn't really a concubine or wife? Am I a servant of the palace? What will become of me now?"

Bathsheba had learned not to meddle in the love lives of her sons, so she refrained from bringing up her suspicions about Solomon's feelings toward Abishag. "Don't worry about any of that, Abishag. You will stay with me until your future is more certain."

The girl smiled, showing her perfect white teeth. Then she took Bathsheba's hand and kissed it. "Thank you, Eema."

Chapter 69

When the people of Israel found out their beloved King David was dead, a cry rose from every house of the city. The men tore their robes, and the women put ashes in their hair and cried. Even the children ceased their games and mourned for their fallen hero. There seemed no end to the line of mourners pouring out through the city gates to the tomb where David was buried. At the tomb, a prayer was offered by the prophet Nathan; then Solomon blessed the entire congregations while tears for his father streamed down his cheeks. When he was composed enough to find his voice, Solomon sang one of David's favorite psalms, and the children of Israel sang along through their tears.

When the family returned to the palace, they found a funeral meal had been prepared for them, but Bathsheba was unable to eat any of the food set before her. Many came to her to offer their condolences, and she responded graciously, but she wanted nothing more than to be left alone with her grief. Bathsheba was numb to everything around her until a strange hand on her shoulder brought her back to reality. It was David's son Adonijah, the very man who had tried to steal the throne from her son.

"Bathsheba, may I speak with you outside?" he asked humbly.

She was very suspicious, but Adonijah seemed sincere. "Do you come to me in peace, Adonijah?"

"Yes, I mean you no harm. In fact, I was wondering if you could help me with something."

Knowing that Adonijah's own mother had been dead for many years and now his father was gone too, Bathsheba felt obliged to listen to his request. She nodded her consent, and he led her to the palace gardens.

"I have a favor to ask of you," he began tentatively once they were both seated on a bench. "You know the kingdom was mine and that all of Israel expected me to be king, but it must not have been what God wanted because He gave it to my brother. I have lost everything, but there is one thing that would make it easier to bear. You see, I've been noticing the beautiful girl, Abishag, who belonged to my father. I was wondering if you could go to Solomon and ask if I can have her as a wife. I'm sure he won't refuse me if *you* ask him."

A cold chill ran down Bathsheba's spine. She knew immediately what Adonijah was up to. If he took a woman who belonged to the former king, what was to stop him from trying to take the crown as well? It wasn't much different from what his brother Absalom had done when he raped David's concubines. She felt as if every drop of blood had been drained from her body. How could she take this request to her son? But if she refused to ask Solomon, what would Adonijah do? Surely Solomon would see through this request and punish his brother for his treachery, but what if he proved to be weak like his father when dealing with family?

Bathsheba thought for a moment then finally replied, "Very well, I'll speak to the king for you."

Adonijah smiled, and for a fleeting moment, Bathsheba saw a malicious glint in his eyes. He stood and bowed low to her, but she wasn't fooled by his mock respect. Without another word, he turned and left. She sat alone in the garden for hours, pouring her heart out to God once again. The sun crawled across the sky, sinking lower and lower toward the horizon. Her prayers were interrupted by the sound of the priest's horn notifying the city that the Sabbath was approaching. Suddenly a terrifying thought came to Bathsheba's mind, and she became frightened for Abishag. What if Adonijah decided not to wait for Solomon's response? What if he took her now? Not only would war break out between the brothers, but the girl who had grown so dear to her was sure to be the first victim.

Bathsheba quickly returned to the banquet hall where everyone was just starting to leave so they could be home before the sun set. She looked frantically for the Shunammite girl, but the crowd was moving toward the door where she was standing, and she found it almost impossible to move forward. Finally, she heard someone calling her name. She turned around and saw the beautiful dark face of Abishag. Feeling relieved, she made her way through the group and took the girl by the arm.

"I would like you to stay close to me for the next couple of days, Abishag," Bathsheba suggested, sounding more maternal than she had intended.

"I will do whatever you say. Is something wrong?"

Chapter 70

Early in the morning on the first day of the week, Bathsheba left her house giving specific instructions for Abishag to stay inside until she returned. As she walked to the throne room, Bathsheba prayed silently with every step. *Lord, please give my son wisdom to see through his brother's plot. Please give him strength to maintain the kingdom You gave him,* she pleaded just before she stepped into the large room where Solomon was seated before a group of courtiers and towns-people who brought their cases to the king.

When Solomon saw her, he held his hand up to silence the young man who stood before him droning on and on about the troubles he was having with a neighbor.

"Eema, please come forward," he said, smiling as he spoke to her. Then he turned and spoke quietly to a servant next to him, who bustled out of the room to do the king's bidding.

She slowly walked toward her son and stopped just in front of his throne, but before she could bow to Solomon showing him the proper respect due to the king, he did something that greatly sur-prised her and everyone else in the room. He stepped down from his throne and stood before his mother, and then the king of Israel bowed low to her! Everyone in the room gasped then started whis-pering excitedly. Just then, the servant returned with another chair and placed it on the right side of Solomon's throne.

"What brings you here today?" Solomon asked as he motioned for her to sit next to him.

"Well, I have a request," Bathsheba replied slowly, thinking care-fully of each word before she spoke it.

"Anything, ask me anything, and it shall be yours."

She cringed noticeably. How could she tell him she didn't want him to grant her request?

"I have come on behalf of your brother Adonijah. He has asked for Abishag the Shunammite to be his wife."

Though she spoke softly to her son, it seemed as though everyone in the room heard her because the room had become completely silent. She saw the color drain from Solomon's face as he absorbed the full meaning of what his mother asked him. He looked at her, his eyes filled first with pain, then with understanding.

"He may as well have asked for my crown," Solomon finally said quietly. Then he stood so everyone in the room was looking at him. "Adonijah is using my father's women to try once again to take the throne. He has been given ample warning to leave the palace and return to his home, but he insists on causing trouble for the one appointed by King David himself and anointed by God. I will have no more of it!"

Bathsheba shook with awe and wonder at the power in her son's voice. If she ever had a doubt about his ability to lead Israel, it completely vanished as she watched him leap into action. Solomon summoned his guards and sent them to immediately kill the traitorous Adonijah and anyone else who still supported him.

Any village disagreements were forgotten as the people in the throne room whispered their approval of Solomon's decisiveness and wisdom. Though many of the Israelites had briefly supported the uprisings of David's rebellious sons, they now fully put their faith in their new king. Amidst all the commotion, Solomon returned to his throne and sat next to his mother and took her hand.

"This must have been very difficult for you," Solomon said quietly so only she could hear.

"I shouldn't have worried. You were put here by the Lord. I know if you continue to seek Him first, He will help you lead His people. You, my son, will bring us into a time of peace and prosperity, and someday," Bathsheba said with tears welling in her eyes, "someday, as the Lord promised, your seed will redeem us all and give us eternal salvation."

Epilogue

As God promised through His prophet Nathan, the reign of Solomon was one of greatness for the Israelites. When Solomon sincerely prayed for good judgment in guiding his people, the Lord blessed him not only with wisdom beyond compare, but also with wealth and a long life.

For Bathsheba, the kingdom's golden years were filled with both joy and sorrow, birth and loss. She sat by the bedsides of her mother and her dear friend Abigail as they breathed their last. She watched with a heavy heart as the stones were rolled in front of their tombs. But, she also rejoiced with her son's wives as they brought forth new lives. Though Abishag the Shunammite was Solomon's third bride, she was the first to give him a child, a girl whom they named Basmath. The daughter of the Egyptian pharaoh, with whom Solomon formed a marriage alliance, gave him another daughter named Taphath. There was much rejoicing in the palace when Solomon's first wife, Naamah, finally gave him a son named Rehoboam.

Eleven years after Solomon was crowned king over all of Israel, he completed the temple his father David had so diligently planned and prayed for. Materials and laborers came from all over the country. Many who came to Jerusalem to find work found so much more. The God of Abraham became real to the thousands of spectators the day the ark was brought from the tent of meeting into the newly finished Most Holy Place in the temple. Bathsheba stood with throngs of other women, holding her granddaughter Basmath on her hip. Again she watched in amazement as the four priests carried the ark using the long poles slipped through rings on each corner. They carried it behind the curtain which separated the Holy Place from the Most Holy Place. Her daughter-in-law Abishag asked questions about everything, and Bathsheba did her best to answer them. The questions came to a sudden end when everyone in the crowd was struck dumb with amazement. The entire temple filled with a cloud of light, the unmistakable presence of God. That distant God of her childhood had become so real to her through her years of heartache and trials that she knew even when she felt forsaken by all, she was never really alone. She noticed a few of the women around her were frightened by the glory, but she rejoiced because it indicated that God was pleased with the temple that David had planned and Solomon had built. Bathsheba closed her eyes but saw the glory even through her eyelids. She turned her face toward heaven and offered up a silent prayer to her Friend and Creator. *Thank You for never leaving me, no matter what. Thank You for Your promise of a Redeemer. Though I haven't done a single thing in my life to deserve Your goodness, I thank You for Your mercy to me.*

Her thoughts were interrupted by the little hand of her granddaughter on her cheek. "Sava," she whispered in awe, "is that the same cloud that led our people through the Red Sea?"

"Yes it is, child. It is the one and only God."

"Is He going to live here in the new house my Abba made for Him?"

"He'll stay in this house and in our hearts as long as we ask Him to stay."

Satisfied with this answer, the girl laid her head of thick dark curls back on her grandmother's shoulder. Bathsheba was filled with peace.

If you found this book inspiring and full of hope, you'll also find God's patience and hand at work in the lives of Peter the disciple of Jesus, and in the life of a successful modern businesswoman.

Peter: Fisher of Men
By *Noni Beth Gibbs*

Peter is the disciple that most of us can relate to. He had his ups and downs. At times he was brave and at other times cowardly. He had problems at home. He had problems at work. He was human. He didn't become a great disciple overnight.

Author Noni Beth Gibbs tells the gripping story of the disciple's spiritual growth in the context of spiritual warfare. Come eavesdrop on the angels and demons competing for Peter's attention. There is a war going on around each of us. We, too, must be alert.

Paperback, 384 pages.

ISBN 13: 978-0-8163-2189-6   ISBN 10: 0-8163-2189-2

Lemons to Lemonade
By *Sylvia Matiko and Pat Moore*

Sylvia had had enough of the "Adventist bubble." Once she had graduated from Kingsway College and Andrews University, she was determined to put all that behind her. She became the vice president of franchise operations for Ripley's Believe It or Not! She was happily married to the man of her dreams. They had a big, beautiful house. They were living "the good life," or so she thought. She had a great salary, furs, fine jewelry, and duties that took here all over the world to meet the rich and famous. What more could anyone want? "God, if You're really up there, help me!" she shouted one day. God seemed distant, but He wasn't.

Paperback, 128 pages.

ISBN 13: 978-0-8163-2190-2.   ISBN 10: 0-8163-2190-6